Next Time

a novel by
Cheryl Matlock

PB Productions

Published by
PB Productions
P.O. Box 81137
Chicago, IL 60681

All rights reserved. No part of this publication may be reproduced, stored in a retrieval system, or transmitted, in any form or by any means, electronic, mechanical, photocopying, recording, or otherwise, without the prior written permission of the author. Requests for permission should be addressed to Cheryl Matlock, P.O. Box 81137, Chicago, IL 60681 or visit www.cmatlock.com.

This novel is a work of fiction. Names, characters, places and incidents are products of the author's imagination or are used fictitiously. Any resemblance to actual events or locales or persons, living or dead, is entirely coincidental.

Printed in the United States of America
Library of Congress Control Number: 2006908657
ISBN: 0-9769468-0-7

Copyright © 2007 by Cheryl R. Matlock

Dedication

To my precious mother, father and brother - words cannot express the deep love and admiration I have for each of you.

To my dear friends Tracye, Verneva, Quentin and Victor for being the first to read my rough drafts. To Quentin, for designing such a lovely web site and for his excellent marketing tips. To Lawrence, the best cameraman in the world - you've always been there for me and you have always believed in me. To Charles, for being so supportive, and for helping me move while I was in the middle of pulling all of this together. To Tony, my ever so suave hairdresser and friend, for his patience and his wisdom. To Arnita, Candis and Scott for all their encouragement and for looking at an endless number of cover drafts. To Pierre for listening and listening and listening. To Robin for telling me to stand tall. To Mr. Powell for his extraordinary photography skills which helped create the beautiful cover. To all the others who helped with the cover design process: Richton and Ted for donating their time and expertise, Rock my gifted cover designer and teacher and Waymond for helping with the final version and for installing DSL on my computer. To John E. Smith for his exquisite author photos. Red, Gary, Snooze and all the other jocks at WHPK who played the great music that helped set the mood for many of the chapters in the novel. To G.L. - my muse. And to First, my most brilliant manager. Thank you. Thank you, one and all!

Reader Comments

I liked the main subject Kahara. The sister had flava! While reading I could see her, the way she moved, the way she spoke, her full ample hips with a banging body to match, a bangin black women's body. I wanted to meet her myself. When I read I like to feel a connection. Please let me know when your next book is coming out.
- Kalum Johnson - Chicago, IL

Words teamed with romance, faith, wisdom and conviction.
- Maurice M. Tonia - Long Island, NY

I really enjoyed reading it. One day I was at the auto repair place and was reading your book. I had to close it quickly. I was breathing hard. When I got back to home I stayed up until 2:00AM to finish it. I could not put it down. I really understand Kahara and her emotions. I get it. Thanks for writing it.
- Beverly Sheppard - Chicago, IL

I had the chance to read this book and was AMAZED at the realness of the characters! This is not a CHICK book BUT a RELATIONSHIP book. The main character, KAHARA, is like so many women that I have come across, that I felt like this was a bio on the women I've dated. The one thing that I truly enjoyed---that the MEN in this book were not painted in a negative image, but in a TRUTHFUL MANNER. If you like Eric Jerome Dickey, then you will enjoy Cheryl Matlock's book NEXT TIME!
- Phinesse - Program Director/Talk Show Host –WPUL, Daytona Beach, FL

To read or leave additional comments visit:
www.cmatlock.com

Chapter 1

No woman is average. Every woman has a unique quality that gives her definition. Something that makes her stand out. Kahara Jenkins had been repeating these words to herself ever since she heard them more than a month before at a Chicago singles meeting.

For the past year, Kahara had done everything by the book. When she met a man, she waited until she got to know him better before making the decision to become intimate. That tactic failed. The few men she did meet never stayed around long enough for anything to develop.

Since forming a meaningful relationship seemed all but impossible, she decided to do the next best thing—have sex. And she felt she had found the perfect subject—Julius. Julius was an event coordinator for the Virginia Beach Black Film Festival, which Kahara would be attending during the third week in April. After almost a month of sexual banter with him, she decided it was time to take care of her sexual needs—something she hadn't done in over a year.

Julius seemed willing enough. A native New Yorker, he had a thick Brooklyn accent that turned her on whenever she heard it. The fact that he lived in New York and she lived in Chicago didn't matter. In fact it was almost a relief. It forced her to keep things in perspective, and not think that their affair could become anything more than an extended one-night stand.

It was after seven that evening when she arrived at the Avenda, a beachfront resort hotel where the festival was based. She phoned her mother and gave her the room number. After unpacking most of her clothes, she took a quick look in the mirror. A healthy 5'7" frame—thick from the waist down as her mother would say. Kahara had a classic black woman's shape—generous behind, full hips, legs thick and firm. Her eyes were penetrating, lips full, her skin tone cinnamon brown and her hair medium length. After applying a fresh coat of lipstick, she went downstairs to the registration area.

After all that sexual banter, she hoped meeting Julius wouldn't be a letdown. As she approached the registration desk, she spotted a tall, brown-skinned man in a stark white short-sleeved knit shirt, and loose-fitting khaki knee length shorts. He was surrounded by three festival employees, two young women and an attractive man. She smiled at him.

"Julius?" she asked.

"Kahara," he said knowingly.

It was a strange experience, the two of them being able to identify each other even though they had never met. They stared at each other for a moment without saying anything. She wasn't sure what he was expecting, but his expression was a dead give away—it wasn't her. For her part, she wasn't exactly moved. He was good looking enough—around six feet tall as he had said. But something about him. As she spoke with him, he didn't have the same presence he had over the phone. He seemed subdued and nondescript. His shoulders seemed to cave in, and his big eyes seemed to sag. In fact, his whole demeanor seemed to sag. Where was the rambunctious, aggressive, native New Yorker she had been coyly teasing over the last month? The man that spoke to her on the phone would have been standing erect with a knowing glint of mischief in his eyes. This man seemed winded and slumped over.

He gave her another once-over, furrowing his eyebrows, his expression a little sour.

"What's the matter?" she asked.

"Nothin', nothin'. Why?"

"You look like you're about to pass a kidney stone," she said.

"No I'm fine. Just—just got a few things to do before I hit this party this evening. Listen, I'd like to stay and talk but I gotta—I need to umm—"

"Don't bother to whip up a reason Julius. I got it."

One of his co-workers motioned to him in the distance.

A look of relief passed over his face. "I need to get over there. I'll be back," he said, rushing off.

"Don't hurry," she said, picking up a few of the film pluggers lying on the exhibition table.

After he left, she peppered his male and female co-workers with questions about the festival, and then watched their expressions change as she turned the subject to Julius. Each of them seemed to almost smirk when referring to him, making snide comments about his work ethic and his delusion that he was a ladies man.

Kahara felt even more of a sense of letdown. She didn't know what it was—maybe the $2,000 price tag for this networking vacation, her age, or both. But she felt a sense of immediacy. How could she have been so wrong about him? She liked men who exuded confidence and a sense of certainty, but Julius oozed none of that. It probably shouldn't have mattered to her since it was only a fling anyway, but it did. It was as though the person on the phone and the person she was seeing now were two completely different people. His apparent disappointment in her didn't help. *Well at least it's mutual,* she thought. She began walking toward the elevator then doubled back to pick up some additional pamphlets. As she headed back, she noticed Julius do a three-sixty, and walk in the opposite direction when he saw her returning. She shook her head and laughed to herself a little as she gathered the pamphlets and left. As she waited for the elevator, she perused the festival booklet, noting that next year's event was being pushed from the third week of April to the middle of July.

She thought about the encounter she'd had with Julius as she rode up to her room. A mutual unspoken rejection. They both seemed to silently agree that the idea of an affair was dead in the water. His attitude toward her didn't help, neither did the age differential. He was thirty-two and she was turning forty. Kahara didn't look her age though, most would mistake her for thirty. Nor was she ugly. She reasoned Julius must have met a stunning twenty-year-old that he considered a better prospect.

After returning to her room, she opened her small suitcase, which contained all her toiletries, including prophylactics. "Won't be needing these," she said out loud, as she resealed the Ziploc bag. She looked lovingly at the lace teddy she had laid out. "This either," she said sullenly, a little sad that her chance for an out-of-town tryst had fizzled. "Oh well, I didn't pay all this money to get screwed, I paid it to network," she said. She took the turquoise teddy and laid it gently in the drawer by itself, as though holding out hope.

After showering, she applied her makeup meticulously, then slipped into a sleeveless form-fitting dress, stark white on the left side and jet black on the right. As she left her room, her thoughts turned to the party. She hoped this affair wouldn't turn out to be like the parties she attended in Chicago, where all the eligible men stood around the wall talking to each other, and only the very young and the very pretty were asked to dance. The only men who approached her at those gatherings were the hungry ones, out for sex. The type who didn't bother putting much, if any, effort into courting a woman. She hated those types. The idea of being thought of as just some indiscriminate hole a man could stick his penis into made her feel disposable. If she was going to be involved with a man, she needed to be romanced, made to feel special—even if the affair was only to last a few nights.

When Kahara arrived at the party there were many people crowded in front trying to get in. She flashed her pass and entered. To her disappointment, the men there seemed just like the men in Chicago. Many of the good-looking ones were standing around talking to each other, not trying to mix with the women. The others, of course, were dancing with the youngest prettiest women.

Is this an interstate disease? she wondered.

She stood near the entrance of the dance floor, absorbing the festive mood of the people dancing. After about ten minutes, she walked around trying to look accessible, reasoning that her mistake in Chicago was that she would often find a spot and stay there all night. This time, she would move around, so that she could be seen and hopefully approached. No luck. Twenty minutes went by and no one had asked her to dance.

I'll be damned if I'm going to come all the way to Virginia to stand here by myself, she thought. She asked an attractive man to dance. He turned her down, but promised to dance with her later. Shaking off that rejection, she walked to another part of the club. Not confident enough to ask another attractive man to dance, she spotted a somewhat unattractive one and made her move. He accepted and they headed toward the dance floor. She remembered what her friend Arnita had said about looking upbeat, and took comfort in the fact that no one knew she had been the one who did the asking.

After that dance, she went to another spot and stood waiting, fighting off that sinking feeling that this event would mirror some of the ones she'd attended in Chicago, where she went the entire night without once being asked to dance. About a half-hour later, she approached another man, tall about 6 feet 3 inches, thin, caramel-colored and rather attractive.

"Want to dance?" she said a little dryly, expecting to be turned down.

He looked at her as though sizing up her intentions. "Sure I'll dance with you sister," he said.

"I guess I passed the test," she said, under her breath, as they made their way to the dance floor.

"No test," he said.

Kahara blushed, embarrassed that he had heard what she said. She stopped short. "I didn't mean—it's just you were lookin' so—oh forget it," she said, shaking her head in frustration. He smiled, took her hand, and led her onto the floor. Kahara smiled to herself as she followed him, admiring the way he gently took control. She drank in his lean body as they began dancing.

After a few records, they headed upstairs where another DJ was spinning old-school cuts. Kahara felt more at home up there listening to Earth Wind and Fire, and the Commodores. She was finally beginning to have some fun that evening. They found seats at the bar, he ordered drinks and they continued to get to know each other. As they chatted, Kahara felt herself becoming attracted to him. His unassuming manner appealed to her. He was very polite, hadn't danced too close, and didn't come on too strong.

His name was Gary Mount, a native of Virginia. He worked at a Fortune 500 company for years before being downsized. It was then that he decided to pursue his dream of owning a video production company. The generous severance he received enabled him to return to school and stay on his feet financially during a rocky first year. As Kahara listened to him describe the slow process of building his customer base, she could tell that, after struggling for years, this man would let little stand in the way of his success. Through word of mouth, he built a network of regular customers in Norfolk, Chicago, and Los Angeles. She sensed a fierce determination lay underneath his cool, almost aloof, exterior. He had a quiet intensity about him, a sureness of purpose. That intensity unnerved her a little. His eyes followed her every move, and she felt at times as though she were being sized up.

"You like to scrutinize people don't you?" she asked.

His gaze softened a little. "Depends on who it is. Why?"

"The way you look at me. Especially when I asked you to dance. It's like you're trying to figure out my motive or something."

He rubbed his chin a little and looked at her. "Did you have a motive?"

"Yeah," she said, leaning forward a bit. "I want you to support me financially for the rest of my life."

"Is that right?" he said, laughing softly. "And just how do you intend to do that?"

"I have my ways," she said. "I don't know. You seem like the conservative type, so throwing my body at you would probably be a turn-off."

"Yeah," he nodded. "I'm not real into sisters that put themselves out there like that."

Kahara smiled to herself. She wondered what Gary would have thought about her dashed plans to jump into bed with Julius.

"So what do you do?" he asked.

"Take a guess," she said.

"I don't know, what are you—a stunt woman? Porn actress?"

"Try financial analyst."

"Damn, and I was going to guess that next," he said.

Kahara told him a little about her background, and about the film she would be shooting when she returned to Chicago.

"So, it's a film about a stormy relationship," he said, grinning at her a little. "You seem like you've been in a few of those."

"What?"

"You seem high-maintenance. Yeah," he said, "I'd bet money you're high-maintenance."

"Why would you say that?"

"What's the longest relationship you've ever been in?"

Kahara frowned. "I've had a lot of long-term relationships," she said lying, trying not to look as uncomfortable as she felt. He had read her right. Her hot temper had driven away many of the men in her life. She could count on her hand the number of relationships she had that lasted over a year. "Anyway, know it all, we were talking about my film—not my love life." *Non-existent as it is*, she thought.

"Do they make it? Are they still together at the end of the film?" he asked.

She looked at him and smiled. "You'll have to see it when it's finished to find out."

He looked at her and nodded. "Is that an invitation?"

"You're good at reading people. I'll let you figure that one out," she said a little coyly. She enjoyed the subtle dance they were doing.

Gary smiled. "I've shot for a number of independent filmmakers," he said, "so I know how much work is involved, especially when you're trying to hold down a full-time job. Must put a strain on your love life."

"Love life! Yeah, right. There's a joke. Please. I can't even get a dance here. I mean like tonight. I came out here thinking things would be different, you know, and—" Kahara stopped short, realizing she was maybe letting off a little bit too much steam. She decided to lighten up a bit, afraid she might scare him off.

"Come out here and what?" he asked, furrowing his eyebrows.

"Nothing. It's not important. Never mind."

He reached in his pocket and pulled out his wallet. "Look, if you or any of your filmmaker friends are ever looking for a cameraman, here's my card," he said, handing it to her.

"I'll keep that in mind," Kahara said. "Listen, I've got a friend in L.A. who is part-owner of a cable station there. He asked me to get some video interviews from the fest. Would you be willing?"

"Sure, why not. Tell you what, why don't I take you to breakfast tomorrow, and we can do the interview after that. That's my cell number on the card. Give me a call in the morning after you wake up."

Kahara was elated. Her first interview. They talked a little longer, then Gary excused himself after spotting one of his friends downstairs. For a moment, Kahara was a little taken aback by his departure, thinking he might have been interested in her. Then she remembered the statement he had made to her about looking for new customers. She was a budding filmmaker, so he probably viewed her as a potential client.

She shrugged off the disappointment, happy that he'd spent at least that much time with her. She felt a little abandoned, though, sitting up there alone. Feeling self-conscious, as though other people may have seen Gary leave her, she couldn't help but feel a little lost. Kahara spotted Julius talking to an attractive young woman. After having struck out the entire night, even he looked appealing at that point. But she saw, from the way he immediately looked away, that he didn't want to have anything to do with her. She sauntered down the stairs, trying to appear unaffected, and went back to her old spot near the tip of the dance floor. Kahara stared out at the crowd.

After a few minutes, she spotted Gary on the dance floor with another woman. A woman much younger than herself. As she watched Gary and his friend both dancing with younger women, she couldn't help but feel a little old. She watched him smile and be as gracious to his young dance partner as he had been to her. How much easier it was for men to be successful at events like this. Her thoughts drifted back to a time when she was younger and more sought-after. Feeling somewhat disillusioned, she bitterly concluded the evening had been a bust, and decided to head back to the hotel.

As she was walking to the exit, she spotted the actor Derrick Johnson. She walked up to him smiling. "Aren't you Derrick Johnson?" she said, reaching out to shake his hand.

"Yeah," he said, giving her a limp handshake. He immediately turned his back to her and began talking to another woman before she could say anything else.

Kahara stood there a little stunned and confused. He did not turn back to acknowledge her. The rejection for some reason didn't sting as much as it normally might have. After not being asked to dance all night, this slight paled in comparison. The experience, however, left her a little shaken. Kahara didn't want to return to the hotel after yet another defeat, no matter how small. She wandered back toward the dance floor. She felt almost numb at this point realizing that she came all the way out to Virginia to be treated the same as she was in Chicago.

She spotted the attractive man she had asked to dance earlier. The one who said he would dance with her later. He all but ran away from her when she spoke to him. Jolted by yet another rejection, she wandered over toward a tall business-like gentleman standing at the tip of the dance floor entrance. She decided to give it one more try.

"You want to dance?" she asked wryly.

He gave her the once-over. "Sure," he returned.

He was plain looking, wore glasses, chocolate-brown, broad shouldered, and stood about 6'2". He had a corporate look about him though that Kahara found a little off-putting. His posture was straight, almost rigid. Dressed in a crisp white shirt, with loose-fitting black slacks and a deep maroon tie, he seemed like a businessman who had just escaped a late night at the office. He led her to the middle of the floor. A Rap song was playing. Kahara wasn't really into Rap, but that was what was being played most of the evening. As they began to dance, she watched his demeanor change. Gone was the stiff, prim corporate executive, and what emerged was a flirtatious, lascivious, hungry-looking predator. None of the polite distance of Gary, he pulled her close to him as they danced.

"What's your name?" he asked brashly.

"Kahara. What's yours?" she returned, a little shaken by his manner.

"Denzel."

"Denzel what?"

He paused. "*Rumppincher*," he said, watching her reaction. He smiled down at her. "It's Taylor. Marshall Taylor."

He spun around, then grabbed her shoulders and pulled her close again. She edged away from him, but he crept closer, leaving only about an inch between them.

"You are awfully mannish," she said.

"Mannish? What's mannish?"

"Where are you from?" she asked.

"Birmingham, Alabama."
"They don't use that term there, huh?"
"No."
"It means fresh, forward, hungry."
"Turn around," he said, trying to turn her body.
"Why? What are you trying to do?"
"Turn around."

She turned around slowly. He edged up behind her, and held her hips against his mid-section. She turned back around abruptly.

"Mannish! See what I mean."

"Aw, come on. Nobody knows you here. I'm single, unattached, and you're…"

"Yeah, I'm single too, but I don't dance like that."

"Where are you from?" he asked.

"Chicago."

"Ah heck yeah, you should know all about it then. I've been there. I've seen them do it. It's all we do in Birmingham. We call it dirty south. Women grind up against the brothers—be breaking them off on the dance floor."

"Well I'm not into that."

He grabbed her face gently with his large hands and pulled it against his. "Get into it."

"Marshall," she said, trying to pull away. "Marshall!"

He let go of her face but grabbed her shoulders again and pulled her close. What was she going to do with this man? He held her close and began to slow-dance with her even as the fast beat thumped on. She became embarrassed, wondering what others were thinking of their strange behavior. "I hope no one thinks we're involved," she said.

"Why not? Nobody here knows you."

"How do you know that?"

"You have that lost look about you. I can always tell," he said, spinning around. He came back toward her. "Where are you staying?"

"The Avenda," she said, caught off guard by his assessment of her.

"Me too. What's your room number?"

"What's yours?" she asked.

"647."

He danced with her for a moment, giving her a little more room than usual. "What's yours?"

She looked up at him coyly. "I'm not telling you."

He shrugged and continued dancing. How brash and forward he was. It annoyed, but tickled her at the same time. He was like a big mischievous puppy that needed to be trained. How completely opposite he was from Gary—who never leered at her once, never moved closer than ten inches, and never said anything out of turn. How completely different—but fascinating. After being ignored all night, she found all this attention a little overwhelming, but in a way titillating. This experience reminded her of how she felt the first time she watched the Q's step—both repelled and aroused at once.

They continued dancing record after record. Unlike the other man she had asked, who seemed ready to end it after one record—Marshall seemed content to stay on the dance floor with her all night. She found it amusing how he knew the lyrics to all the current Rap songs, and laughed as he waved his hands up in the air as he recited the words. It seemed so incongruent to the proper dignified image he projected when she first saw him. This mischievous new playmate. She never knew what to expect next—a refreshing change for someone whose life had been all too predictable lately. He turned around, backing against her midsection, then bent over, holding his head with both hands. She smiled, finding his brashness entertaining. Looking around feeling a little embarrassed, she placed her hand gently on his back, not knowing what else to do. He was like a big uncontrollable dog. She spotted a woman dancing the way he wanted her to dance. The woman was tall about 5'11", attractive with velvety cocoa-brown skin, a small waist and full round hips, dressed in a stark white tank-top and hip-hugger jeans. Kahara tapped him on the shoulder. He turned around.

"How about her," she said, motioning to the girl. "She's doing that dance you like."

He watched her and nodded his head, looking unfazed. Kahara was a little surprised—the girl was gorgeous and young, something she thought he would leap towards, but he seemed completely unmoved by her. He grabbed Kahara's shoulders and tried to turn her around again, but she wouldn't move.

"Turn around."

She laughed mischievously, twirling around quickly before he could grab a hold of her hips to pull her against him. He shrugged and pulled her close again for their third slow dance to a fast record.

"What do you do for a living?" she asked.

"Can't tell you—you're too mannish." he responded.

She laughed. *He has a good sense of humor,* she thought. *Even if he is mannish.*

He bent over and spoke softly into her ear. "I'm a computer analyst," he said.

A slight shiver ran down Kahara's spine as his lips brushed against her ear. They were dancing so close now that their perspiration was mixing, and she could feel his penis pressing against her. She wasn't sure if it was hard, big, or both. It felt wide and warm against her stomach. Although the titillation was amusing, she was becoming more and more embarrassed and concerned with what people around her might think of their intimate display on the dance floor. What if proper Gary had seen her? What would he think? She decided she'd had enough.

"Marshall." He continued holding her close ignoring her. "Marshall. Marshall Taylor!" she said, in a commanding tone. He immediately let go and dropped his hands to his side.

"Okay," he relinquished. And with that, he walked away. She stood in the middle of the dance floor and watched him as he made his way to the spot he was originally standing in when she first approached him. She shook her head and laughed to herself. More amused than embarrassed, she headed outside to get a cab.

Chapter 2

It was 3:00 a.m. when Kahara entered her hotel room. As she undressed, she laughed softly to herself, thinking how completely off-the-wall Marshall was compared to how staid and reserved Gary was. It was fun meeting two such completely different men in one night. As she sat on the toilet, she pushed back the bathroom door, which had a full-length mirror on the other side. She had never been able to watch herself use the bathroom, and found her reflection a little amusing.

As she looked at the curve in her full round hips, her thoughts wandered back to Marshall. She could tell his type—hungry—out just for sex. She was not about to be his next victim. Then she thought for a moment about the idea of sex itself. No holds barred, no strings attached, good unconditional sex. Not a bad idea—but not with him. He was too hungry, a bit too brash. But if she were to meet someone else, she wouldn't rule it out.

She put on her oversized Angela Davis t-shirt and climbed into bed. As she lay there she found herself becoming aroused as she thought back to the way Marshall danced with her—how close he held her—their sweat mingling—how tall and how supremely confident he seemed, how brazen and lascivious he was. Pulling her close—spinning her around—pressing up against her in the most intimate way. His hands everywhere—her face—her waist—her hips. Slowly tracing the satin material of her string-bikini panties, she slid her fingers beneath the material, gently rubbing her pubic hairs. Teasing her clitoris lightly with her middle finger, she began a slow, gentle stroke back and forth, back and forth, until she was unable to hold it in any longer. A gentle explosion, as she called out Marshall's name.

Kahara awoke early the next morning, too restless to sleep in. She pulled out her computer and continued to work on a feature-length version of the half-hour short she would film when she returned home. The screenplay told the story of a young couple trying to adjust to each other in the early stages of their relationship. Their love affair collapses however, under the weight of their intense arguments. Kahara drew from her own experiences while creating the script. Her seemingly calm exterior hid a hot temper that surprised and sometimes scared off the men in her life.

After years of working in the field of finance, she threw herself into film—the love of her life since high school. She went to Columbia College and took courses in screenwriting and digital film editing. She purchased the necessary equipment, including a DV camera and a computer editing system, then completed her first film. It was a short about a cold-hearted businessman who wakes up one day and discovers that he has become the homeless man he ignored every day on the way to work. She won an award for that film two years ago. But due to the demands of her job, she was not able to start production on her new film until recently.

After showering and changing, she decided to call Marshall, only to see if he had given her the right room number. She remembered after dialing his number that she was supposed to call Gary to have breakfast and do the interview, but she decided to call him after talking to Marshall. He answered the phone half asleep.

"Oh, I woke you up," she said regrettably.

"Naw, that's okay. I need to get up. What are you doing?"

"Getting ready to find a cheap place to eat."

"Why don't you come over and give me a good back rub?"

"Marshall, I am not going to give you a back rub."

"Then why don't you let me give you one? What's your room number?"

"1043," she said hesitantly, not sure if she should have surrendered that information. "Look, I gotta go. I just called to say hi."

"Alright, suit yourself," he said. "You don't know what you're missing."

She hung up and shook her head. "Mannish. Mannish!" Kahara couldn't help but smile at his brashness. About five minutes into her shower, the phone rang.

Kahara jumped out and answered it. "Hello?"

"Yeah, it's Marshall. Listen are you in a rush?"

"No, I was just in the shower. Why?"

"Why didn't you tell me, I could've come up and scrubbed your back."

"Scrub my back, then give me a massage, then what?" she asked.

"You're over twenty-one, you fill in the blanks. Listen," he said, "I was thinking we could go to breakfast together. I'll call you when I'm ready, and you can come down to my room."

"How about this. I'll meet you in the lobby instead." Kahara hung up the phone a few minutes later smiling. "Nice try Marshall," she said, heading back to the shower.

Twenty minutes later, Kahara stood in the lobby waiting. The elegance of the resort hotel impressed her. The spacious waiting area was graced with beautiful chandeliers, a set of plush, deep maroon-colored couches, separated by a cherry-wood coffee table. A marble staircase led to the mezzanine level, where the festival seminars took place. A consortium of black celebrities and black business owners purchased the Avenda over a decade ago, transforming the once-dilapidated beachfront resort into a four-star hotel. A sense of pride filled her as she watched the well-trained staff busily tending to their various duties.

While waiting, she spotted some young women in bikinis on their way to the pool. Kahara felt a little envious of their youth. They seemed so carefree and at ease, as though they didn't have a care in the world. She remembered back to a time when she felt that way. A time when an event like this would leave her feeling full of possibilities. But as forty loomed closer and closer, she felt as though she were being backed toward the edge of a cliff, and that if something didn't happen soon she would fall off. A few moments later, Marshall arrived and they set out to find a restaurant. They settled for a small outdoor cafe called The President. He let her pick the table.

"I'm going to sit next to you," he said, taking a seat next to her at the small table. She found this peculiar, but cozy. They ordered the same meal; pancakes, hash browns, scrambled eggs, and bacon. During the meal an older gentleman, a festival attendee from New York, struck up a conversation with them. The old man began to dominate the conversation, and Kahara noticed Marshall became quiet and a little sullen. She tried to draw him into their discussion, but he seemed unwilling. The man told her about an independent film company he started in Brooklyn. He and Kahara exchanged cards. Marshall lightened up after the older gentleman left. He told her about a friend of his that was starring in a women's prison film playing at the festival. She would be arriving on Thursday with some friends. Kahara found herself feeling a little jealous without knowing why. After the meal she sat back, stuffed from all the food she had just eaten.

"I love going to breakfast and having men spend all their money on me," she said cheerfully. She looked over at him, his expression a little glum. Marshall motioned for the waiter. "What's the matter?" she said. " I was just joking. I can pay my own way if that's a problem."

"No, I have it."

"I don't need you to pay for me," she said. "I don't need a man to do anything for me. I don't need a man period," she said smiling.

"Who are you kidding?" he quipped as the waiter walked up. "Look, I'll have another cup of coffee and the check please," he said to the waiter.

Marshall's statement caught Kahara off guard and left her feeling a little insulted. "You know these assessments you keep making about me are getting a little irritating."

"What assessment—what are you talking about?" he asked, looking confused.

"The one just now, and the one you made last night about me not knowing anyone."

"Do you know someone here?"

"No, but that's not the point—*you* don't know that."

"Alright," he said calmly.

"So you can't jump to any conclusions about me."

"That's right." he nodded.

"You need to get to know me first," she said with finality, sitting back in her seat and folding her arms.

"Ok," he said, pausing. "I'ma get to know you real well before the weekend's out."

"No you're not," she said sternly.

He sighed. "Yeah, this is pretty much wrapped up. I can always tell." He looked her directly in the eye. "You're hungry."

"Listen, I don't like your attitude," she said, frowning as the waiter walked up.

Marshall ignored her, counted out his money, and paid the waiter.

"Look, you know something," she said, "you're arrogant as hell—don't flatter yourself."

"Ok, I won't," he said. The waiter left, smiling to himself. "I'd give it to Friday," he said, under his breath.

"You're about to get slapped."

"If I was wrong you wouldn't get so mad," he said, taking a sip of his coffee.

"We better change the subject before you get hurt. What's the name of the movie you were talking about seeing?"

"Gaming. Yeah listen, we better get going if we're going to catch any of the films."

Kahara decided to pay her own tab. She was hoping to be treated, but she didn't want him to get the idea that he was paying for future sex.

"Here," she said, handing him a $10 bill. "That should cover my meal."

"What are you doing? I said I'd treat," he said.

"Yeah, but after the conversation we just had I think I better."

"It's really not necessary."

"No, I insist."

They left the restaurant and started walking toward the theatre, which was about five blocks away.

"So what brought you to the fest?" he asked.

"I'll be filming my second short soon," she said.

Marshall nodded, saying nothing.

"There are also a couple of seminars I want to attend," she said, noting that he, unlike Gary, did not ask her to elaborate on her film.

Marshall stopped short. "Let's go back to the hotel," he said abruptly.

"What?"

"Afternoon lovemaking—it's the best kind," he said, pulling her close.

"I'm not having sex with you," she said, pulling away.

"Ok," he said, letting go of her.

He looked ahead as they continued walking, saying nothing.

"So what do you do for a living again? Do you work, or do you just go around sniffing for women?"

Marshall gazed over at her and shook his head. "Just had to get that one in didn't ya," he said calmly. "I work as a consultant. I design and install computer systems."

"You work for a consulting company or are you on your own?" she asked.

"I'm independent."

"What's your rate?"

"I usually bill out between sixty to eighty dollars an hour."

"Really," she said. "So you're on your own. Don't you ever get nervous about where your money's coming from?"

"Don't you?"

"No, I work for a corporation."

"Yeah, but you can be laid off," he said.

"Yeah, that's true, but there's less certainty in what you're doing." Kahara, being a frugal financial analyst, had set up a portfolio for herself years ago. She had a substantial retirement account, and enough extra money saved up to live without working for at least five years. Yet she was still afraid of branching out on her own. "The idea of floating like that scares me," she said.

"Learn to fly baby. Learn to fly."

"Someday," she said, looking off thinking. "Say, guess who I met at the set last night?"

"That asshole Derrick Johnson?"

"How did you know?" she asked.

"He was the only real star there."

She walked in front of him and stopped. "Okay, look, you be me and I'll be him." Marshall looked a little startled. "Now say 'Aren't you Derrick Johnson?' then reach out to shake my hand. Go ahead. Go ahead."

He hesitated for a moment. "Aren't you Derrick Johnson," he repeated slowly, reaching out his hand.

Kahara took his hand. "Yes," she returned nonchalantly, giving him a limp handshake before turning her back to him.

Marshall looked a little stunned. "He did that to you?"

"Yesssss. I mean he physically turned his body completely away from me. Like I—I didn't exist. Like I wasn't even there. I didn't have to speak to him. I was being polite, because to be honest, I really don't care for his work. I just figured I'd give him some props since hardly anyone else seemed to be paying any attention to him. That character he plays on that cop drama is dead on point. He's not acting—that's who he really is. That asshole. 'Hi, I'm Derrick Johnson, and I don't have time to talk to unimportant people, so please don't approach me. If you do I'll just ignore you.'"

"I met him two years ago at a festival in L.A. He was sitting at a table with some people. I asked him if he would take a picture with me." Marshall said.

"Did he do it?" she asked.

"Are you kidding? He said 'Well, if I take a picture with you, everybody in here will want to take a picture with me.' I said okay. Then as I was walking away I said 'beeeyotch!' He stood up and said 'What did you say?' I just kept walking."

"I can't believe you called him that!" she said, grabbing his arm. His arms were huge and firm. Kahara let her hand linger on his arm for a moment before letting go. As they continued walking, the idea he planted in her mind about afternoon sex began to sink in. She imagined what it would be like to have sex with him—having that big, tall, country mass weighing down on top of her. Her legs went a little weak just thinking about it. She liked him in spite of his arrogance. In fact, it made him more appealing. Kahara thought back to the amusing image of him waving his arms up in the air like a Rap artist as they had danced the night before, and juxtaposed that against how at ease and serene he seemed now.

"You're different," she said, as they continued walking. "I'd never guess you'd be into Rap. You're like a mixture of corporate and Hip Hop."

He looked ahead saying nothing. He put his hand up in the air and started flipping it the way he did the night before, reciting suggestive lyrics. He looked over at Kahara. She blushed. They reached the theatre about twenty minutes later. As they stood in line, Kahara looked around and noticed most of the women were there without men. Having taken his company for granted up until now, she began feeling a little privileged to have a man with her. Marshall found seats in a secluded section of the balcony. The movie began with a heated sex scene. A man was vigorously humping a woman in a number of different positions.

"Oooh that's a good one," Marshall said, as he watched the man hold the woman's leg high up in the air as he thrust into her. The woman reached behind her head, and held onto the bedpost as the man pushed her leg farther and farther back, pumping furiously. "Humph, he's getting all in her shit," Marshall said, easing his large hand between Kahara's thighs, squeezing gently. Kahara jumped a little, startled by his forwardness, but raised no objection. He continued squeezing her thigh, his fingers inadvertently pressing against her vaginal lips each time he caressed her. He stopped, after a moment but did not remove his hand. She let it stay there between her legs without saying a word, as they continued watching the movie. He looked over at her and she looked down, blushing. A woman came in their row, crossing in front, taking a seat next to Kahara. Marshall removed his hand. Kahara, feeling a little angry, looked over at the woman, whose expression registered embarrassment, apparently realizing what she had just interrupted. She stared ahead, not looking at Kahara, who would periodically glare at her. Marshall nudged Kahara.

"Stop that," he said softly.

Kahara sat back, still mad at the woman, but realizing things were heating up a bit too much. About ten minutes before the end of the movie, Kahara realized she might be late for the "Pitching to Cable" seminar that was being held back at the hotel in less than a half-hour. She stood up abruptly.

"I've got to go," she said. "I don't want to miss the Cable seminar." Marshall nodded, looking visibly disappointed. Kahara left a moment later.

Kahara felt bad for leaving so hastily, and while she enjoyed Marshall's company, she felt she'd paid too much money to miss one of the main seminars she came to the festival for. As she walked hurriedly back to the hotel, she smiled, thinking back to their interlude. She wasn't sure why she didn't remove his hand from between her thighs. Then again, she knew exactly why. She didn't want to. It had been over a year since she'd had sex, or had even been touched by a man in an intimate manner. His large hand felt good between her thighs. He was awakening a lust in her that until that day had remained dormant. The realization that her actions probably made her seem risqué, especially after the speech she'd made about not having sex with him, didn't seem to register. She was too drunk with the feeling to pay attention to the inconsistencies of her behavior.

Her mind flashed to what might have happened had she been wearing a skirt instead of jeans. The fantasy left her feeling extremely aroused but with no one to act it out on. Her fortress was slowly being peeled away.

Back at the hotel, she freshened up and headed downstairs to the seminar. As she stepped off the elevator, she remembered that she was supposed to have breakfast with Gary. He was standing outside the seminar room when she arrived.

"Hi Gary," she said apologetically. She felt guilty for running off with Marshall instead of calling him as she said she would.

"Stood me up, huh?" he said.

"No, no, no, I'm sorry. I got wrapped up—got in late last night. My whole day just got thrown off. How about after the seminar?"

"Sounds good. I'll meet you out here."

Kahara felt guilty for standing Gary up, but she didn't regret running off with Marshall, especially when she thought about their little adventure inside the theatre. She walked in and took her seat in the front row and pulled out her camera and her tripod and taped portions of the seminar.

During her screening two years ago, Kahara had befriended a newspaper reporter named Craig Adams. He wrote a favorable article about her film in the *Los Angeles Central* newspaper. He and his business partners were owners of the local cable station, KBTN, in Los Angeles. Kahara promised him footage and interviews from the festival.

After the seminar, she edged up to the panelists' table. One of the speakers, who Kahara thought favored Bob Marley, was accepting cards from various people. Kahara succeeded in getting him to agree to an interview. He gave her his card, which contained the number to the cable station where he worked. He instructed her to call the station, explain her project and see if they would grant him clearance to do the interview. None of the other panelists were available, but Kahara floated outside, happy she had scored at least one interview.

She had again completely forgotten about Gary, who was waiting patiently outside with another gentleman.

Gary introduced her to his business associate, Phil Rodgers. Phil was about a foot shorter than Gary, medium build, and rather rugged looking. Kahara suggested they do the interview in the area outside the conference room where the panel discussion had been held. Kahara set up her tripod and mounted the camera, but the lighting was inadequate.

"Why don't you try adjusting the exposure?" Gary asked. "Here, let me show you." He walked over.

Although Kahara's focus at Columbia had been on writing, directing and editing, she knew how to adjust the exposure, but she coyly decided to let Gary show her anyway. She stepped aside and watched as he took control of her equipment. He had an assuredness about himself that impressed her.

"Come over here. I want to show you something," he said, motioning to her. She walked over obediently. He moved over, placed her hand on the camera, and stood behind her.

"This is how you adjust the exposure and the aperture," he said, leaning his tall body over hers, moving her fingers over the mechanism. This was the closest he had ever come to her. He had been so careful the night before not to get too close. He was as tall, if not taller than, Marshall, but rail-thin. "You press here," he said, as he adjusted the exposure. The light was still not adequate so she suggested they do the interview in her room, since she had another light there. Kahara felt a little wary about inviting two men she didn't know into her hotel room, but decided to chance it. She had gone with her instincts so far and had been okay. Once inside, Gary helped her set up the special light she had brought with her.

"I want to show you a trick for bouncing light when you don't have a lot of room. Come over here for a second," he said.

She walked over, and he let her take control of the light, as he stood close behind her. *Never too far,* she thought, smiling to herself. *Is this man flirting with me or what?*

"See, if you move it over here and bounce it off the corner, you can get just the amount you need. He put his hand over hers and helped her cock the light down at a sharper angle. Kahara studied his face for a moment, still trying to figure him out. Gary, as though sensing he might be too close, moved away from her slightly. Kahara did her introductory speech, then let Gary introduce himself.

"Hi I'm Gary Mount, director of Camera Ready Productions, located in Norfolk, Virginia. We've been around for about six years now. I previously worked for a Fortune 500 company as a systems analyst for eight years right out of college. I decided I wanted to work with the creative side of my brain instead of the technical side—haven't looked back since. And this gentleman here," he said, motioning to Phil. "This is my production assistant, help in the time of need, etcetera and so on, Mr. Phil Rodgers. He helps me with a lot of different projects—especially on location—organizing, getting the crew together whenever we have gigantic shoots. He's my second AD on all shoots."

Gary paused to let Phil interject. "For the laymen out there, an AD is assistant director of photography. I've been working with Gary now for about three years. I've known him since college. We both went to Hampton. I'm a photographer. I've been freelancing now for about five years."

"So what are your ultimate goals? Phil, we'll start with you."

"Well, like I said, I have my own photography business. Gary and I often exchange clients. My goal is to continue to grow my business and expand my studio."

"Gary?"

"Well, my ultimate goal is to own a production company."

"You already have one," Kahara said.

"No, I'm talking about on the level of a Steven Spielberg Dreamworks. I want to be able to green light and produce major motion pictures."

Kahara was impressed. *Very ambitious,* she thought. "So what was your motivation for coming to the festival?"

"I've always understood that when you come to festivals you meet people from all over the country. I understand there are other significant film festivals such as Sundance and others, but I wanted to attend one that was focused on black cinema. That's my interest," he finished.

His voice carried an air of conviction that Kahara found appealing. He had an unwavering poise and coolness that made him very attractive. She was seeing a flavor of black men at the festival she'd not seen before. These black men had an edge to them that even successful black businessmen she'd met in Chicago didn't have. Gary, Marshall, and even the old man she and Marshall met at the restaurant. Their entrepreneurial status gave them an air of mastery. They seemed, even in a bad economic climate, to have clear control of their destinies. She found this inspiring.

While Gary dismantled the special light from its stand, Kahara dialed the phone number panelist Gil Davis had given her, and left a message asking permission to do the interview. They left shortly after that.

"So, where you headed?" Gary asked as they stood outside the hotel.

"I was going to go to the Caribbean Café. The attendant said it was to the left of the hotel."

"It's on the next block," Gary said. "Sounds like a plan. You game man?" he said, looking over at his partner.

"Yeah, that sounds good," Phil said.

On the way there, the group ran into Shelia, an old friend of Phil's. She decided to join them for dinner. Kahara felt good walking to the café with her newfound friends. It felt good having people to eat with, especially since she had been alone most of the time since her arrival, save for the time she spent with Marshall. As they walked to the café, she began to wonder where Marshall was, and if she would see him later, craving those large hands.

The outdoor café had several inviting patio tables randomly spaced, just beyond the pickup window. They purchased their meals and began eating. Kahara struck up a conversation with Shelia. She told her a little about the screenwriter's seminar she attended. Kahara was going to take the course, but the 8:30 a.m. start time for the class would have put a serious crimp in her late-night partying, not to mention the additional $250. After not being asked to dance the entire night at the party the previous evening, she began to regret her decision not to take the course.

Gary got up. "Listen, I'm gonna get another drink. You all want anything?"

"Yeah, I'd like another mango frost please," Kahara said. She leaned forward to Phil as Gary got up to leave. "So Phil, give us the skinny on Gary. You mentioned you both went to Hampton. What was he like in college?"

Phil leaned back. "What was he like?"

"Did he have a stable?" Kahara asked, smiling as Gary looked back at them.

"Stable? Oh, you mean of women." Kahara nodded. "Ah man, you gonna put me on the spot," Phil said. "This brother," he said, exchanging glances with Gary as he stood in line. "Well, you know he had that height thing going. He was always skinny, but tall. And he was so laid back you know, so they'd come after him thinking he was shy. That brotha's not shy—just reserved." Gary returned and handed Kahara her drink and sat down. "They would come up to me and say, 'Introduce me to your friend with the big sad eyes.' All he had to do was look at 'em, boy, and they'd melt."

Kahara looked over at Gary and took the tip of his chin in her hand. "Yeah, he does have some pretty sad eyes," she said, smiling.

"And he played that to his advantage, trust me."

"Okay, let's move past college to today," Kahara said.

"Ah, he's a cold-hearted businessman today. I gotta admit, in college this brother played the field tough. He ain't got that kinda time now. Too busy collecting clients."

"Ambitious entrepreneur," Kahara said, shoving Gary's shoulder leaning back in her seat.

"Anybody ever told you you talk too much?" Gary said, cutting Phil a mean stare.

"She asked Man. She asked."

"I think that's good that he's devoted to his work," Shelia said. "It shows determination."

"I do get complaints," Gary admitted. "I've had more than one woman complain about my work."

"And what do you do when that happens?" Kahara asked.

"I gotta have people in my life who understand what I do. Most people wake up knowing where their money's coming from. I have to go *to* mine."

"So the women get left behind," Kahara said.

"No." Gary looked uncomfortable. "Some may have viewed it that way. But if there's an opportunity—I have to chase it. If she can't get with that program—there'll be friction."

"I guess that's fair," Kahara said, shrugging.

"Let's get off this subject for a minute," Gary said. "I want to show ya'll something." He reached into his festival bag and pulled out a folder. He opened it and produced a five-by-seven shot of him and Lisa Fayson, the actress.

"Wow," Kahara said, feeling a little jealous, observing the big grin on his face in the picture. "When did you take this?"

"Today at the hotel," he said beaming. "There was a photographer there who snapped it for us. I was surprised at how approachable she was."

"Yeah, that's exactly how you look. Surprised," Kahara said. She looked over the picture. Lisa Fayson was dressed elegantly, her fashionable red dress hugging her tiny figure. Kahara's clothes never seemed to fit her quite right. Even her very best garments seemed to be either too loose in the waist or shoulders. She always found herself readjusting her clothes so they would hang right. She passed the picture slowly on to the others with a slightly defeated look on her face.

"Yeah, that grin is spread pretty wide," Shelia said.

"I'm framing this when I get home," he said. "I hope she shows up at the party tonight. Who knows, maybe she'll give a brother some play."

"You'd just be another notch on her belt," Kahara snapped.

"I'm more than happy to be her notch."

"Seems a little shallow to me," Kahara quipped, resting her chin in her hand, looking away.

Gary looked at her. "Listen, the most she'd probably do with me is have fun for one night, then move on. I'm not playing myself down, but I'm a realist."

"But if she came at you, you'd go for it."

"Damn right I would! Wouldn't you? If Derrick Johnson came up to you—"

"HELL no!" she said, cutting him off. She leaned forward to Shelia. "Do you know what he did to me?"

"What?" she asked.

"Okay, pretend you're me. Wait, wait, wait. Get up. Stand up. Stand up. Come on," Kahara commanded, rising from her seat. The woman got up slowly, looking over at Phil as though uncertain what was coming next. "Now pretend you're me, and I'm Derrick Johnson. Walk up to me, extend your hand and say, 'Aren't you Derrick Johnson?' Go ahead, do it. Do it."

The woman did as Kahara asked. Kahara repeated exactly what she did for Marshall, giving the woman a limp handshake before turning her back to her.

"He did that to you?" Shelia asked.

"Yesssssssss," she said, looking over at Gary, as though for reassurance. "It was like I didn't exist. Like I wasn't even there. That self-important asshole." She plopped back down in her seat folding her arms.

Gary looked at her. "Did you sleep with him?"

"Hell no," Kahara scoffed. The mere idea of that turned her stomach.

"I could see if you slept with him and he did that to you," Gary said.

"You seem really upset about it," Shelia interjected.

"It doesn't bother me. Really. I just don't—you don't treat people that way. You don't just ignore people like they're not there. I didn't have to walk up to him. I could have kept going."

"You probably should have, then you wouldn't be so bent out of shape about it now," Gary said.

"I'll file that away for future reference," Kahara said. "Don't worry, it won't happen again."

They finished their meals and got ready to head to the comedy show, which was being sponsored by the festival. The show was located less than a block away from the café, so Kahara brought her mango frost drink with her. They walked up to the entrance and were greeted by a tall man who looked like a weight-lifter.

"She can't come in with that," he said sternly.

Kahara continued sipping her drink. "You all go ahead. I'ma go back to the hotel," she said.

"You sure? We can wait while you finish," Gary said

"Thanks, but no. I'm fine."

Gary and the others continued inside as Kahara headed back to the hotel. The idea of sitting through a two-hour comedy show didn't appeal to her. She was more interested in the party after the show. Kahara felt a slight sense of regret being separated from Gary, but in a way, she didn't mind. With Marshall, things were pretty black and white, but Gary was harder to read. She liked him, but sensed only a slight interest on his part; an interest she felt was mainly fueled by the prospect of her being a potential client. And while Gary was fun, Marshall was fun in a different way. She was hoping she'd run into Marshall later that evening, still hungry for those large hands.

Chapter 3

After returning to the hotel and showering, she gave Marshall a call but got no answer. She watched a little TV, then returned to the arena for the last portion of the comedy show. As she sat there, she saw Marshall leave, but he didn't see her. She figured he was probably returning to the hotel for a bit before the party, as she had done.

Her first impulse was to follow him. But she checked herself, not wanting to seem too anxious. If they were meant to be together, he'd find her. After a while, she became bored and walked to the rear of the club. In the back was an exquisite amber-lit fountain, surrounded by a coral-green brick seating area. Kahara took a seat in front of the fountain. A few moments later, an attractive woman dressed in a long cream-colored sequined gown walked up and stood in front of her. She stood so close to her that her gown was touching Kahara's knee. Kahara shifted her body slightly to the left in order to get out of the way, but the woman moved over with her. Kahara breathed in hard. The least the woman could do was say excuse me. Kahara started to say something, but decided to bite her tongue. The woman turned around after a moment and looked back at her, as though expecting her to move.

"Excuse me," the woman said.

"Finally," Kahara returned a little testily, not moving.

A photographer and four other people walked up to the woman. The woman looked back at Kahara again.

"Look, we're going to need this space. I want to take a picture in front of the fountain. Can you please move?" she commanded.

Something in her manner irritated Kahara. That entitled tone.

"Yeah sure, no problem, go ahead," Kahara quipped. She moved over an inch. The woman looked at the group and then shook her head in disgust. The photographer adjusted the settings on his camera, snapped the picture, and the group left.

Kahara smoothed her hands over her thighs and looked around. She resented all the so-called 'important' people at the festival who had entourages with them. She didn't mind being alone when she was back in Chicago, but there was something very isolating about being alone there. It made her feel more like a misfit, and the little run-in she had with the woman didn't help. Angry with herself for letting Gary buy her that mango drink, she now regretted the fact that she was not with him, enjoying herself. The social side of her wanted to be with Gary and the others, but the carnal side wanted to be with Marshall.

Bored and a little restless, she walked up to the second level. The upstairs wrapped around the club in a semi-circle, and the area was sprinkled with small tables and chairs. People were seated or standing by the railing, overlooking the level below. She hiked up to the third level but still didn't see anyone she knew. No Gary. No Marshall. No one. Kahara suddenly felt very isolated and very alone. It was now that she wished she'd stayed with the original group, instead of separating herself from them in hopes of running into Marshall. Everyone else there seemed to know someone—seemed to be connected.

The moderator announced the last comedian. Kahara hurried down to the first level, and walked over to the bar and stood. As she looked around at the thinning crowd, a man walked up beside her without her knowing it. She turned, and there standing next to her, was Marshall. Kahara's face registered her surprise and delight at seeing him. They both surveyed the crowd.

"This looks like it's going to be a dull party," she said.

Marshall leaned over and mumbled something suggestive in her ear. Kahara blushed.

"Let's leave and go back to the hotel," he said.

Kahara smiled saying nothing.

He leaned closer to her and spoke softly. "You know that's where we're going to wind up anyway. Why you fightin' it? You need it to happen."

Kahara bristled as he continued.

"That's why you didn't move my hand when I put it between your legs earlier. You're ready lady, just admit it."

She scowled at him. "Look, lower your voice. I don't like other people hearing my business." His statement made her angry. How did he know what she needed? What really annoyed her though, was that he could see through her motives better than she could. She felt incriminated for having let him put his hand between her legs. But he was caressing her inner thigh, not her genitals. She began to wonder what she would have done if he had caressed more than her thigh. Probably nothing, especially if the lady hadn't sat next to her and interrupted them. He was right. She did need it. She needed his hands on her—had been craving it all day. She didn't realize just how much until now. Her actions had told him what her words didn't. That was why she isolated herself from Gary and the others. She wanted to make sure nothing spoiled the possibility of them "bumping" into each other. She needed it all right, and she marked him as the one to give it to her. But he wouldn't get it tonight—not all of it. They stood and talked for a few minutes. The dance floor was empty.

"You want to start this off?" He asked, looking over at her.

"Yeah, why not," she said.

They both approached the floor. He seemed more subdued that evening.

"What happened to dirty south?" she asked.

He shrugged, his eyes twinkling a little as he began dancing. Back was the mischievous leering smile. He turned around and backed into her.

Now this is the Marshall I was waiting for, she thought. She began rubbing his massive back with her hands caressing the sides of his broad shoulders. He turned around and held her body close to his, beginning his unique slow dance to a fast record. He caressed her face in his hands and held it against his.

She smiled, delighting in all of it. "What are you doing?" she asked.

"I just want to feel you close to me."

Grabbing her by her upper waist, he let his hands slip down to the exposed skin between her tank top and her jeans. He squeezed her waist, lifting her two feet off the ground with his large hands and let go of her suddenly. Kahara's body jolted as it hit the dance floor. She smiled, imagining him lifting her up in the air that way while making love. Marshall looked down at her. "This DJ doesn't know what he's doing. Let's go."

"Not yet," she said.

Marshall sighed and continued to dance. Kahara knew he wanted to leave, but she was enjoying the control she had over him. His friend Raymond came on the dance floor a few minutes later with a partner. Raymond, as though noticing how far apart Kahara was dancing from Marshall, took her arm and moved her closer to Marshall. Marshall grabbed her and held her close. His dancing was so intimate. There was something decidedly sensual—sexual, about the way he held her—the way he moved his body. She couldn't help but wonder what he must move like in bed. As her thoughts drifted to that image, she found herself becoming more and more aroused. He held her close, squeezing her back as he pressed his body against hers, over and over. She placed her hands gently around his neck and traced down his body, squeezing his shoulders, rubbing his arms, and caressing his large biceps. His hands rubbed down the sides of her hips and thighs before sliding up over her ample buttocks giving it one long squeeze. Kahara went weak as he pressed his groin against her. His penis felt full and firm. She swallowed. "That's a lot," she said. He looked down at her and smiled. "It gets better." He continued rubbing against her as they swayed in rhythm to the music. Kahara's head was spinning, she was so aroused.

I'm not having sex with him tonight, she thought. *Tomorrow, but not tonight.*

They continued their sensual embraces. Kahara broke out of her trance momentarily, looked around at the other couples, and wondered how many other people came together like this. She was hoping Gary had left, and hadn't seen the way she was dancing with Marshall. He seemed so straight-laced he might not approve. Marshall turned around and backed into her again. His back was sweaty. She rubbed her hands all over it again, stopping to caress his shoulders. As she moved closer to him, she pressed her breasts against his back. He reached back, grabbed her hands and pulled them around his waist. Kahara had had enough of dancing.

"You ready?" she said.

He leaned over and said something in Raymond's ear and they left.

The night air was still warm, but not nearly as humid as the previous evening. A slight breeze was blowing. As they came into the lobby, Kahara smiled as the cool breeze hit her face, making it tingle. It felt so nice returning *with* someone. They got on the elevator, she punched 10 and then looked at him. He looked at her and smiled, not making a move to press his floor.

When they got in her room, she noticed the message light blinking. She went out on the terrace and Marshall joined her. She sat in the chair and looked out over the beach. The moon was gleaming over the pitch-black water.

"Rub me here," she said, squeezing the area behind her neck. He began massaging her, gripping her neck and shoulders with his large hands. "Harder," she said. "Squeeze harder."

He continued rubbing her stiff neck. Kahara relaxed, feeling the warm breeze blowing against her.

"Get up," he said, motioning to her. He walked back inside the room. Kahara reluctantly followed.

"What are you doing?"

"Come here," he said softly through the darkness.

He motioned to the bed. "Lie on your back."

"I'm not laying on my back so you can get on top of me."

"I'm not going to do anything to you," he said, his face taking an "are you kidding" kind of expression.

She lay down apprehensively. He removed her sandals and began massaging her feet. After a moment, he eased his body on top of hers.

"Get up off of me Marshall, you said you wouldn't."

He rolled over on his back, unbuttoned his shirt, and cupped his hands behind his head. Kahara leaned over and kissed him. His lips were full and firm.

"Lie on your stomach," he said.

She did as he asked. He sat lightly on her butt and began massaging the back of her shoulders. Marshall pulled up her top and began unhooking her bra. Kahara thought back to his hand between her legs at the theatre. She didn't try to stop him then, and she didn't try to stop him now. He had little trouble getting it undone. Kahara lay there motionless, anticipating his next move. He began tracing the outer part of her body lightly with his fingers—her arms, her shoulders, then her waist. A chill ran up her spine. Kahara rolled over on her side as he began kissing and sucking her breasts. She let out a long sigh. It felt so good to be touched by a man, especially such a big man.

"You're sensitive there, aren't you?" he asked, stroking her nipples lightly with his fingers.

"Yeah, my nipples especially," she said blushing.

He lay on his back after a few minutes, and Kahara began kissing him on his chest. She licked and circled his nipple with her tongue until it became erect.

He rubbed her head gently. "You can touch my penis if you like," he volunteered.

She placed her hands over his trousers and squeezed it. "It's hard as a brick."

"Yeah," he sighed, unzipping his pants.

She didn't want to get that intimate that night, but decided to go with the feeling. She eased his thick penis out from his briefs and held it in her hand. The skin was soft and warm.

"It feels like calves' leather," she said. He smiled as she stroked it. "Is this how you like it done?" she asked. "It's so thick it's hard to maneuver."

"You're doin' fine," he said. He began to moan after a few minutes. "It's coming," he said.

"That's okay baby, let it shoot. Let it shoot out all over my hand."

He continued moaning as she worked it. "Ooh, there it is," he said, lifting his torso up a little as he climaxed. The white liquid spurted out the tip of his penis, spreading warmth all over her hand. Kahara went to the bathroom a moment later and returned with a warm cloth and gently wiped the semen from his penis and his pubic hairs. A few minutes later, he zipped up his pants and fastened his belt buckle. He got up slowly, looking a little embarrassed, and began buttoning his shirt. When he got to the door, he pulled her in his large arms for a hug. "Talk to you tomorrow," he said softly.

She watched him as he walked down the hall toward the elevator.

That's not all you're going to do to me, she thought, smiling to herself as she closed the door.

She checked her messages. One was from her friend Sergio in Chicago, and the other was from Gil Davis' assistant. Gil was the Bob Marley look-alike Kahara had tried to secure an interview with earlier that day. The woman left Gil's cell phone number and said the interview had been okayed. Kahara smiled at hearing the news.

Kahara walked over to the dresser a moment later, then opened the drawer containing the lace teddy. It was her favorite, and part of an expensive collection of nightgowns. When she originally purchased them, she vowed only to wear them on a special occasion, with a special man. That was four years ago.

As she neared her fortieth birthday, it began to dawn on her that maybe that special occasion would never come. Perhaps she had missed her chance, and was past the point of being able to establish a meaningful relationship. Maybe a sexual interlude would be the most special occasion she'd ever have. She felt most men her age wanted younger women, and younger men only wanted to have flings. What was so wrong with wearing a lace teddy for a fling? As she took off her clothes and slipped on the teddy, she thought about Marshall. How tight he held her that night on the dance floor—his hands all over her—the way he brazenly squeezed her ass and how skillfully he teased her in bed. Kahara stepped in front of the full-length mirror, and viewed her image. She wondered what Marshall's reaction would be if he saw her in the sexy gown. Then, she thought back to her friend Sergio's comments about how gorgeous Jasmine was. Jasmine was the stunning 23-year-old lead actress in the short film Kahara was shooting when she returned to Chicago. As Kahara looked in the mirror, she wondered what it must be like to be that beautiful and sought-after. After a moment, she removed the gown, donned her Angela Davis t-shirt, and climbed into bed.

Chapter 4

She slept well that night, but woke up feeling a little depressed without knowing why. She phoned Gil and left him a message to call her back, then browsed the festival schedule and marked a few movies she wanted to see that day. The idea of going to the movies alone didn't bother her before yesterday. But after spending all morning and part of the afternoon with Marshall the day before, the idea of going to the movie alone left her feeling a little lost.

She went to the bathroom, showered, dried herself off and looked at her naked body in the mirror. "You're going to finish what you started," she said, thinking back to her rendezvous with Marshall the night before. She smiled, thinking about the possibilities. Kahara was determined to see Marshall that day, and wasn't going to leave it to chance. Marshall was so nonchalant about things. Here it was ten o'clock, and she hadn't heard from him. She called, got no answer and decided against leaving a message. "No, no, I'm not going to do this," she said to herself. "If he wants me he can come after me. I'm not going to beg a man to have sex with me."

Kahara took her camcorder with her and went to the diner where she, Gary, and the others had eaten the evening before. She spotted two men wearing festival badges having breakfast. She always felt uncomfortable approaching very attractive men, feeling they would think she was out of her league. While she didn't think of herself as ugly, she knew she wasn't drop-dead-gorgeous either—the kind of woman these two were probably used to.

She introduced herself to them and began conversing. Both were from New York, one an actor, the other a comedian. After a few moments, the comedian left. The actor remained at the table with her. He was about six feet tall, chestnut-brown, medium build with large brown eyes. He agreed to an interview. Kahara began with basic questions, but after a while began to probe deeper. She wanted to see what lay beneath that cool façade.

"Is all this a front? Or do you really have balls strong enough to make it in this industry?"

He looked a little startled. "Oh no doubt, no doubt," he said, shifting in his seat. "I've got talent. I mean, it's not a question of that. Everyone who's anyone out there knows it, and those that don't—don't matter."

"Oh really," she said, laughing a little from behind the camera.

"Really," he said, his expression serious.

Kahara admired his confidence, especially working in an industry that had such little regard for black actors.

"I'm trying out for a part in a film next month called *The Missing Day*," he said.

"Good luck getting the part."

"It's not about luck, but thanks."

"You're a cocky SOB. You know that?" Kahara said.

He smiled nodding slowly. "I've been told that before."

She wrapped up the interview, ate, then returned to her room with her sandwich. After eating and watching TV, she called Gil and left another message. She called Marshall again, but got no answer. She still did not leave a message, because she didn't want his roommate to get the idea she was chasing him, even though at this point she was. Deciding that if he was anywhere he'd be at the Cineplex, she decided to go check out one of the movies she had marked on her schedule.

Marshall had mentioned wanting to see *Chains* the night before, but that film was sold out when Kahara got to the theatre. She tried using her feminine wiles to get the attendant to let her in, but he stood guard in front of the theatre entrance like a sentry. Kahara stood on her toes and peeked inside as he talked to other disappointed patrons. Marshall was in there—she could feel it. Forced to settle for another movie, she sat begrudgingly by herself in the cold theatre, thinking back to how much more fun it would be if she were there with Marshall. A melancholy feeling swept over her as she thought about what she'd be returning to once she left Virginia.

Chicago was a big city, but with few venues in which older black professionals could meet. Sure there were the clubs, but she had long since outgrown them. The truth was, she didn't know how to meet men. She tried going to different events, but they were usually crowded with single females like herself, couples, but few, if any, desirable men. Why couldn't she meet a Marshall in Chicago? That question left her feeling depressed. As she sat there with arms folded, a pensive look etched over her face. The film she was watching was not registering.

After the movie, she walked slowly back to the hotel, wishing—hoping she would run into Marshall. When she got back to her room, she checked to see if there were any messages from Gil or Marshall. Nothing. She called Marshall, but again got no answer. Still too scared to leave a message, she hung up. As she thought more and more about how bleak her prospects were at home, she became more and more depressed.

She left her room a half-hour later to attend a seminar entitled "The Next Stage." The write-up on this workshop boasted that it would cover every aspect of movie-making from A to Z. This workshop, as well as the seminar the day before, were the main reasons Kahara had attended the conference. Taking a seat in the front row as she had done the day before, Kahara sat with her tripod and camera, feeling drained and a little sad. Why would not running into Marshall cause her to feel this way? She hadn't felt like this prior to meeting him. If she did, she managed to hide it from herself better than she was doing now. Finally mounting the camcorder on the tripod, she filmed the panel for about five minutes and then stopped.

After the seminar, she did a few interviews, realizing that she had to show Craig something, since she'd promised him footage. She went through the motions, filming five different festival attendees, pumping them up by feigning enthusiasm in order to get good responses, but her heart wasn't in it. Her spirit felt drained as she slowly made her way to the elevator to return to her room. When she left for the seminar, it was five o'clock. Why hadn't Marshall tried to contact her by now—or searched her out the way she did him? Why was it always she that had to do all the work—all the coordinating, all the planning? Why didn't the men in her life ever go out of their way or make more of an effort to hunt her down and get with her?

Kahara got on the elevator with two men, and listened as one spoke of his 9/11 experiences. He recounted how he woke up anxious to get to work for an important meeting, only to be made late by a tardy friend. That tardy friend saved his life. He got there just as the plane flew into the first building. From that moment on, he vowed to stop feeling sorry for himself. Kahara's eyes grew wide as she listened. She felt like a deflated balloon being slowly filled up with helium.

As she headed toward her room, she felt a new resolve. Once inside, she picked up the phone and dialed Marshall's number. "Marshall this is Kahara. I'm going to see the Anthony Harris documentary, and I thought that maybe after the movie we could hook up. Give me a call."

A sense of relief passed over her as she hung up, no longer ashamed or worried, if Marshall's roommate thought she was chasing him. She was going after what she wanted. Her head erect, her shoulders back, she felt a sense of calm as she walked to the theatre. She still had no solutions to her dating problems, but at the moment, that didn't matter. She was determined to enjoy herself.

Chapter 5

Anthony Harris was a famous actor turned director, who was teaching an actors' workshop at the fest. Kahara felt a little nervous approaching him, but was pleased when he agreed to do an interview the next day. She agreed to meet him after class at 11:30 a.m. Jubilant over her success, she floated to the ladies room. On her way there, she passed by Lisa Fayson who was standing in the lobby talking to a few people. Kahara sat in the corner of the lobby watching her, trying to decipher why Gary was so enthralled by her. She was about an inch taller than Kahara, slim and shapely with butterscotch colored skin and long silky jet-black hair. A trophy. Just the kind of woman she'd expect to see someone like Gary with.

Kahara was very apprehensive about approaching the actress, but decided she had nothing to lose. She walked up to her, introduced herself, and to her surprise, Lisa agreed to do the interview right there. Kahara conducted the brief interview, and then went in the bathroom stall for a silent scream. She couldn't believe the luck she was having. *Craig is going to be so proud of me,* she thought. *Wait till he sees this footage.* She decided to stay for the second film and ask the director if he would grant her an interview. The next movie would not start for another half-hour, so she decided to treat herself to a chocolate sundae.

A 31 Flavors ice cream parlor was only a few blocks away. As Kahara wandered back inside the theatre, she heard someone call out her name.

She turned and saw Marshall walking toward her. He was wearing a pair of black slacks and a long-sleeved pullover maroon shirt. A sight for sore eyes. She smiled, delighted to see him.

"You sitting with anyone?" he asked.

"No," she said, the words music to her ears. As they headed toward the front of the theatre, Marshall ran into two women he knew. The women smiled as they greeted Marshall. One of them shot Kahara a cross look. Kahara did not feel intimidated by either of the bland, nondescript looking women. The blander of the two eased up to Marshall and delicately touched the sleeve of his shirt.

"This is nice," she said, feeling the light material.

"Thanks," he returned.

The woman's tone and her demeanor let Kahara know that she was talking about more than his shirt.

"We're going to that party at the Hilton later. Maybe we could hook up," she said, easing her body forward to him a little.

Kahara moved closer to Marshall almost instinctively, pressing her body lightly against his, guarding her territory. Marshall looked down at Kahara then back at the woman. "We'll see. I'm kinda partied out now—I've been out late every night since I got here."

The woman looked over at Kahara as though finally understanding. Kahara felt triumphant, but was miffed that the woman made no attempt to hide her attraction to Marshall, especially since she didn't know the nature of their relationship. But she could tell by the expression on her face that she got it now.

Nice try, she thought. *But this is mine! All MINE!* Kahara wanted to yell it out as the two women walked off. Happy to finally be with her prize, she followed him toward the middle of the theatre where they took their seats. Kahara scrunched down in the seat as did Marshall, resting her knees against the back of the empty chair in front of her. It felt so good being there with him. She contrasted this with how lonely and isolated she felt inside the multiplex earlier that same day. The film being screened told the story of two Rap artists who start out as best friends but wind up bitter enemies.

During the Rap music segments, Kahara made the Rap artist hand motion Marshall had taught her. He repeated the motion during the film, helping her to perfect it. She leaned her head back and smiled, thinking how at ease she felt with him.

After the movie, Kahara approached the director and secured an interview for the following day. He was only available at 8:30 a.m. though. Kahara felt the early start-time would not allow her the luxury to languish in bed with Marshall after a morning lovemaking session. But she had an obligation to get Craig footage, and she would let nothing—not even Marshall—stop that.

"So what do we do now?" she asked, as they left the theatre. "Well," he said, rubbing his hands together speaking in his usual relaxed tone. "How about dinner, a glass of wine, a walk on the beach and the breeze from the terrace blowing in on us as we make love."

She blushed saying nothing. Marshall had a way of making her blush. She remembered how earlier that day she was worried she'd have no one to spend the evening with. But now, she'd be treated to dinner, something that hadn't occurred in quite a while. And then after dinner she'd make love, something else that had not occurred in quite a while—over a year. They continued walking in silence, the evening sealed. Kahara looked over at him. "You know that woman was hitting on you when she complimented your shirt."

"Yeah," he said nonchalantly, "I'm used to it. Happens a lot."

"It does?"

"Yeah. I get approached a lot by women. Men too. Maybe it's because I'm tall," he said, smiling to himself.

"What do you say to them?"

"Tell them I'm not interested," he said shrugging.

This scared Kahara a little. She never thought of him as being that sought-after. His plain looks had relaxed her into thinking she wouldn't have to compete with other women. Her confidence tumbling as she approached her fortieth birthday, the idea of going head-to-head against other women for the attention of a man scared her.

They continued walking. The night air was humid and there was a soft breeze. Kahara became melancholy as she realized that tomorrow was the last day. She pushed those thoughts out of her mind and stayed in the moment. Marshall seemed a little preoccupied now—not as attentive as he had been before the lovemaking proposal. It was almost as though he knew the evening was a foregone conclusion and now his mind was on some other business—as though the challenge was gone. She pushed this thought out of her mind too, figuring he wasn't distracted, just easygoing.

They perused a few outdoor spots and finally settled on a quaint outdoor cafe. Kahara excused herself and went inside upstairs to the bathroom. A blues singer was performing on the upper level. Kahara noted as she exited the bathroom, that the audience was made up primarily of women. As she scanned the sea of black and white faces, she couldn't help but feel lucky that she had someone, even if it was just for that night. She and Marshall clicked so well though, that she saw no reason why they couldn't continue to see each other even after the fest. When she returned, he was waiting patiently at their table for her. He was so easygoing and easy to be with. So unaffected. She decided to see if she could shake up their relaxed conversation a little. She took her seat, propped her elbows up on the table, clasped her hands together, then looked him square in the eye.

"What are you thinking?" she asked, smiling mischievously.

"Well, let's see," he said, leaning into her. "I like your shoulders and your smile."

"My shoulders?" she said, a little surprised by the statement. "You like my shoulders?"

"I'm sure someone else has commented on them."

"No, not really."

He studied her for a minute. "Maybe because you don't wear clothes that accentuate them."

"Sure I do," she said lying. The clothes she wore on this trip had been in her closet for months. She always considered it a waste to wear her good clothes to work or to events where the number of men would be scarce. She found herself saving her clothes the same way she saved her sexy nightgowns, for special occasions that never occurred.

"So tell me Marshall," she said, "what do you think of in your quiet moments? What are you really like?"

He looked at her and said nothing.

Kahara wanted to see if there was more beneath the surface of this calm, soothing exterior. "Tell me," she said. "Don't be afraid. I won't hurt you."

"That's too bad," he said sighing. "Okay, let's see. Well, I'm a pretty laid back person, affectionate."

Kahara thought back to the previous evening, nodding her head in agreement.

"It gets me in trouble sometimes," he said. "I'm very demonstrative in public when I'm in a relationship. I like to hold hands, kiss, hug, that kind of stuff. That puts some women off—makes them feel self conscious."

Kahara caught that qualifying statement "when I'm in a relationship." So she figured she need not expect him to be that demonstrative when it came to her. And as she thought about it, he hadn't been. While he had been intimate with her on the dance floor and in her hotel room, he was, at best, neutral every place else.

"And I expect to be the only person having sex with my partner when I'm in a relationship," he finished.

"Me too," she nodded.

He expects to be the only person? What was he telling her all this for? She began to wonder maybe if he was sizing her up for a possible relationship.

"I really like kids, can't wait to have some," he continued.

Oh no. It's all spilling out now. Well that definitely disqualifies me, she thought. Kahara decided she better come clean about her age. Most men didn't realize how old she was, assuming she was in her early thirties. With all this talk of relationships and babies, she felt it was only fair to let him know her age, and see if he would hopefully still be interested. *Why couldn't he have already had kids?* she thought.

Their food arrived.

Kahara toyed with her French fries, then looked up at Marshall. It felt so good being pursued by someone that she liked. The evening was ripe with possibilities—possibilities she didn't want to see fade away once she told him her age. She didn't want to tell him, but she felt it was only fair. He was opening up, so she felt she should as well. "How old do you think I am?" she said, too nervous to look him directly in the eye.

"Hmmmm," he said. "I always seem to attract older women for some reason. I don't know, forty? Fifty?"

"Fifty!" she exclaimed.

"What's wrong?"

"Fifty? You think I could be fifty!" She looked away for a moment then turned back toward him. "I'll be forty June 30th."

She watched his facial expression drop. He looked down at his food as though searching for words.

"This fish is dry," he said, picking at it with his fork.

Kahara began to think he must have been sizing her up for more than just a brief fling or he wouldn't look so disappointed. If sex were all he was after, then her age wouldn't matter. She was certain he had affairs with older women—he had just admitted that. *Just my luck,* she thought. "What's the matter?" she said, watching him trying to cover up his disappointment. "You guessed fifty."

"I was kidding. Seriously I would have guessed thirty-one."

"Oh," she said, her voice dropping.

"*I'm* thirty-one," he said.

His tone seemed to imply his anticipation of getting involved with someone who was closer to his age—

someone who could have children. *Timing,* she thought. *My timing has always been off. I'm always too late to get something. Why couldn't I have met you years ago?*

They continued eating in silence. Marshall finished his meal first.

"I hear sex is more fulfilling for women in their forties," he said.

Back to sex again, she thought. "I never thought about it but I guess it will be—more intense." *The few times I'll get some,* she thought. She continued struggling with the huge turkey burger she ordered.

"You having a problem finishing that?" he asked.

"No, I'm just a slow eater." She could tell he was getting impatient. Probably wanted to hurry up and get her back to the hotel so he could fuck her and then leave. A moment ago, before revealing her age, he was opening up, telling her how affectionate he was, how much he liked kids and how he expected his woman to be monogamous. Now, he just wanted her to hurry up and finish her meal so he could get what he wanted. That's all she was good for at this point.

"You know it's not as unusual anymore to see—"

"To see what?"

"Never mind. Forget it. What's the point." She thought of bringing up examples of women who were nine years or more older than their mates, but she remembered many of them had babies before the age of forty. Kahara made up her mind years ago that forty was her cut off for having children. "Have you ever had a threesome?" she asked, bringing the subject back to sex.

"Yeah," he said matter-of-factly.

"Did you enjoy it?"

"Not really. It was a lot of work. I kept looking over at the other woman thinking—I gotta do you too?"

She laughed and felt a little relieved that it didn't appeal to him. Kahara hurriedly finished her meal and they left.

"If we're going to the beach, I'm going to have to change clothes," he said.

"We don't have to go," she said.

"No, let's do it."

They arrived at the hotel and got on the elevator.

"I'll meet you back at your place," he said, pressing his floor.

Kahara was relieved. Now she could shower and change. She knew exactly what she would wear. She rushed into her room, quickly removed her clothes, and then jumped in the shower. She washed all the major areas extra well; her ears, her breasts and nipples, and of course her vagina. Kahara dried herself off quickly, then changed into a black tank-top and a short flair-skirt with an elastic waist—no panties. About fifteen minutes went by. Ordinarily she would be anxious, but she wasn't worried. He wanted it and she wanted it, so there was no way this evening would not take place. She walked over to the terrace and looked out. The beach looked empty and dark. Marshall called a moment later.

"What's your room number again?" he asked.

"1043," she said.

He arrived a moment later with a blanket.

"The beach looks dark," she said, closing the door.

Marshall walked over to the terrace and went out. "No need to let that stop us," he said. "Let's go."

Kahara grabbed an extra blanket from the closet and they left. There was a gentleman waiting at the elevator when they arrived. He looked knowingly at Marshall and smiled. "Looks like a night on the beach," he said to them.

"Not the whole night," Kahara said, leaning forward a little. She looped her arm through his. Marshall looked down at her and smiled.

When they arrived at the beach it was practically empty. They walked to a secluded spot where no one could see them.

"I haven't been on the beach with a date in years," Kahara said, regretting she let that slip out.

They spread out their blankets and sat down. Marshall began massaging her shoulders. Kahara leaned her head back and smiled.

"This is heaven," she said, as the breeze blew against the back of her neck.

He kissed the side of her neck and nibbled at the back of her ear. He continued the massage, and then laid her down on the blanket. He traced her arms from her shoulders down to her fingertips with his fingers. A shiver ran up her spine.

"No one's ever done this to me before," she said, closing her eyes. "It feels good." She turned on her side and faced him. He continued stroking the length of her arm and then down her waist. He cased his hand back up the side of her skirt and caressed her buttocks, his face registered surprise as he realized she wasn't wearing any panties. He traced a circle around her buttocks, squeezed it, and then let his hand travel under her skirt. The moment she had been waiting for. He pulled lightly at her pubic hairs, slid his finger between her lips, and began making slow circles around her clitoris. She put her leg up on his waist so he could get to it better. He pulled up her tank-top, exposing her breasts, her nipples standing eagerly at attention. He licked them carefully, as he eased his hand back between her legs and continued stroking her clitoris. She had a vicious climax.

"Fuck me Marshall," she hissed.

He reached in his pocket, pulled out a rubber, and put it on. He climbed on top of her, easing the blanket over them, but the sand from the blanket began falling on her body.

"Oh shit," she said, trying to brush it out of her pubic hair.

"You okay?" he asked.

"Yeah, I just don't want the sand to get inside of me while we're doing it," she said, brushing furiously. "How do people do this?"

He rolled back over on his side brushing more sand off of her thigh. "You got a lot of hair down there," he said, as he tried to remove the sand from her bush.

She felt the top of her head. "My hair! Is there any sand in my hair?"

He looked at her and nodded. "A little."

"Oh no, it's time to go," she said. "It'll take all my hair out. We gotta go."

"Are you serious?"

"Yes I'm serious. I can't let it stay in there it'll break all my hair off. When I was in fourth grade, me and my brother were in the sandbox in the playground. Some kids threw sand at us, and it got in my hair. In a month, it all broke off. It took me over a year to grow it back."

Next Time

Marshall sighed, removed the rubber, zipped up his pants, and got up. He gathered up both blankets, and they headed back to the hotel. Kahara walked quickly with Marshall trailing behind her.

"I gotta wash this stuff out of my hair," she said, motioning with her hand for him to walk faster. He continued at his same relaxed pace.

When they returned to her room, Marshall clicked on the TV and sat in a chair, as Kahara rushed into the bathroom. She emerged twenty minutes later and walked over to him. He got up from the chair and edged her over to the bed.

"I still need to blow dry it," she said.

"Dry it later, I got somethin' else you can blow," he said, pulling her into his arms, kissing her on the lips.

"Marshall," she said, in between kisses.

He squeezed her ample bottom as he inserted his tongue deep into her mouth. He pulled open her robe feeling her bare flesh. He caressed her buttocks, laid her down on the bed, and then lay next to her. He probed her ear lightly with his tongue, blowing hot air into it. Kahara's body went weak as he continued tonguing her ear. He rolled her over on top of him and began gripping her buttocks with one hand, while holding her breast with the other, sucking feverishly at her nipple. She eased down, straddling him, and began grinding against his penis. He squeezed her behind with his large hands and began moving her body in a rhythmic motion.

"Ooh I can't wait for this dick," she said, sticking her tongue in his ear, licking and blowing hot air on it. "That's payback for earlier."

He smiled and rolled her over, removing his pants pulling out another rubber.

"This time we'll get it right," he said, edging the rubber over his huge penis.

She touched it gingerly as he finished putting it on. He scooped her legs up in his arms and pulled them open and up towards her head.

"See how deep we can go," he said breathily.

He pressed his penis against the entrance but it was too wide to fit in.

"Oooh, ouch!" she said.

He began making slow, steady circles, inching it in slowly until it filled her up. She threw her arms around his neck and bit it. "Work this pussy," she hissed.

He began to thrust deep in and out. Kahara clasped a hold of his huge arms, squeezing them and moaning as he continued to stroke. He stopped after a few minutes and turned her over. She got on her knees and tooted her butt up in the air. He inserted from the rear and held on to her buttocks.

"Ouch, it hurts," she said, as he tried to enter again.

"Put your legs down," he said softly. She eased her legs down and lay flat on her stomach. He stayed on top of her gently easing his penis in and out. He reached around the front and began playing with her clitoris.

"Ooh shit," she said. "I've never had a man do it to me like this. Shit, I'm being fucked."

"What'd you say?"

"I'm being FUCKED! I'm being fucked. I'm being fucked," she kept repeating it. He continued making steady slow strokes in and out, speeding up as he neared orgasm. He had a shattering climax and lay next to her afterwards. She went in the bathroom a few minutes later to freshen up, and when she returned, she found he had fallen asleep. Kahara went back into the bathroom, returned with a warm washcloth, and wiped off his penis and his balls.

"I'm not through with this," she said, massaging it until it became firm.

"Nice way to wake a person up," he said, rubbing her head.

She eased down and positioned herself between his legs. "You know what I've got?" she said.

"No, what?"

"Fruit flavored condoms," she said, reaching in the drawer pulling one out.

"Ummm, what do you do with those?"

"You'll see." Kahara removed it from the package. "Strawberry," she said, holding it up. He smiled down at her. She eased the condom gently over his stiff penis, put her whole mouth over it, and began sucking voraciously. His penis was so wide that her jaws became tired after a few minutes. She ran her tongue down the shaft toward his scrotum and began licking his balls feverishly. She took one in her mouth and sucked it gently. His moans let her know how much he enjoyed it. Marshall pulled her on top of him.

"I'm not that good on top," she said.

"I'll guide you," he said softly. "Squat."

She squatted as he eased his body under the right spot. "Now come down on it," he said, grabbing her cheeks, guiding her slowly down the shaft. She did as he told her, squeezing her vaginal muscles as she came up and down on it.

"That's right, that's right," he said, leaning his head back. "Keep going up and down just like that."

As he got ready to climax, he grabbed her cheeks and pulled her down hard. "Oh my gosh," she said, feeling the full length of his penis. She crumpled on top of him then rolled over. "I'm done," she said, curling up in a ball. He removed the condom and let it fall on the floor, then curled up in a spoon behind her.

They slept in that position for about fifteen minutes, and then Kahara pulled away. Her shoulder was becoming sore. She wasn't used to spooning. None of the men she had been involved with in the past had been that affectionate. She woke up two hours later realizing that she had pulled all the way to the other side of the bed and eased back toward him, remembering he wasn't like the others.

After about three hours of sleep, she felt him rubbing his body against her buttocks. She knew what that meant. Kahara looked over at the clock. It was 6:00 a.m. She had to be up in less than two-and-a-half hours to interview Carl Henderson. She lay there, motionless, exhausted. He began stroking her body with his fingertips, tracing the area where her buttocks cupped in. "Feels good," she said, clutching her pillow, wanting to sleep longer. She looked back, realizing he was putting on a condom.

"You're sleepy, and I want to have sex," he said, hoisting himself up on his elbow, turning her onto her back. She made no objection as he eased his body on top of hers and tried to insert his penis. She held onto his arms as he entered her. It felt so good to have a man this size on top of her. All of her ex lovers, except for one, had been bone thin. She never experienced what it was like to have a massive, toned body on top of her. She drank it up. *All this man on top of me,* she thought. *All this big—country—on top of me.* He thrust deep.

"You can take it all now huh?" he said. They rocked back and forth in each other's arms until he climaxed. He rolled over and turned onto his back. After a few moments, she heard him sniffing the air.

"Smells like sex in here," he said. He got up after a few minutes and walked over to the terrace and looked out.

"Marshall, people can see you," Kahara said, jumping up heading for the closet.

"Even way up here?" he said, turning to her. She walked up to him and handed him a robe. He put it on but didn't close it, and walked out onto the terrace. Kahara went to the bathroom. When she returned, Marshall was motioning to someone in the other tower on the other side of the pool.

"What are you doing?"

"There's this chick on the balcony. I think she's white."

"She's coming on to you?"

"Yeah," he said, laughing softly. Kahara was not laughing. She walked up behind him and peeked from behind his shoulder, trying to get a good look at this new threat. The woman was tall and thin. She pulled her hand through her long brown hair, and tossed her head back like the white women in the TV ads.

This is MINE, she thought. "Who's this white tramp think she is?" she said out loud.

"Five minutes," he said, holding up five fingers and then pointing to his watch.

"Close your robe!" she said.

"She can't see it from here."

"Still," Kahara said, her voice showing her disgust. She walked over to the bed and lay back down, looking over at him. "You going over there?"

"Hell no!" he scoffed, looking back at her. He came back over to the bed and lay down next to her. He let out a long sigh. "Man, my vacation is almost over," he said. They lay there for a few more minutes, saying nothing. He got up a little later and went to the bathroom. She walked over to the window, but the woman was no longer there.

"Fool!" she said to her vanished competition. Marshall came out the bathroom a few moments later and got dressed.

"Guess I'll get back before my roommate wonders if I'm still alive," he said. She walked him to the door. He took her in his arms and gave her a hug. She looked at him, still drunk from their encounter.

"You want to hook up after the party tonight?" she asked.

"I don't know, I'm so beat. I don't think I'd be any use to you tonight. Unless I left early."

She didn't press it any further. Him mentioning the possibility of leaving early gave her all the hope she needed. After he left, she called Carl Henderson to firm up their eight-thirty interview. She dashed into the bathroom to take a shower.

"Of course we'll get together," she said, as she sudsed up her body. "Who's more convenient? He already said that most people staying here had roommates. How many other women here have a room all to themselves? We're in the same hotel too. Of course he's coming over." She was in much better spirits today. Gone was the depression of not knowing if she would run into him. After what they did all night and into the morning, she had no doubt he'd search her out. Kahara fixed her hair, applied her makeup and put on her prettiest summer dress—a sleeveless, sleek bright yellow print that played well off her cinnamon brown skin.

Chapter 6

After interviewing Mr. Henderson, Kahara returned to her room to take a nap before her eleven-thirty interview with Anthony Harris. She called Gil before laying down, but got his answering machine again. She didn't sleep well, and woke up still exhausted.

The interview with Anthony Harris could not take place until the Actors' Workshop he was teaching let out. Kahara realized that this meant she'd be unable to go to the movies with Marshall, who had mentioned wanting to see Grace, the one she had watched by herself the day before in her depressed state. Although she had already seen the movie, she felt seeing it again, with him would somehow erase the bad memory. Almost like rewriting history—erasing the loneliness and isolation she felt as she watched it alone the previous day. Besides, she could think of no better send-off for her vacation than to return to the scene of the crime. The possibility of him easing his hand between her thighs again would hold an even greater significance, after what they shared the night before.

But she had obligations. She had an obligation to Craig to get him footage. Kahara understood that life meant not just doing what she felt like doing. If that were the case, she would run to the theatre, wait in the back, and run down and sit with Marshall when he came in. But she wasn't too worried. They'd hook up later. They had to.

The festival ended mid-afternoon the next day. This was the last night, and they had such a good time the night before. She readied herself—tripod, camera, and extra battery, and then went downstairs to wait for the Actors' Workshop to let out.

After interviewing Anthony Harris, Kahara decided to head to the theatre, realizing Marshall would more than likely want to see the new film by Terrance McGaw. On the way there, she ran into Thomas Johnson, the actor from New York she had interviewed the day before.
"So, did you get a lot more interviews?" he asked.
"I interviewed Lisa Fayson and a couple of directors since your interview," she said proudly. "I'll let you know when the footage airs on the web."
"Do that. Please." He paused and eyed her for a moment. "You know, I kept trying to place your face that day you interviewed me, but it just clicked."
Kahara became a little nervous without knowing why.
"You were the one on the dance floor the last couple of nights with that big cat. Yeah," he said, nodding his head. "Ya'll had a little soft porn thing goin' there for a minute," he said, grinning at her.
Kahara blushed. "Oh, oh, that. We—we were just actin' silly."
"Is that what you call it," he said wryly. "Okay, well listen, I'm supposed to be meeting with a producer in a few. Maybe I'll catch you at the awards this evening," he said.
"Yeah, that should be fun," she said, as he walked away. His comments about their antics on the dance floor caught Kahara a little off guard. She didn't realize their behavior had been that noticeable. She shrugged off the

embarrassment though, thinking about how much fun it would be going to the awards banquet with Marshall, then to the closing night party for another intimate dance session, then back to her room for another lovemaking session.

When she arrived at the theatre, she was disappointed to see that the line for the McGaw film wrapped around the entire upper lobby. She reasoned Marshall must have decided not to come, since she didn't see him in line—either that, or he was wise enough to get there early and was already inside the theatre. Feeling a little dejected, she decided a little shopping might lift her spirits.

She stopped in a small, quaint clothing boutique a few blocks from the theatre. On both sides of the shop, along the walls, hung a variety of summer tops and delicate wispy summer dresses. Kahara tried on a pair of sexy caramel-colored sandals with four-inch heels. While waiting for the attendant to ring up the shoes, she glanced back at the wooden showcase. There, draped across the glass, was a long, braided twenty-eight inch black leather belt. Kahara walked over and stood there, almost transfixed. She gently lifted the thick belt. Hanging from the end of it was an additional 18 inches of thin leather straps. Kahara slid her hand under it, letting the leather strips fall between her fingers. She walked back to the mirror and tried it on over her summer dress—the dress she hoped would impress Marshall. As she twisted and turned in the mirror, she was tickled by the way the cat-o-nine-tails fringes slapped against her curvaceous thighs. The belt was completely out of character for someone so conservative, which is exactly why she decided to buy it. It was time for her to break out of that safe box she was trapped in.

The attendant convinced her to try on some sexy cologne while she stood in the checkout line. Kahara decided to purchase it as well. The attendant wrapped the cologne in white tissue paper and tied a pink ribbon around it. Kahara thought about how she'd feel that evening, untying the ribbon for her date with Marshall. She'd wear the perfume and the turquoise gown that night, and they would make love on the terrace. Kahara regretted the fact that she hadn't worn it for him the night before. No problem, she'd have a chance to wear it that evening. She could hardly wait.

As she sailed out of the store wearing her new shoes, she slowed her pace as she spotted Marshall and his roommate Raymond walking a few yards ahead. Marshall looked crisp and clean, draped in a white gauze, loose-fitting shirt, a matching pair of knee-length shorts, and a pair of tan canvass shoes. He was such a sharp dresser. The shirt flowed nicely against his wide frame as he sauntered along in his usual relaxed gate. Kahara hoped he would be turned on by her sexy new sandals, and the sensuous summer dress she was wearing.

She sped up until she was only a few feet behind them. "Your money or your life," she growled, trying to disguise her voice. Neither of them turned around. She said it again. Raymond looked back first, then Marshall, who turned back around as though unaffected.

"I was wondering what that noise was," Marshall said, staring straight ahead not looking back at her.

She walked behind them for a few moments. Marshall made no move to let her in next to him, so she walked next to Raymond instead. The three chatted about the Terrance McGaw movie that she arrived too late to see. Kahara watched Marshall as he ambled along. He seemed so nonchalant, almost too nonchalant—not like someone who had spent most of the night making love to her. And while she didn't expect him to refer to their tryst the evening before, especially with Raymond present, she would have still appreciated a wink, a smile, or something that would acknowledge what had happened between them. For some reason, he seemed a little distant now.

When they got a half a block from the hotel, Marshall and Raymond stopped to watch a street hustler, who was performing card tricks. Kahara stopped with them, but after a few moments, began to feel that she should leave. The last thing she wanted to do was hang around Marshall uninvited, especially after letting him have sex with her the night before. Kahara knew how squeamish men could be after sex, so she decided to get away from them—separate, and give him some space. She excused herself, saying she was headed to the seminar. Marshall told her he'd be there shortly.

She noted that he seemed concerned that she was leaving, but something about him seemed different. After arriving at the hotel, she went upstairs and looked over her new purchases. Kahara looked lovingly at the perfume wrapped in tissue paper, and laid it gently next to the turquoise gown, hoping that before the evening was over, she'd be wearing them both.

Chapter 7

By the time she made it to the seminar, Marshall and Raymond were already seated in the back. She sailed past them knowingly, tripod and camera in hand, to her usual spot in the front. As she sat there, she began to feel a little guilty for not at least speaking to them when she came in. Kahara wasn't sure why she didn't say anything. Maybe it was because she sensed a little distance on Marshall's part. Maybe this was her unconscious way of asserting her independence—showing him and his roommate that she didn't need his attention. Feeling a little restless, she decided to leave the room and get some last minute interviews. Kahara walked by Marshall and Raymond and gave them a smile, trying to make up for her purposeful snub a few minutes earlier. Marshall mouthed, "You leaving?" Kahara bent over and told him she wanted to catch some additional interviews.

He seems concerned, she thought, as she went outside. Kahara returned after a few moments because there were only a few people outside, but mainly because she wanted to be near Marshall. She took a seat directly behind them. Marshall's six-foot-two frame was sprawled across two seats in a semi-reclining position. Kahara leaned over after a minute, and jokingly asked Marshall if he needed a pillow. He shrugged without looking back at her. She didn't know if he was just tired, or ignoring her. After a moment, he turned around and looked at the camcorder she had lying in the seat next to her.

"That a camcorder?" he asked.

She nodded. "Digital, with a built-in stereo mike."

He looked at it, and then down at her thighs smiling. "It's too bad we could've—" he stopped short before finishing his sentence, but she knew what he was thinking.

Don't worry, she thought, *We'll get a chance to use it tonight.* She relaxed a bit now, figuring she'd see him for sure later on. Gone was the doubt that had crept in as she walked behind him earlier. Marshall was just nonchalant, laid back, Southern comfort. He wasn't ignoring her. They clicked mentally and physically, so there was no way he was not going to be with her that evening, and beyond that if she wanted. Birmingham was not that far away from Chicago.

After the seminar was over, Kahara decided to test Marshall to see if he would wait for her. She purposely lagged behind and waited while he and Raymond made their way toward the front to speak to the panelists. Marshall ran into a woman he knew and stopped to talk to her—a very attractive woman. Kahara stood in the back of the room, arms folded, watching as he continued what she felt was an overly lengthy conversation. Where did she come from anyway?

Kahara was in no mood to compete with another female for his attention. She realized now that no matter how cavalier she tried to act, her whole perspective changed once she had sex. Her footing was always less certain. Seeing Marshall talk to another woman for that length of time, especially such an attractive woman, left her feeling nervous and on edge. Kahara continued to watch, as

Marshall looked at his watch as he talked with the woman. What was he planning? *He can't make other plans for tonight, not after last night. No way,* she thought.

"Hey stranger," a voice called from behind her. She turned around quickly, irritated at the interruption, only to face Gary. His lean body was draped in a pair of loose-fitting black dress slacks and a black, short-sleeved linen shirt. Ordinarily, a tall gaunt man like this would send her into orbit. She had gravitated toward tall, thin men most of her life. But at this point, Gary was nothing short of an annoyance—interference with her plans to monitor Marshall. Her voice was cordial but strained.

"Hi Gary," she forced.

"I didn't see you at the set last night."

"Yeah, yeah," she said, still trying to keep an eye on Marshall. "I—I didn't make it. I—wasn't feeling—wasn't feeling well."

"You going to make it to the awards tonight? If so, I was thinking maybe we could—"

"Yeah, yeah I—I—I might. Yeah, yeah I should. I paid for it, so I should."

Gary looked in Marshall's direction then back at Kahara, as though realizing what had her preoccupied. "Well, your attention seems to be somewhere else, so let me let you go. I've got something for you." Kahara did not look at him. "I'll try to get it to you before you leave," he said. He stood there for a moment as though waiting for a response.

Kahara had barely heard a word he said. "Yeah, thanks. That's great," she said, hardly looking at him.

"Take care Kahara," he said stiffly, as he walked away.

She could tell from his tone that he was miffed, but she couldn't be bothered right then. She was obsessed with this woman. Kahara turned briefly and watched Gary as he walked away. He had a nice gait; his tall, sleek body seemed to flow like liquid as he strolled. She turned back around and noticed with relief that the woman Marshall was talking to was leaving. But as he continued toward the front, he was stopped by yet another woman. Another attractive woman.

"Where did they all come from anyway?" she said, under her breath. Realizing she couldn't hang back there forever, she headed toward the front to collect business cards from the panelists. Kahara walked past Marshall, who hardly noticed her, and stood behind the others who were waiting their turn. She spotted Raymond standing off to the side and walked up to him.

"You're not going to go talk to them?" she asked.

"Naw, I don't like approaching people cold."

She studied him for a moment. He was much more reserved than Marshall and seemed somewhat shy. He would not look directly at her.

"What type of work do you do?" she asked.

"Video/film, primarily editing now. I work for an editing shop."

She gently took his arm. "You better get up there!" she said, nudging him the same way he nudged her two nights ago while she was dancing with Marshall. "You're missing out on too many contacts. Don't worry about how awkward it feels. Come on."

Kahara held onto his arm, guided him toward the line and made him stand in front of her. He exchanged information with one panelist and got into a somewhat lengthy conversation with another. She talked to two of the panelists at length. She lost track of Marshall and Raymond, finally doing the networking she had originally come there to do. By the time she finished talking to the last panelist, she looked around and realized that her ploy failed. Marshall did not wait for her.

She returned to her room and brushed off that uncertain feeling. Kahara decided she better get some of her packing done, reasoning there wouldn't be enough time to pack everything later, since she'd hopefully be locked in a lovemaking embrace with Marshall. He was just probably tired and needed a nap or something. After packing many of her items, she took her tripod and camera and went outside to shoot some footage of the outer hotel area. A large tent had been set up outside on the hotel grounds where drinks were being served. There was a large crowd gathered outside the tent, and many were milling about. Kahara began taping the crowd.

As she panned the camera, she spotted a man she had met earlier that she wanted to interview. He was with an attractive woman, who was wearing a tan suede bikini top and a brown wrap skirt. The woman had long micro-thin braids and mocha chocolate-brown skin. Kahara found the contrast between her dark skin and his light skin striking, and decided to ask them for an interview. They both agreed. After the interview, she clowned around with them while the camera was still taping.

Kahara had spotted Marshall a bit earlier outside the tent. He seemed a little distant, so she decided to give him some space. As she mugged for the camera, she hoped Marshall observed how much fun she was having with the couple. She wanted him to think she was popular—not needy. It was important to her, that he not think she was lonely, waiting for him to come rescue her.

Once their taping session was over, she wandered over to where Marshall and Raymond were. A man she had interviewed earlier was standing not too far from them. Still wanting to appear popular, she struck up a five-minute conversation with the man and his friend, hoping Marshall would catch this too. As she laughed and joked with the two of them, she sensed after a while that they were ready to move on, so she politely ended the conversation.

Trying to appear as unassuming as possible, she eased over to where Marshall and Raymond were and asked them for an interview. Kahara was not really trying to interview them; she just wanted to get Marshall on tape, as a remembrance. Marshall looked a little annoyed muttering something about having had a few drinks but agreed to do it. She set up the tripod and began taping both of them as they held their champagne glasses.

"Hi, my name is Marshall Taylor and this is my friend Raymond."

"Better known as Romeo," Raymond said pretentiously, nodding his head at the camera, taking a long sip from his drink.

Marshall looked over at him and smirked. "Yeah, better known as Romeo. Anyway," he said, "we've produced a couple of sitcoms, and have now branched off into making our own films. Our most recent feature is called the Cornbread Monster."

Kahara smiled, a little surprised to see this side of him.

"Umm, it's a story about people who've thrown large quantities of soul food into this radioactive pit, which subsequently produces a monster made of cornbread. It has a cornbread body, pinto-bean eyes and macaroni lips. Yeah, and it has crab claws and legs made out of ham hocks."

The camera viewer went black. "Oh no, the battery's dead," Kahara said, biting her lip, scared Marshall might use it as an excuse to get away from her.

A relieved look passed over Marshall's face. A moment later, a woman wearing a long, brassy-colored wig walked up the driveway, diverting their attention. The woman was huge, but well proportioned. She had an enormous chest, and was dressed in very tight-fitting denim shorts, with white lace trim that barely covered her robust bottom. Marshall nudged Raymond and mumbled something to him. They both broke out in loud laughter. A few people turned and looked over at them.

"That's not nice," Kahara said. "How would you like it if you were her and people were laughing at you?"

"If I was her?" he asked incredulously. "If I was her, I'd kill myself." His expression gave away his disdain for the woman.

Kahara felt a little shaken by his bluntness. This was a side of him she had never seen before. She couldn't help but feel curious as to why he was so hard on the woman. "That's kind of harsh isn't it?"

"Some people bring it on themselves," he said, shrugging, not looking at her.

Some people bring it on themselves? She couldn't help but wonder if some of this might be directed toward her, but she brushed it off as she had done everything else that day.

"You guys got time to wait while I run upstairs and get my other battery?"

"Naw, we're gonna have dinner then head out to the awards banquet."

Kahara looked down at her watch and realized they were running short on time. "Yeah, I guess you're right," she said. Marshall and Raymond headed back into the hotel. Kahara stood there alone, watching the woman in the daisy duke shorts as she tried to blend in with the large crowd of people milling about. The woman was not successful however, and every time she walked up to a group, the crowd would part and leave. Kahara felt sympathy and a certain connection with this woman, who, much like herself, was just trying to be accepted by a class of people she felt a little inferior to.

She began to resent the crowd as they continued to move away from the peculiar woman. She felt a little abandoned by Marshall, and began to wonder whether they would get together after all. Why didn't he invite her out to dinner or to the awards banquet? Kahara began to feel very self-conscious standing there alone with her tripod and camera. She wondered if any of the crowd remembered her antics with Marshall on the dance floor during the last few nights. It was silly of her to even think anyone cared, but after being seen dancing with Marshall as though they were rabid lovers, she was worried people would get the impression that she had been dumped by him. She felt a little despondent, but she wasn't going to show it.

After packing away her tripod and camera, she walked proudly toward a Kentucky Fried Chicken, trying to appear unaffected by Marshall's change in behavior. Her bravado, however, was more for her own benefit than the crowd of unconcerned people.

As she waited in line, she noticed two attractive men in front of her talking. They were wearing their festival badges. As a rule, Kahara didn't talk to exceptionally nice-looking men because she figured they would only ignore her. She had tried it successfully the day before, when she interviewed the actor from New York. But her confidence was a little shaken now, and after suffering what she hoped was a temporary rejection by Marshall, she was in no mood for another.

Miffed by her own lack of confidence, Kahara decided to stop being a wuss. She spoke to both of them, but they both gave her a dry greeting. Ignoring their initial rejection, she asked what brought them to the festival. Their eyes lit up and they began to pour forth about their video production company. On the surface, these men appeared stuck up and aloof, but after a little probing, Kahara realized that the aloofness was just a façade—a protective cover. Kahara filed that away for future reference. She conducted a brief outdoor interview with them then returned to her room.

After looking over some of the footage from her interviews, she clicked the TV on and began eating dinner. The movie, Charlie's Angels, was playing. Kahara felt a certain amount of resentment toward the perky Caucasian women on TV, whose dating prospects seemed endless compared to her own. She watched as Cameron Diaz proceeded to seduce a man. "Boy, if you're a black man or a white woman you got it made," she said sighing. She picked at her now-cold chicken, not bothering with the corn on the cob or the ice-cold mashed potatoes.

Kahara pushed away her meal and set about the task of finishing packing. She opened the drawer containing the gown and the perfume, feeling tempted to pack them away, but didn't. Still holding out hope. Of all the gowns she had purchased, but never worn, the turquoise gown was her favorite. She sighed wistfully as she tossed different items in her suitcase. Realizing the packing would take her too long, she abandoned it and decided to leave for the awards banquet.

Next Time

The banquet was a short cab ride from the hotel. Kahara arrived twenty minutes late, but she was in such a malaise she didn't care that she had missed part of the program. As she sat there alone in the huge, chilly theatre, she felt a little melancholy. These affairs were always better when you were there with people you knew. The woman on stage was singing a Jill Scott song. The song instantly catapulted Kahara back to the lovemaking embrace she and Marshall were locked in the night before.

Kahara pulled out a pad of paper and a pen, and began writing a poem about her lovemaking experience with Marshall, appropriately entitled, *Fucked for Real*. The Jill Scott song filled her full of possibilities. She read the poem back to herself and thought about how good their lovemaking session would be that night if she and Marshall got together. As she sat there influenced by the romantic lyrics, the idea of a weekend tryst in Birmingham with Marshall brought a smile to her face. She made a note to check on the airfare once she returned home. After the Jill Scott song ended, so did her trance. As the awards presentation droned on, Kahara became a little sullen. Sitting there alone, she thought about Gary and Phil, how much fun they were probably having now, and how she had foolishly shoved aside Gary's friendship to chase Marshall. Kahara became despondent and decided to leave.

Foregoing a cab ride, she decided to walk back to the hotel instead. As she walked back, a heavy depression crept over her. Feelings of isolation and aloneness set in again.

When she got back to her room, she finished packing everything—except the turquoise teddy and the perfume. Now she had to decide what to wear to the final party. At first, she thought of going all-out sexy, and pulled out a sleeveless, clingy red dress. As she stared down at it, she thought back to the nasty comment Marshall made earlier that day about the woman dressed in the daisy duke shorts. She decided against wearing the dress, and began feeling incriminated for having sucked his penis, and for having sex with him so soon. Kahara winced at the thought of being lumped in the same category as the woman in the nasty shorts.

She walked to the party wearing the same dress she had worn all day. When she arrived at the club, she found it dark inside, and the dance floor empty. *Good,* she thought. *Maybe when Marshall gets here he'll see this is dead and want to leave.* She wandered over near a group of people seated on a bench against a wall in the back of the club. Her eyes still adjusting to the dark, she didn't recognize Raymond at first when he reached out and grabbed her hand. Two seats over from him sat Marshall. He gave her a polite but lifeless wave. There was no room next to Marshall, so Kahara sat next to Raymond. Her stomach dropped as she viewed two women sitting between Marshall and Raymond. *What if they came with them?* she thought fearfully. How completely embarrassing that would be. Kahara tried to play off her discomfort by appearing nonchalant. She realized after a few moments though, that they were not together. Marshall, for his part, did not seem too happy to see her. Quite the opposite—he stayed in his seat. She leaned forward, sensing something was wrong. Marshall got up after a few minutes and went to the bar. When he returned, another woman was sitting in his seat. She offered it back to him, but he waved her off, and went and stood next to Kahara.

Next Time

He leaned over her. "If you want to leave your credit card with the bartender, there's a $100 minimum," he said, referring to a practice some bars had of letting patrons leave their credit cards with the bartender.

So what! she thought. *How about this evening? Let's talk about that.* The woman got up and left, and Marshall returned to his old seat. Everything's changed, she thought. She couldn't believe it. She watched as an attractive woman came over and began talking to Marshall. He looked at his watch during the conversation, said something to the woman, who then left.

Another female came up to him and spoke to him briefly. The woman said something that was apparently funny, and they both laughed. Kahara did not find any of it funny. She looked around the club searching desperately for someone—anyone she knew who could acknowledge her existence and make her feel even slightly important—like she belonged—like she was connected the way Marshall apparently was. Where did all these beautiful women come from anyway? No one was talking to him like this a few nights ago. She felt almost as though she were vanishing—eclipsed by this sea of beautiful women. She spotted Gary over by the bar talking with a male friend. Tempted to get up, but afraid to lose her spot near Marshall, she stayed there still holding on to all she had at that point still hoping that Marshall would reach over and say, "This is dead let's get out of here" as he did two nights ago. She watched as one woman after another walked up to Gary as well. *What gives with all these women?* she thought. Even though she never felt Gary was really that interested in her, she prayed he would at least look over at her, acknowledge her, come over, and make even a small fuss around her, to show Marshall he wasn't the only connected person there.

A feeling of powerlessness gripped her. A few moments later, yet another woman came up and spoke with Marshall. This one, an absolute stunner. Full-figured, light-skinned, shapely and tall. She was dressed in a tasteful, yet sexy, sleek crimson-colored sequined gown. She leaned in close to Marshall. Her attire was very classy—unlike the woman in the denim daisy dukes, and much more appealing than the drab dress Kahara was wearing. The dress she thought would impress Marshall. He never even noticed it.

She recognized the woman from two nights before. The snotty one with the entourage, who all but demanded Kahara move aside so she could take a picture in front of the fountain. Marshall looked at his watch again as he talked with her. Kahara began to feel angry, thinking he had lined up something with these women. Maybe some special hot-shot party that only the privileged were invited to.

Raymond got up and left after a few minutes. The women sitting between them left a moment later. There she and Marshall sat with a huge space between them. The space seemed as big as the Grand Canyon to her. There was no way she was going to move over next to him. He made a move to scoot over, but a man came and sat between them. Marshall got up and moved over next to her anyway. The gentleman moved over, giving him room. Kahara felt a sense of relief as Marshall sat down next to her, as though things would soon return to normal. But she was still insecure as to how the evening would turn out. She pressed her hands against her tired knees, still trying to appear unaffected. "I'm going to get out of here in a bit. I leave tomorrow morning," she said, trying not to sound as drained and dejected as she felt.

Marshall's expression looked disappointed, but he didn't say what she had been hoping, praying he would say ever since she arrived—that he wanted to see her that night. Her last night. There they sat, saying nothing to each other. After a few minutes, he asked her to dance.

Finally, she thought. She became hopeful as she followed him onto the dance floor. Maybe they could rekindle what they had nights before—go back to the point when he was avidly pursuing her. Perhaps he didn't have another date after all, and the woman was just a friend he was giving the time to. Maybe the dance floor would melt away any doubts—the uncertain feeling that had stayed in the pit of her stomach all day. Maybe now, finally.

But once on the dance floor, Marshall was not the same person he had been nights before. He danced the way he should have danced when he first met her—distant—no intimacy whatsoever—no face holding—no backing his massive body into hers—none of his unique slow-dancing to a fast record—only the stupid hand movement he taught her. Two nights ago, he could barely keep his hands off of her. Now he wouldn't touch her. She might as well have been the woman in the nasty shorts.

For the first time, it really registered. He had indeed cooled towards her. She watched his expression as they danced—no smile—no leer—no holding her close—no rubbing up against her. Very formal—very dry. On his best behavior, as though he thought people were watching. Her heart sank into her stomach. His abrupt change led her to believe that there must be someone there. Someone he wanted to make sure didn't get the impression that there was anything going on between them. She tried a few times to ease up to him smiling, but he did not engage her. Instead, he turned his back to her, and eased away from her. She got the message and didn't do it again.

Once the song ended, he decided to stop. This was a change from the man who danced for over a half-hour with her Wednesday and Thursday night. When they returned, their seats were taken. Kahara understood now why he asked her to dance. He knew, as she did, that when they returned their seats would be occupied, and used it as a way to get away from her. He didn't have to bother when Raymond was wedged between them. But once Raymond left, he was stuck without a buffer. He could find no other polite way to get away from her, other than to ask her to dance. Marshall drifted away towards the bar. Kahara stood there not knowing exactly what to do with herself, feeling lost.

The man she interviewed earlier that day came up to her and asked her to dance. Kahara gratefully accepted. The middle-aged man made a good attempt to match Kahara's stamina but his efforts were lost on her. What a letdown he was from Marshall. Is this what was left for her? Fifty-plus-year-old men trying to act young? She became more depressed at the prospect of this. The man became tired after two records and stopped. It caught Kahara off guard that the man would want to stop dancing with her. But she was in no mood to put on a happy face after being snubbed by Marshall.

Kahara wandered awkwardly toward the bar, trying not to look like she was following Marshall, even though she was. She bought herself a drink and strolled about, attempting to look carefree. As she walked toward the back of the club, she practically bumped into Gary. He looked handsome in his tan linen shirt and tan loose fitting slacks.

"How you doin' lady?" he said, giving her a long hug. A woman passed by and greeted him. He spoke to her, then turned his attention back to Kahara. "You enjoy yourself? Make a lot of contacts?"

"Yeah, yeah," she said. "How about you?"

"I gotta say, this has been a good experience for me. Did a lot of networking, made a lot of new contacts, couple of new projects lined up." He studied her expression. "You alright?"

"Yeah, why?" Kahara was a little annoyed that he could tell something was wrong.

"I don't know, you look like you lost your best friend."

Kahara shrugged off the comment without responding.

"Listen, what's your room number?" he asked.

"What?" Kahara said, caught off-guard. Was he interested in her after all?

"Remember the thing I said I had for you?"

"Yeah?" she said a little eagerly.

"Well it's a t-shirt with my company name and logo on it—I wanted to give it to you as a memento."

Kahara wasn't sure how to take this; then again, she was never quite sure how to take Gary. Was the shirt really a memento, or an advertising tool for his company? She decided not to be so cynical—no one else was offering her anything.

"1043," she said, looking around to see if she could spot Marshall with someone.

"I'm driving back to Norfolk tomorrow morning," he said. "If it's not too late, I'll drop it by tonight, or I'll leave it at the front desk."

She still couldn't see Marshall. "Okay, Gare," she said, drifting away from him. She lost sight of Marshall and reasoned he was probably with the woman in the sequined dress. Kahara got a sinking feeling in the pit of her stomach that he had probably already left with her. She was tired, it was too crowded, and she couldn't take another evening of standing around all night not being asked to dance. Her spirit was so worn down at this point, that she couldn't bring herself to ask anyone to dance anyway.

As she made her way toward the exit, she ran into Marshall. He was, to her relief, alone. Kahara told him that she would be leaving soon, but wanted one last dance. Marshall asked her to dance, probably, she thought, to get her out of the way so he could move on to his new conquest. His demeanor was still cooler and more formal than the previous nights. He barely looked at her as they danced. She tried to catch his eye a few times by doing a mock belly-dance. He looked down at her, his expression a mixture of amusement and sympathy—the kind of look you give someone you know is trying too hard to impress. After one song, a vulgar Rap record began playing. The woman in the song was giving graphic instructions on how she expected to be pleasured orally. Marshall's face scowled in apparent distaste, and he stopped dancing.

"All right, well I'm leaving," Kahara said abruptly, praying he'd say what she wanted to hear.

He bent over. "I'll call you if I get back in time," he said. He walked off without waiting for a response, and disappeared inside the crowd.

Kahara stood there for a moment, feeling abandoned and foolish for thinking he would ever leave with her. No more dirty south. She looked anxiously for the exit, just wanting to get away. The front exit was blocked by a crunch of people waiting to get in, so she was forced to exit from the rear. Kahara stumbled over some cans left in the dimly lit gangway.

She walked back to the hotel completely numb. Everything had changed. There was no way he was calling or coming over now. She felt stupid and used. She never waited long enough to find out if the men were sincere, always afraid they'd lose interest if they had to wait too long to have sex. They usually did lose interest however, a hard lesson she never seemed to learn. This letdown was worse than usual. Although in the past she may have had sex in the first few weeks, she never did it on the third night, and never so far away from home. Maybe that was why she gave in. Maybe the isolation she felt drove her to intimacy. Next time, she'd wait, so that she wouldn't have to deal with feeling used and disposed of—a hard lesson to learn so far away from home.

After arriving back at her room, she undressed slowly, packing away the dress she was wearing, along with her shoes. She eased into a pair of shorts and her Angela Davis t-shirt, and then went out on the terrace and stood. It was cool, so she went back inside, put on a robe and then walked back out.

Kahara sat in the patio chair motionless for a half-hour, her thoughts drifting wistfully to how romantic it could have been if Marshall were there with her. She folded her arms and looked out at the beach they had been on the night before, a single tear rolling down her cheek. Kahara replayed the events of the day, from the time she ran into Marshall on the way back from the boutique, to the nonchalant way he treated her at the seminar, and the annoyed look he gave her when she asked for the interview. How could she have missed all those signs?

She pulled out her laptop and made an attempt to journal her thoughts, but she was such a jumble of emotions she couldn't sort through them all. The thoughts passed through her brain so quickly, they all seemed to merge together. She felt angry, sad, dejected, obsolete, old, unwanted and discarded. She read over what she had written a half-hour later, but could make no sense of it, so she stopped typing. For the next two hours, she sat dozing off and waking up. When she finally came back inside the room, it was well after two-thirty in the morning. Her heart sank more, realizing there was no way Marshall was coming over now. Probably screwing the classy woman in the sequined gown. Again, where did all these beautiful women come from? They certainly weren't approaching him the two nights they were dancing together. The tears she had fought off began to flow now, as she realized she had been nothing more than a weigh station, until something better came along.

She pulled out her suitcase and placed it on the other twin bed in her room. She opened the drawer containing the turquoise gown and the perfume she thought she was going to wear that night. Tears fell on the gown as she picked it up, soiling its satin finish. Kahara tried wiping away the tear stains with her thumb, but they would not come out. She took the gown and the perfume, walked them over by the suitcase, but then dropped them in the trash can by the bed. What a joke—the idea of her wearing the gown and the perfume and making love on the terrace.

What a joke. She slid into the other bed—the same bed they made love in the night before, curled up in a ball and tried to go to sleep.

Less than three hours later, she awoke. Unable to sleep, Kahara decided to settle her hotel bill. As she waited in line in the lobby, she struck up a conversation with an attractive young man standing in front of her. He was another aspiring actor from New York. After he stepped up to the counter to check out, Kahara stood there feeling alone, a heavy feeling pulling at the pit of her stomach. She wondered if Marshall would call her before she left. The least he could do was call, and wish her a safe trip home—at the very least he could do that.

She checked with the front desk, remembering Gary telling her he would leave the t-shirt there. He didn't. As she walked down the hallway on the way back to her room, she spotted the attractive woman she had told Marshall to dance with that Wednesday night—the hippy one with the small waist. She was coming out of a young man's room two doors down from Kahara's. Kahara remembered him—he was in his twenties, very cute and rugged looking.

The woman giggled self-consciously, and practically stumbled as she exited his room, rushing off as he reached for her, his open shirt revealing his well-toned frame. It was five-thirty in the morning. Kahara assumed they must have had sex. The young lady was wearing the same killer jeans she had worn a few nights ago. Kahara envied her. The young woman's tight body made her feel even more non-existent, which wasn't hard to do at that point. The girl nodded to her as she went by, giving her a knowing smile. She had that afterglow, the same afterglow Kahara had two nights ago. But even if the woman's affair with the young man was just a brief fling, she had at least twenty years on her side that Kahara did not have, and the chance for future prospects. Kahara was returning to a life of dateless weekends. *At least somebody got some,* she thought.

Kahara went into her room, undressed and crawled back into bed. Hoping she would be awakened by Marshall's call, she fell asleep. She awoke at eight forty-five that morning and jumped up to get ready. No calls. He knew she was leaving that morning, but no calls.

After showering and getting dressed, she went to Kentucky Fried Chicken once again, but saw that it was closed. The sky was overcast and it looked as though it might rain at any moment. It matched her mood. She walked over and videotaped the Caribbean Café. The place where she, Gary and the others had dinner, the night before she had sex with Marshall. Everything was in reference to the events that took place between she and Marshall. The café seemed like an oasis to her now. Her memories of the dinner she had there with Gary and his friends, were the most enjoyment she had during her stay in Virginia.

On her way back, she ran into the actor from New York she had interviewed a few days prior. He was sitting outside having breakfast at the hotel, which stood next to the Caribbean Café. She smiled faintly at him, stopped, and videotaped him again from the distance. He was so full of confidence and bravado—completely opposite of the way she felt. She admired his resilience. She wished she could muster up some.

"What's up?" he called to her as she neared him.

"Not too much," she said.

He watched her as she neared. "You seem different today," he said, as he finished up the last of his burger. Kahara stood in front of him. "Different how?"

"I don't know like—"

"I lost my best friend?" she said, repeating Gary's words from the night before.

"Did you?"

Kahara scoffed at the idea of even remotely considering Marshall her friend. "Hell no," she said, plopping down in the seat opposite of him. She bit her lip not wanting to verbally admit what he probably read from her body language. "Some of the people—some of the people here were really quite nice," she said, thinking back to Gary and his friends, her voice breaking a little.

"Yeah, yeah, some of them are, but not everybody here got your back." He studied her for a moment. "I guess you probably already found that out." He leaned back in his chair then looked off to his right for a moment. "You know, years ago back when I first started out, I auditioned for this part in a film and this big-shot producer—female—took a liking to me, you know. Next thing you know I'm hittin' it—every week, two or three times a week. It went on like that for about a month, then without warning she just cut me off cold. Wouldn't return phone calls—nothin'. Found out a few weeks later the part went to another cat she had started doing the same thing to." He looked at her. "Yeah, men get burnt too. I was more pissed off at myself than I was at her though."

Kahara smiled, looking down.

He leaned forward and took the tip of her chin in his hand. "You fall down, you get up—you move on."

Kahara repeated those words to herself as she headed back to the hotel. She understood now that most of her depression stemmed from the rut her life was in. It would be different if she had the brief fling with Marshall, and then returned to a life that was full and rich, but that was not the case. Her life was mediocre and dull—Marshall was the most excitement she had had in over a year. The thought of this depressed her even more.

It was amazing to her how rejection from one man could open up all these feelings of isolation and depression. It was as though she was, for the first time, facing some facts about her life that she had kept beneath the surface up to that point.

Maybe when she was younger, connecting was optional—good sex was an end in and of itself, because she had youth on her side. So what now? Since she was approaching forty she should just settle for good sex and expect nothing more? Be grateful a man would spend even one night with her? Is that what her life had been reduced to? Maybe if Marshall had acknowledged her existence the day after, or the day after that, it would have been okay. Or would it have? Should a man ignoring her plunge her into such a deep depression? She realized now it wasn't the man, but her feelings about her place in the world, now that she was nearing forty.

When she was younger, if she was rejected, it hurt, but she always felt she had time on her side. Someone better would come along in a few months and things would usually work out. But that had not been the case during the last five years. Once a relationship ended it would be months—sometimes more than a year—before she would meet anyone else. It was easier to push this realization out of her mind before Marshall. But Marshall's coldness lifted the lid off of all that she had been insecure about. The wound that had never really healed. His rejection pulled back the scab, leaving an exposed sore.

A wistful feeling came over her as she walked back into her hotel room. She videotaped the inside of the room, a habit she had developed years ago, then walked onto the terrace and taped the beach area. She sighed, remembering their tryst on the sand. A knock came at the door. A strange voice mumbled something, but she couldn't make out what it was. Kahara's stomach dropped. "Marshall!" She rushed to the door.

"Who is it?" she yelled before getting there. The strange voice came back with another response. As she peered out the peephole, an unexpected figure stood there.

"Gary?" she said.

Kahara pulled the door open slowly. Gary walked in holding something red in his hand.

"As I promised," he said, handing the t-shirt to her.

Kahara forced a smile as she took the shirt from him.

"You remembered," she said, slowly trying to hide her disappointment. She held it up to her shoulders to see how it would fit.

"Yeah, it's just a little big." He took the sides of the shirt and pressed it against her waist. "It'll barely make it past those hips." He paused for a moment. "Those hips," he said slowly, grinning, as though trying to picture her in it. "Yeah, that would definitely work," he said, the smile still on his face. He let his hands drop to his side, clearing his throat as though remembering himself. "Well, look, I'm ummm—parked illegally. You got my card, give me a buzz sometime." He reached over and gave her a slightly awkward hug, then headed toward the door.

"Thanks Gare," she said, smiling a little. His Southern gentlemanliness amused her.

He looked down at her luggage. "You look like you got most of your stuff packed. You need a lift to the airport?"

"Naw, that's okay I got some things I need to—that's okay thanks anyway."

"You okay?" he asked, studying her for a moment.

"Sure. I'm fine," she said.

"Come here," he said softly.

She walked forward hesitantly. He pulled her into his arms, gave her a long solid hug this time, and then let go of her. "Look, you take care of yourself okay," he said, looking down at her, giving her a sad smile. "Give a brother a call."

Gary left a moment later. A lift would have been nice, but there was no way she would have been able to sustain an upbeat mood during the ride. She really just wanted to be alone to sort through what had happened over the past few nights. Kahara let out a long sigh. Of course it wasn't Marshall. He was probably sleeping with his arm draped around the bitch in the red dress. She checked the room one last time, then lugged her things down to the lobby and took the shuttle to the airport.

On the plane ride home she leafed through her notepad and read over the poem she had written while she was at the awards banquet. As she thought over what happened after their sexual encounter, the title *"Fucked for Real"* took on a completely different meaning. A pang went through her as she read it to herself:

"Large Southern hands know just where to touch, just how to feel, just how to please. Large Southern mouth knows just how to suck, just how to lick, just how to tease—me my Southern comfort. My Southern comfort.

Wide as a doorway—succulent, smooth, Southern dick—pushin', shovin', probing. Banging me into oblivion." *Then dumped my ass like I was a piece of shit,* she thought wryly.

Chapter 8

The forty-story twin tower looked like an oasis in the distance as the cab driver neared her home. Hyde Park/Kenwood was one of the most affluent neighborhoods on the south side of Chicago. The doorman met Kahara in the driveway to help her in with her luggage. Once inside, she called her mother, then immediately checked her answering machine, hoping to have a message from Marshall. To her disappointment, she had none. As each day passed, the dull ache in her stomach grew worse.

By midweek, she was in a total funk. She asked herself that night, and the night before, whether she needed that phone call from Marshall to feel good about herself. Did she want the call from him because she wanted to hear from him, or because she wanted to feel wanted, admired—worth something? Did a man's feelings about her dictate how she felt about herself? *How sad,* she thought. *No more.*

She remembered thinking as she sat on the plane. If only he had called, how much more upbeat her mood would have been. If only he had picked up the phone and made that ten-second phone call. She became angry thinking about it. *What was the big deal?* she thought. *If you get in late you call the front desk and ask for a wakeup call. Then you call the woman up and say "I know you're busy packing, but I just wanted to say I really enjoyed the time* we spent together. Email me when you get a chance, and have a safe trip." That's non-committal. That's not saying, "Kahara I love you and I want to marry you." It's just an acknowledgement that I had some impact. Instead of just being some anonymous hole you stuck your dick into.

And even if he had spent the night in someone's room he eventually came back to his, and at that point he could have left her a message that she could have received at home when she returned—a ten-second message. She wasn't even worth a ten-second message.

Jackie, the administrative assistant, passed by Kahara's desk with the mail cart that Thursday, but noting Kahara's downcast expression, backtracked. Jackie was like a second mother to Kahara. She could share things with Jackie that she couldn't talk to her mother about. When Kahara told Jackie about her upcoming trip over a month ago, Jackie warned her against leaving town and losing her head. Jackie cautioned her about sex demons, which she felt could possess a person, and cause them to do carnal things they would later regret. The idea that an outside force could cause a person to jump into bed with someone haphazardly amused Kahara back then, but not anymore.

"Hey you, what's up?" Jackie said, leaning against the cart.

Kahara was hoping Jackie would just pass by, not much in the mood for an interrogation. She did not want to let Jackie know that the sex demon had won, in no mood to hear an "I told you so."

"Hey Jackie. How you doin'?"

"What's been up with you? You've been actin' weird ever since you came back from Virginia."

"Nothin'. I'm okay."

Jackie gave her a knowing look. "Tried to warn you," she said, shaking her head. "Tried to warn you." She continued pushing her cart, not waiting for Kahara to respond.

How did Jackie know? How could she tell? Was it still that obvious? Kahara dragged through the rest of the day then went home. Still no messages.

As her first week back came to an end, Kahara decided to send Marshall an email. As the days passed with still no response, she moved from sadness to anger. On Thursday of the following week, Kahara decided to call him. Her stomach knotted up as the phone rang. She had no idea what she would say if he answered. She was almost relieved when his voicemail picked up. Still nervous, she began speaking. "Marshall, this is Kahara. Just wondering how everything is going. If you want to get in touch with me here's a number where you can reach me." She recited her home number, then hung up. It hurt her pride to do this, but in the event that he changed Internet providers and/or had lost her number, she didn't want to leave him any excuses. If he didn't contact her now, she'd know it was because he definitely didn't want to.

Chapter 9

Kahara spent the first part of the weekend capturing the festival footage into her computer. She purposely skipped over the segment containing Marshall, too angry to look at him, her wound still fresh. She burned the final piece onto a DVD and mailed it off to Craig, the reporter from the *Los Angeles Central*.

The final rehearsal for her film would be held that Sunday. Kahara was nervous about her two temperamental leads, Charles and Jasmine. She knew the two had become involved, and found out that Charles had recently dumped Jasmine. He called two days prior to rehearsal to ask if there was any way he could back out. Kahara, irritated by his lack of responsibility, insisted he complete the project.

Charles fell for Jasmine the moment he saw her. She was a stunning beauty. Her hourglass shape, sculptured features, full bow-shaped lips and large, searching eyes captivated the men on the set. Jasmine was likewise drawn to his tall good looks. But Kahara knew of Charles' reputation, and suspected from the beginning that he had no desire for anything long-term, just pulling a drive-through. Another Marshall. It angered her at how disposable some men viewed women.

When Kahara spoke to Jasmine, she assured her that nothing would prevent her from completing the film.

But when Jasmine arrived for rehearsal, Kahara noted a coolness in her demeanor. Jasmine looked over at Charles, who was slumped on the couch and gave him an icy hello. He barely mumbled a response.

Most of the intimate love scenes were implied, but there were three scenes that involved kissing. Kahara decided to direct the camera angle so that it would look as though they were kissing, even though their lips weren't touching. They were both awkward at first, but with Kahara's gentle direction, they were able to finally make it through the love scenes. Kahara breathed a sigh of relief after everyone left. It would be a huge setback if either Charles or Jasmine abandoned the project. Kahara took a week off from work to complete the shoot, which would start Monday and last five days.

Her film told the story of the young couple's breakup, via a series of flashbacks. Each character tells their best friend their own version of the beginning, middle and end of their affair. The first three days of the shoot went well, with the exception of a few mild arguments between Charles and Jasmine. As they made it midway through day four, things began to unravel. Charles' repeated indifference towards Jasmine made her increasingly hostile toward him. Their bickering grew worse, and Kahara found it increasingly difficult to direct them.

"Charles, would you put your arm around her again," Kahara said, sighing.

Charles put his arm around Jasmine's rigid shoulder. She glared at him without moving. "Jasmine, you still look like you want to split his head open," Kahara said, after the seventh take. "Charles, pull her close to you and kiss her—pretend to kiss her. You know, the way we practiced it."

Charles pulled Jasmine's stiff body close to his. He let go of her after a moment and got up. "I can't do this," he said, walking away. Kahara dropped her clipboard down onto an empty chair.

"Charles, come with me," she said, heading for the bedroom without looking back. Charles reluctantly followed her. He came in the room but did not close the door. Kahara walked behind him and slammed it. She turned to him.

"Listen, I'm going to get this picture done. Now I don't give a damn if you don't want to kiss her," she said, her voice loud, "but you're going to kiss her. And no more of this fake, shoot it from the side, bullshit. You're going to kiss her flat on the mouth. You made the decision to fuck her then dump her, that's your shit to fix—not mine. You ruin this for me, and I will put the word out to every independent filmmaker in this city. Choice is yours."

Charles headed for the door. "Ask Jasmine to come in here, please," Kahara said. Her stomach was balled up in knots. She was angry and frustrated. Her love life was a disaster, and the one thing she thought she could count on was falling apart in front of her eyes. She was in no mood for excuses. Jasmine walked in and closed the door.

"Listen, I want my piece *done*. You said you were a professional—then act like it. I've got a lot of money and time tied up in this. We're going to finish this film and you're going to kiss him on the mouth and you're going to pretend to like it. Some day when you win an Academy Award, you'll think back to this moment. Then again, you may not. I don't give a damn. I just want my picture done. You don't have to like kissing him—you don't have to like letting him hold you. FAKE IT. Are we on the same page?" Jasmine nodded reluctantly. "Alright, let's go back out and finish this scene."

Kahara opened the door and walked out with Jasmine. She wasn't sure if Charles would still be there, or if he had walked out. To her relief, he was seated on the couch. They resumed the shoot and made it through the scene. Jasmine and Charles seemed awkward at first during the bedroom scenes, but after the third take, they settled into a rhythm and by the fifth take, Kahara had what she thought was a convincing scene.

After everyone was gone, she reviewed the footage, as she had done every day prior. The last day of the shoot went by without any surprises. As they wrapped up, Kahara thanked the cast and the crew, and let them know how soon she would have a rough cut of the film ready. As the cast filed out, she overheard Charles talking to Jasmine. Kahara noted the softness of Charles' tone as he offered the leading lady a ride home. *Here we go again,* Kahara thought as they left.

The following day, Kahara phoned Craig Adams, the reporter from the *Los Angeles Central*, to find out when the interviews she shot for him at the Virginia Beach Black Film Festival would air. The local cable station, which Craig and his partners owned, aired footage gathered from volunteers from the US, the Caribbean, and different parts of Africa. A simulcast was also played over the web.

Craig told her the segment would run that following Monday, along with a web simulcast. Kahara pulled out the business cards she had collected from the festival and began calling all the participants to let them know when they could view the interviews on the web. As she sorted through the last three cards, she smiled when she got to Gary's. He wasn't home when she called, so she left him a message.

Three full weeks had gone by and Kahara had still not heard from Marshall. She realized now how foolish she was to even care if he called at that point. Kahara took refuge in the fact that her film was now completed, and she began the task of capturing all the footage into her computer. Soon, she would begin logging the portions of the scenes that she would use in the final piece.

Chapter 10

Exhausted after working eleven hours, Kahara plopped down on her couch that Monday evening. She reached into the brown paper bag, and took out an egg roll and shrimp fried rice she'd purchased from a nearby restaurant. After finishing her meal, she relaxed back on her couch and took a long look around her living room. It looked as drab as she felt. The floors were bare—no carpet, just ugly brown tile.

When Kahara purchased the condo, she decided to wait before decorating because she wanted to make sure she would hold onto it for at least two years. She had lived there for five. As she sat on the dark blue sofa she had bought from an old landlord more than seven years ago, she realized how worn and faded the fabric looked. Kahara hated dark colors—dark browns, deep maroons, dismal purples. Pastels had always been her favorites. Peach, turquoise. Why then was her apartment so drab? What was she waiting for? Kahara decided it was time to change her environment. Maybe that would pull her out of the slump she was in. She called Carol, an interior designer who lived in the building, and set up an appointment for the following day.

Her spirits lifted, she smiled as she thought of what her newly redecorated apartment might look like. She went into her office and brought up the website that was airing the festival footage. As she sat there watching the portion that contained her interview with Gary, she smiled thinking back on him. Gary, who had tried so hard to impress her even after she ignored him. Why had she ignored him? She had found his personality vexing, not certain whether he was interested in her, just being friendly, or just looking for another client. But why didn't she try to find out? She remembered back to how good he looked that Saturday afternoon at the seminar, dressed in his black slacks and black linen shirt—so tall and so lean.

There he was, offering to treat her to breakfast and she passed him up to chase Marshall. Did she ignore Gary because he was too nice? True, he was nice, but not like the self-effacing nice guys she had run across in the past. He exuded confidence and a reserved Southern charm. And as she thought about it, the most enjoyable times she had at the festival were with Gary. What was the matter with her? Why didn't she even probe to see if the man was interested?

Kahara decided she would now. She pulled out the business cards she had collected from the festival and sorted through them until she found his. She dialed his number. An anxious feeling bubbled in the pit of her stomach as his phone rang.

"Hello?"

"Gary?" she asked a little nervously.

"Yeah, this is Gary."

"It's Kahara from Chicago. Remember, we met at the Black Film Fest?"

"Oh yeah. How have you been?"

"Fine."

"Thanks for the message," he said. "I just saw the interview on the web. I thought I came off sounding a little cocky."

"No, no, not at all. You sounded confident, not cocky. There's a distinct difference—I know enough cocky men—believe me, you are not cocky," she said, trying not to gush too much. "Listen, when do you think you'll be in Chicago again?"

"In a few weeks actually. I've got some gigs lined up there. I'll be in Chicago on a somewhat regular basis for the next six months."

Kahara was elated. She sat up in her seat, excited at the prospect of seeing him soon. "Well, when you get in town, we should get together. Maybe have dinner."

"Yeah, we might do that," he said, his voice taking on a reserved tone.

"You like jazz?" she asked.

"Of course."

"Well, we've got some real nice intimate jazz spots. The Jazz Showcase, and this nice little getaway called Lights Out."

"Yeah, I've heard of that place." Gary cleared his throat. "Look Kahara, I feel it's only fair to tell you. You know at the time I met you at the festival, I wasn't involved with anybody."

Kahara felt her stomach drop. "But you are now," she finished for him.

"Yeah."

"How'd you meet her?" she said, sounding completely disinterested.

"Some friends introduced us, not even a week after the festival. We're both alums of Hampton," he said.

"That's nice." She was trying to keep her tone upbeat but it was hard. "You've got something in common," she said, with a trace of sarcasm. She slumped back down in her chair feeling deflated, but not surprised that he was already snatched up. "Maybe we could have a cup of coffee or something when you get in town," she said a little stiffly. Kahara paused for a moment, scared to say what she felt she had to say next. "Gary, do you mind if I ask you a question?" Kahara didn't want to do this so abruptly, but figured, given his tone, that she would not have time to blend it into the conversation.

"Naw, go ahead."

Kahara swallowed. "Were you ever interested in me?"

He laughed. "You couldn't tell?"

"Uh—no."

"Yeah, I guess you were too busy being felt up by that brother to see it."

Kahara's stomach dropped. "Oh, you saw that huh?"

"You kiddin'? Couldn't help *but* see it. Hey, you know but it's all right. You still seeing him?"

"Uh—no. No we're not—no."

Kahara quickly ended the conversation moments later, feeling completely embarrassed. She had an inkling that people could tell what was going on between her and Marshall, but to have it confirmed by a man she was trying to get together with was a little more than she could take. Especially, since Marshall dumped her. Her once upbeat mood was shattered. The depression she felt at the festival and in the weeks afterward crept in again. As Kahara looked around her apartment, she realized that remodeling would not be enough. She needed to change more than just her furniture.

In the days that followed, she became introspective as to why she hadn't met anyone. Kahara evaluated what she did after work, and on the weekends, and began to realize that she didn't have a lot of free time. She was being spread too thin. Her involvement with various committees in her apartment complex, the independent filmmakers organization, the video work she did for Craig, plus her own film projects, siphoned away most of her time. It was no mystery to her anymore why she hadn't met anyone.

After being honest with herself, Kahara also realized that the number one factor that prevented her from linking up with any eligible men was her hopeless attitude. She was very insecure about her age, her looks and her ability to attract and keep a mate. This was hidden by the upbeat attitude she displayed to friends and coworkers, but underneath that façade, lay a woman who felt past her prime and obsolete. This was an attitude Kahara realized she had to change.

In the weeks that followed, Kahara shed many activities that sucked away her time. She dropped off of all but one condo committee. She had a long conversation with Craig and told him that it would no longer be possible for her to hunt down current event stories, gather, edit, and send footage to him on a regular basis. He thanked her for the work she had done for him. He even baited her by telling her that if she ever decided to quit her job, she could move to L.A. and work for his organization on a part-time basis. Kahara thanked him and told him she would consider the offer.

With the help of Carol, the interior decorator who lived in her building, Kahara spent the next week shopping for paint, furniture, vertical blinds and other items she would need to redo her apartment. She spent her evenings spackling, applying primer to the walls, and then painting. Although she could more than afford to hire someone to do the painting for her, she found doing it herself relaxing. It allowed her to unravel and focus. She paid a contractor to install the cream-colored vertical blinds in the living room and the two bedrooms.

By June 5th, the decorating was complete—the L-shaped apartment transformed. The foyer now covered in ceramic tile, and beyond that, a thick blanket of plush eggshell carpet. The ugly dark blue couch replaced with a caramel-colored Italian leather sofa trimmed in rich mahogany. A beautiful marble coffee table sat between the couch and the matching loveseat. The bedrooms and the bathroom were redone in dusty peach, her favorite color.

As Kahara sat in her new living room, she thought back to the festival and to Marshall. The sting was gone now, as she realized what caused her to choose him in the first place. She examined and let go of a lot of the negative beliefs she had about aging, and after a while began dating again. The woman who at one time felt obsolete, now felt empowered.

On June thirtieth, she begged off of going out with her friends, and spent her fortieth birthday alone. Kahara chose to bring in her milestone birthday in solitude. At around seven o'clock, she poured herself a glass of red wine, turned on some jazz and made a toast to herself. No need for an audience of onlookers and well-wishers. She felt content to be alone, and finally at peace.

Chapter 11

Toward the middle of August, Kahara and her friend Arnita attended a gathering sponsored by the National Black Accountants Association. Arnita and Kahara had been friends since college at Northwestern University. Arnita obtained a degree in journalism and Kahara in finance.

The affair was held at the Hyatt Hotel, located in the downtown area of Chicago. They arrived at the event around 9:00 p.m. Kahara wore a sexy pale yellow A-line halter dress that hit her just above the knee, while Arnita looked svelte as ever in her fuchsia pink chiffon dress. Arnita was the same height as Kahara, but a petite size seven. As they sauntered in, Kahara smiled and nodded as she passed a few gentlemen. The party was not completely underway at that point. The huge banquet hall had only about fifty people in it. The DJ was spinning easy-listening jazz sounds. Kahara and Arnita ordered drinks and sat at one of the many empty tables.

"I need to call my sitter," Arnita said, taking a sip of her drink. She pulled out her cell phone and began dialing. Arnita was divorced with two children, a boy five years old named Kenny, and a twelve-year-old daughter named Darlene. "Yeah CJ, this is Arnita. Are they sleep yet? What? She did what?" Arnita leaned forward in her chair. "Put her on the phone." She looked at Kahara. "Fighting again. Listen little girl," she said to her daughter. "I don't care what he did, you don't hit him. He acts up, you tell CJ. You hear me? Naw, but nothing. Don't hit him unless you want me to hit you."

Kahara smiled as Arnita continued to chastise Darlene.

"I'll be back," Kahara said, tapping her arm. Arnita nodded. Kahara got up and wandered by a group of men engaged in conversation. In the past, she would never approach a group of men she didn't know, afraid it would make her seem lonely and desperate. But now she relished the challenge. She strolled up to the men, waited for an opening and then introduced herself. Two of them looked a little surprised, and one looked annoyed, by her interruption. Their reaction only spurred her on. To get over her apprehension, she made it a point to approach at least two men cold at any affair she attended. After a few minutes of conversation, she exchanged cards with some of them, then returned to her table. Arnita was still on the phone with her daughter.

"No you are not having any boys over if I'm not there. So what about CJ. CJ is nineteen years old. She's babysitting you and your brother—not you and Tyrone. Look, goodbye."

Kahara laughed as Arnita put her cell phone back into her purse.

"That child of mine," she said, shaking her head. She took a sip of her drink. "You never told me what happened to that guy you were dating."

"I don't know, it seems like the last few guys I've been out with expect sex after the second, third date. They take you to a nice restaurant a few times then feel they're entitled. I'm sorry, after Marshall, it ain't happening. I wouldn't care if it was Gary."

"Gary. You still think about him?"

"Yeah, sometimes," she said, sighing. "Oh well, blew that opportunity. So, what you got up for tomorrow?"

"Tony's taking me to see my girl Jill Scott."

Kahara leaned back. "Now that's romantic," she said wistfully. Kahara rested her chin in her hand and looked around the hall, observing the different suits milling about. "You know, I was at a singles meeting last month and this guy kept going on about how black men are a commodity, because there's a shortage of black men and how sisters better get it together or else we'll be passed over, because black men are in demand by women from all races, blah, blah, blah, blah, blah."

Arnita looked at her in surprise. "Really? I know you checked him on that." Arnita was all too familiar with Kahara's tendency to be outspoken.

"Oh yeah, I told him that kind of talk just encourages black women to be desperate and stay in bad relationships. Hell, most women can get laid, so it's not a question of quantity, it's quality. There's a shortage of quality on both sides, male and female. No disrespect to the brothers, but I feel I'm just as much of a commodity as they are," Kahara said, picking up her drink.

"I like that," Arnita said, clinking her glass against hers.

Chapter 12

Arnita's babysitter backed out at the last minute so Kahara agreed to fill in She and the children attempted to make tollhouse cookies. At the end of their cooking session, the kitchen was a mess of unused batter and burnt cookies.

"Well," Kahara said, looking around sighing, "that didn't work. Why don't I read you guys a nice bedtime story."

"Bedtime story," Darlene said, scrunching up her nose. "I'm too old for that."

Kahara took Darlene gently by the arm, and Kenny by the hand, and led them out into the living room. "You're never too old to learn a lesson," she said.

They settled down on Arnita's huge, plush, dark green sofa, and Kahara began to read from Kenny's black fairy tales book. Kenny was just learning to read and followed along diligently, as Kahara read to them. Kahara turned the page and studied the artwork, chuckling to herself.

"This really is an ugly ogre," she said, under her breath. "Okay well, in the land of Nod, there lived a mean, ugly ogre named Marshall."

"That doesn't say Marshall, it says Remella." Darlene said.

Kahara shrugged. "Marshall, Remella, same difference. Anyway, would you let me read the story? Alright then," she said, sitting back. "Marshall, I mean Remella, tricked the beautiful princess into coming away with him to the land of Nod, where he held her captive against her will for six long years." Kahara looked at Darlene. "See what happens? She should never have followed him there. She was naïve. Very naïve. Very stupid—too trusting. She should have found out more about him—checked him out better before running off with him. Remember that Darlene," she said, pointing her finger at her. "Never ever give up your power to a man. You hear me?"

Darlene gave her a strange look. "Yes, auntie Kahara."

"Me too?" Kenny asked eagerly.

Kahara laughed. "Well sweetie, in a different way, yeah. In your case it will be women. But you really shouldn't give up your power to anybody. Anyway, we're getting away from the story." She tweaked Kenny's cheek and hugged him close to her. "Alright, the beautiful princess used her scepter stone to hypnotize the ugly, disgusting, smelly, stupid, ignorant, dirty, lowlife ogre in order to make her escape."

"Auntie K, I don't see all those words there," Kenny said.

Kahara closed the book for a moment. "Of course you don't. That's called ad-libbing. Anyway don't interrupt the story-teller. Now, in today's terms the scepter stone would be the princess' verbal skills." She looked at Darlene. "This is important Darlene. Pay attention. She used her verbal skills to manipulate her oppressor in order to escape from him. That's what you have to do Darlene. Remember, your tongue, not your booty, is your greatest asset. It can get you out of a lot of trouble. Into a lot of trouble too if you're not careful," she said, under her breath.

"Yes, auntie," Darlene said laughing. "You a trip."

"Yes I am," she said. "Now I hope we're all learning a good lesson here. I know I am," she said.

She finished the story and then watched TV with the children. After putting Kenny to bed and finally convincing Darlene she needed her beauty sleep, Kahara spent the next hour cleaning up the mess she had made in the kitchen. Arnita arrived a little later. She checked on the kids, then sat in the kitchen with Kahara and told her about her night out with Tony. Arnita and Tony had been dating for over five months. She met him at the Tribune newspaper where she worked as an editor. He was an entertainment reporter.

"So where'd you go to dinner?"

"He took me to Lavenia's on twenty-second street. I had the soul food special—turkey, dressing, mustard greens, candied yams, macaroni and cheese."

"Stop it. You're making me hungry. How was Jill Scott?"

"Amazing. The sister is so on point. Tony's in love with her. Oh girl, you should have seen him. He wore a suit Kahara, a dark chocolate-brown suit to match that dark chocolate-brown skin of his. We went back to his place afterwards."

"And?" she said, nudging her.

Arnita blushed. "And what? I'm not tellin' you what happened. What do you think happened?"

Arnita was a little prim when it came to discussing sex. Jackie, the administrative assistant at Kahara's job, was just the opposite. Kahara and Jackie had more than a few down-and-dirty discussions about men and sex.

Chapter 13

After a long soak in a gently scented lavender bubble bath Monday evening, Kahara went into her office to continue working on her film. Having captured all the footage onto her computer, she continued editing the scenes together. About two hours later, the phone rang.

"Hello?"

"Hello Kahara? It's Gary."

"Gary," she said smiling, leaning back in her seat. "How are you?"

"Fine, how have you been lady?"

Kahara couldn't help but smile. "Great, just great."

"It's Labor Day weekend, what are you doing home?"

"I'm editing the film I told you I was shooting. I'm supposed to go to a barbecue tomorrow, if it's not too cool."

At first Kahara thought he was calling just to touch base, but as the conversation continued she could sense he was fishing for something more. She had to get used to men like Gary—the ones who put out feelers instead of being blunt and physical the way the Marshalls of the world were.

"So when are you coming back to Chicago?" she asked, trying to prod him along.

"As a matter of fact—next week. I've got a shoot next Friday."

Kahara leaned forward. "Really," she said. "How long will you be here?"

"I get in Thursday night. The shoot will last all day Friday and Saturday morning. I leave Sunday evening."

That left Saturday. Kahara waited to see if he would ask to see her before making any suggestions herself. The air was silent for a moment.

"Say, if you're not busy Saturday, I was thinking maybe we could check out a movie."

"Perhaps, if I feel like it. I'm high-maintenance, remember?"

He laughed. "Yeah, that's right. In that case I guess I better let you pick it."

"Alright, well how about—"

"Naw, don't tell me. Wait until I get there. I want to see if I can guess it."

"Oh, so you're tryin' to get in my head now, huh?"

"A good place to start."

"Mannish," she said.

"Mannish? What's mannish?"

"Oh no, not again," she said, under her breath. "Never mind, I'll explain it to you when you get here."

After hanging up, Kahara leaped from her seat and danced her way into the living room. After nearly tripping over the marble cocktail table, she regained her composure, returned to her office and continued working.

As the week came to a close, Jackie commented that there was a certain sparkle in Kahara's eyes that hadn't been there before. "This must be a reeeeal special one because I don't think I've ever seen you like this."

"Like what?"

"Lit up like a Christmas tree." Jackie grinned, then leaned over her desk, speaking softly. "Listen, just don't give him some on the first date and mess up like you did before."

"I never told you I gave Marshall some on the first date."

"You were only there four days girl. Told you to keep your damn legs closed. Don't listen to nobody. Hardheaded. Giving that man all your eggs and bacon."

Kahara laughed. "All my eggs and bacon?" She smiled at her shaking her head. "Look Jackie, I won't slip again. I do like Gary, but I'm not gonna—not after Marshall." She shook her head. "Don't worry."

After spending the first part of Saturday morning viewing the rough-cut of her film, Kahara rewarded herself with a visit to a day spa. She arrived home a little after six, which left her less than an hour to get ready.

At six-thirty, Gary called to let her know the shoot had run long, and he would be there around eight o'clock. After getting dressed, Kahara went in her dresser drawer and pulled out the T-shirt Gary had given her at the festival. She went into the living room, stood in front of the mirror, and held the shirt up to her shoulders. A smile spread across her face as she thought back to how sweet Gary looked that Sunday when he gave it to her.

The doorman called a moment later to let her know that Gary had arrived. She draped the shirt over the couch, and ran back in front of the mirror to take one last look at her outfit. The sleeveless black and white polka-dot dress hugged her full hips gently. The sexy high-heeled, black-strapped sandals topped off the outfit nicely. A few moments later she heard a light knock at the door. Kahara breathed deep trying to contain her excitement. She opened the door slowly. Gary stood in the doorway giving her a faint smile.

Still got those beautiful sad eyes, she thought. "Hi Gary," she said, reaching up to hug him. He slid his long arms around her waist and gave her a solid embrace.

"How you doin' lady," he said softly, as he slowly let go of her. Kahara blushed.

Gary held her chin up with his finger. "You're blushin'," he said, smiling.

Kahara stepped back, feeling embarrassed, and allowed him to enter. "How did your shoot go?" she asked a little nervously.

"Except for a few last-minute glitches, fine," he replied as he walked in. Gary strolled around the living room taking in the view of downtown Chicago. "This is nice," he said, looking out the window. "Is this a two-bedroom?"

"Yeah. What do you have?" she asked.

"A house," he replied nonchalantly.

Nice, Kahara thought to herself. They left a few minutes later. As they waited for the elevator, Kahara could feel Gary's eyes on her.

"You're sizing me up again," she said, nudging him playfully.

He smiled. "Just admiring what's in front of me." He nodded, as she walked in front of him to board the elevator. "You are definitely wearing that dress," he said.

"Thank you, I guess, if you meant that as a compliment," she said, looking back at him.

"Definitely," he replied.

When they reached the driveway, Gary walked her over to a midnight blue Lexus. The car belonged to his cousin

Darren. Kahara found out Darren owned a town home about a half-mile from her apartment complex. As they drove, Kahara asked Gary more about his business.

"On small shoots, I'll usually handle the lighting, audio and camera. But for larger jobs, I'll pull from a list of free-lancers, cameramen, audio technicians, etc. I just purchased a high-definition editing suite."

"That's nice," she said, rolling her eyes back in her head, pretending to be bored.

Gary gave her a strange look and then continued. "I brought some tapes with me, if you want to see some of my work," he said.

Kahara sighed heavily. "For what? I know what you do. I don't have time to be lookin' at no damn tapes. You don't have to impress me Gary, I'm going out with you. Isn't that enough?" She looked over at him and smiled. "Of course I want to see your work," she said.

Gary laughed. "You got a sense of humor," he said. "I like that."

Kahara smiled. In spite of her pretext, she was indeed impressed. She knew a state-of-the-art high definition editing suite could run well over six grand.

As they continued chatting, Kahara caught Gary watching her as she smoothed her dress down over the curve of her thighs.

He looked back at the road. "I'll bet I can guess which movie you picked," he said. *"Urban Love."*

"How'd you know?" she said, looking over at him.

"You seem like you're in the mood for some romance."

She nodded and smiled. "From the way you were just looking at my legs, I'd say you're the one who's in the mood for something."

Gary laughed. "You caught that huh?"

"I catch everything."

Kahara looked down, admiring Gary's long legs.

He looked over at her. "Ahh, what are you lookin' at?"

"Same thing you were looking at a few minutes ago."

Gary smiled as he continued driving. The Italian restaurant was located on the northern part of town, about thirty minutes from Kahara's place. It was a small, cozy establishment with red-and-white checkered tablecloths. As Kahara dug into her four-inch mountain of lasagna drenched with tomato sauce, she tried to maintain her poise as Gary continued to study her.

"So why haven't you ever been married?"

"Well that was sudden," Kahara said, trying to think up an answer. She didn't really have one. "Let me ask you a question," she said. "Why did you say I was high-maintenance?"

He looked at her and smiled. "A man can always tell when a woman is going to be work. I can take one look at you and tell you're not the compliant type."

"And that's bad?"

"No, it's not bad, but the complete opposite isn't good either."

"You think I'm the complete opposite?"

He looked at her skeptically for a moment. "Close."

"So why did you take me out then?" she asked.

"Something about you," he said, "you just stuck in my head."

She smiled, feeling complimented by his last statement. During their conversation, Kahara found out that Gary had been married in his early twenties, and then divorced when he was twenty-seven. He was now thirty-six. His ex-wife moved back to L.A. shortly after they divorced. He reached in his pocket, pulled out his wallet, and flipped to a picture of his son. "This is Calvin," he said. "He turned thirteen in July." His son had the same caramel brown complexion as his father, with the same rugged chin and deep-set sad eyes.

"He's adorable," she said.

Gary smiled. "I do a number of shoots in L.A., so I get to see him regularly, or else I fly him up to see me." He put his wallet back in his pocket. "You said you finished your film?"

"Yeah. We had an incident with the two leads the forth day of the shoot," Kahara leaned back in her chair, not sure whether she should make her next remark, thinking it might feed into his impression of her being high-maintenance. "I had a slight explosion though, and that seemed to get them back in line."

"You have a temper?"

"Welllllll, maybe," she said, biting her bottom lip. "Let's just say I'm spirited."

Gary smiled, taking a bite of his ravioli. "That's code for bad temper," he said.

"You don't like spirited women?"

"Depends on how spirited," he said. "I'll have to see you when you get mad."

Kahara leaned forward, smiling coyly. "So, you're obviously interested in me."

"You think so, huh?" he said, leaning back in his chair and resting his chin against his knuckles, staring at her.

Kahara became uncomfortable under his gaze. "What are you thinking when you stare at me like that?" she asked.

Gary took a sip of his drink. "How much I'm enjoying all of this," he said softly.

Next Time

Kahara smiled. They finished dinner then headed to the theatre.

As they stood in line to get their tickets, Kahara reveled in how good it felt to stand next to someone so tall. Gary's 6-3 frame towered over her. She liked that. They took their seats in the middle of the theatre. Gary sat deep in his seat with his elbows propped on the armrests, his legs gapped open. Kahara looked down at his long, lean legs and became aroused. She loved tall slim men—it was like an instant aphrodisiac. As they watched the movie, her knee accidentally touched the side of his thigh. He looked over at her, smiled, and then put his arm around her. Kahara leaned her head on his shoulder and breathed in the scent of his Polo cologne. They returned to her apartment after the movie. Gary parked a few blocks from her complex, reached in the back seat, and gathered up three tapes.

"One is a documentary I shot a few months ago, the other is for an event held in North Carolina for the NAACP, and the third is a video shoot for that group—"

"Yeah, yeah, whatever," Kahara said impatiently. "Just give me the damn tapes so I can get upstairs please."

He looked at her and shook his head as she took the tapes from him. "You a trip," he said, as they got out of the car.

"Yeah, I know," she said.

The couple continued chatting as they walked to her apartment building. Kahara looked through the tapes he gave her as they rode up the elevator. When they reached her door, she took her keys out of her purse. She looked up at him just as he came toward her and planted a deep kiss on her mouth.

"Gary," she said hesitantly.

"Yeah?"

"Are you still seeing that woman you told me about a few months ago?"

He looked at her and smiled. "Took you this long to get up the nerve to ask me that, huh?"

"Kahara poked his shoulder lightly. "Just answer the question, smart ass," she said, turning to open the door.

He laughed. "No. Why, you got somebody in mind?"

"Oh, so we're gonna play it like, hah? No, to be honest, I can't think of anybody who'd put up with you."

She opened the door and walked in with Gary strolling behind her. She placed the tapes on her entertainment center and took a seat next to Gary on the couch.

"So tell me why you don't think anyone would be able to put up with me," he said, draping his long arm around her shoulder. Kahara felt her insides go weak.

Breathe. Breathe. Breathe, Kahara said to herself, as he pulled her in his arms for a long, soulful kiss. "Well," she said, sighing heavily, pulling away from him a little afterwards. "You seem very exacting."

"Hmph. Yeah, I guess I am. I know what I like. And I don't usually waste time if I see it's not going to work."

"Usually."

"You caught that huh?"

"Told you, I catch everything," she said.

He looked over and noticed the t-shirt draped over the couch and smiled. "Almost forgot about that," he said. "What's it doing out here, were you going to wear it?"

"I haven't worn it yet, but ever since you called, I bring it to bed every night and press it up against my body before I go to sleep."

He looked at her skeptically. "If you really did that would you tell me?" he asked.

She smiled. "Maybe I would. Maybe I would."

Next Time

As they sat talking, Gary discussed his future plans to relocate to Los Angeles, in order to take advantage of the numerous contacts he had there. Although he had a number of contacts and clients in Chicago, he wanted to move to L.A. to be closer to his teenage son. Kahara told him about her desire to write and direct films full-time. They talked for about an hour before saying goodnight.

After Gary left, Kahara watched one of the tapes he gave her before going to bed. She smiled as she saw his name listed in the credits. His work was impressive. She went into her bedroom a few moments later, undressed, and slipped into the long, white satin gown that she had stashed in her drawer for over four years. The cool satin felt good against her skin. Just as she was about to climb into bed, the phone rang. She snatched it up thinking it was Gary.

"Hello," she said, in her sexiest voice.

"Alright cut it, it's Arnita. I couldn't wait until tomorrow. Did you give him some?"

"I'm not going to tell you that," she said, mimicking Arnita.

"You did it?" Arnita asked.

"No. I told you I wouldn't." She climbed into bed and pulled up the sheet.

"Did he look as good as you remembered?"

Kahara stretched her arms up over her head and sighed. "Better. Girl, I love his eyes. I caught him staring at my legs in the car. He kissed me—damn he's got some soft lips. He looked so good and he smelt so good. I just wanted to fold up in those arms of his and—"

"Slow down. Slow down. Don't go off the deep end yet. So, did he say when he was coming back in town?"

"No."

"Did he say when he was going to call?"

"No."

"Did he say he was going to call?"

"Yeah, but they always do." Kahara smiled, thinking back on their spirited exchange. "I got a feeling he will though."

After hanging up, Kahara went into the living room, took the t-shirt Gary gave her off the couch, and took it back to bed with her. As she relaxed, processing the events of the evening, her thoughts drifted to their conversation. While relieved that he wasn't seeing anyone, Kahara began to wonder about a few things. Gary said he usually didn't embark on affairs that he knew were not destined to work. Usually. Where did that leave her? Was she someone he felt he could establish something long-term with, or was she to him, as she was to Marshall—a weigh station until something better came along? And what did he mean by "I'll call you?" When? Why didn't men ever tell her when they would call? Kahara caught herself going down that old insecure road, and stopped herself before she went any further.

"Not tonight," she said. "No more. If it works, it works. If it doesn't, like Thomas from New York said—move on." She rolled over, pushing all other negative thoughts out of her mind, and fell into a deep and restful sleep.

Kahara had lunch with Jackie that Monday in the company break room, and recounted her evening with Gary.

Jackie leaned in, speaking softly. "So you didn't have sex with him."

"No. I told you already."

"Just making sure. Did he say he'd call you?"

"Yeah," she said, looking away.

"When?"
"When?"
"Yeah, when?"
"I don't know. I didn't ask."
"Well why not?"
"He didn't volunteer it so I didn't press it. I don't want to seem too anxious."

When Kahara arrived home from work that evening, she went into her office to continue editing her film. As she waited for her computer to boot up, her thoughts drifted back to her date with Gary a few nights ago. She rested her chin in her hand and began daydreaming about the event. Almost ten minutes went by without her noticing.

Shifting her focus away from Gary, she turned back to the film project. She was in the process of fixing sound problems. Kahara listened to the film without watching, to make sure that she focused only on the sound. Hours zoomed by as she worked tirelessly. When she had first looked at her watch, it was just after six. It was now nine forty-five. There was more work to be done, but she decided to call it a night, as she had not had dinner yet.

Gary called her the following evening. Kahara let him know how much she enjoyed the video tapes he'd left with her. He told her he'd be back in town at the end of September. As she lay in bed that night, she cupped her hands behind her head and sighed. After their first date, Kahara was hopeful, but still not sure whether Gary was really interested in her. Her doubts were erased, though, by the fact that he was flying in, twice in one month to see her. For their next date, Gary surprised Kahara by spiriting her away in a limo to an expensive restaurant, then off to see the August Wilson play *Fences*.

That Sunday, Kahara walked to the Ramada Inn. She, Arnita, and two of her filmmaker friends, Sergio and Keith, met there once a month for brunch. Keith owned a tax preparation company, and like Kahara, was also a filmmaker. Sergio was a screenwriter who taught classes at Columbia College. Keith's cousin Al joined them. He lived in Evanston, a suburb of Chicago, and taught African American Studies at Northwestern University.

Keith and Sergio looked visibly bored as Kahara and Arnita huddled together discussing her limo date of the previous evening. Al talked on his cell phone. Keith read the Sunday paper, while Sergio sorted through the magazine section. Both men were in their mid-forties and both had receding hairlines. Keith was thin and stood about five feet ten, while Sergio weighed about two-hundred-and-forty pounds and was a little over six feet. Keith's cousin was a tall, attractive man, of medium build, but unlike Keith, had a full head of salt-and-pepper hair.

"So what happened after that?" Arnita asked Kahara excitedly.

"Well," she said, leaning back, "the *limo* driver took us to Medici's restaurant for dinner."

"That's so romantic," Arnita said.

"You should have seen all the people watching us as we got out of—the *limo*. I have never felt so special in my life. He is such a sweetheart. You should have seen him Arnita. He looked so handsome in his navy suit."

Keith looked at his cousin Al and sighed, shaking his head, and continued reading.

"I'm serious. I—am—*still* blown away. And the play." She sat back in her seat. "The play was awesome, absolutely awesome."

"Which play was it?" Keith asked.

"*Fences*," Kahara replied. "When we pulled up in front of the theatre and got out of—the *limo*. I swear, I felt like a movie star."

"You act like you've never been in—a *limo* before," Sergio quipped. "Oh, I keep forgetting, you're so cheap."

"Frugal," Kahara said, correcting him.

"Yeah, right. Like I said, you're so *cheap*, you probably haven't."

"Have you?"

Sergio huffed a little. "Of course I have."

"Why'd he take you in a limo anyway?" Keith asked.

"Because it's romantic," Kahara said, "And besides, his friend owns a limo service and gave him a good rate."

"Alright. Alright. So tell me again. Tell me again," Arnita said. "How did you feel when you *first* saw that limo."

Sergio groaned loudly.

"Girl, my mouth almost *fell* open. I swear the whole evening, I've got this stupid grin on my face."

"You mean like the one you got now?" Sergio said, his impatience showing.

"Man, shut up. Let her finish," Keith said, sighing. "So we can talk about something else."

"What's this guy do for a living anyway?" Sergio asked.

"He owns a video production company. He shoots film, video, does sound, lighting, editing."

"Really? You seen any of his work?" Keith asked, leaning forward, his interest now peaked.

"Yeah, he's very good."

"Hmph, maybe I can use him on my next shoot," Keith said. Keith was in the process of finishing up a screenplay for his third short film.

"He shoot any porn?" Sergio quipped, grinning.

"No he hasn't shot any porn," Kahara said, shoving his arm.

Sergio smirked as he continued leafing through the magazine. "Hmph, look at this," he said. "Kahara, you're forty. Arnita you're near forty."

"What's your point?" Kahara asked, sensing something controversial was coming. Sergio had a knack for raising controversies.

"This article explores the question of why older men prefer younger women. In case you were wondering."

"Not really." Arnita said.

Sergio scanned the article, then began reading out loud. "In the case of mating, what the male is looking for at an instinctual level is the likelihood of reproduction. Since a woman is visually less stimulating when she's less likely to reproduce—wrinkles around the eyes, sagging breasts—certain clues to the inability to bear children, the male is more likely to choose her younger more appealing counterpart."

"Give me that," Arnita said, snatching the magazine away from him. Her eyebrows furrowed as she began reading.

"Did he make it up or is it really in there?" Kahara asked, peering over her shoulder.

"Yeah, it's in here," Arnita said, as she continued reading. "And it blames us when they can't get it up."

"No it doesn't," Sergio insisted, grabbing the magazine back from her. "Let me see. Okay here it is. It says a younger woman is more likely—more apt—to cause an erection than the older, less attractive female."

"Sergio, you're opening up a can of worms," Keith said.

Next Time

"What he's saying may be painful to hear, but it's true," Al said.

Kahara and Arnita looked at Keith's cousin with stunned expressions.

"Man don't get in this, please," Keith said.

"No, it's alright. I can use myself as an example. A woman in her twenties is more stimulating to me sexually than a woman in her forties—or her thirties for that matter."

Arnita looked at Al. "How old are you?"

"Fifty-eight."

"My mother's sixty—you probably wouldn't even look at someone her age would you?" Kahara asked.

He laughed softly, shaking his head. "Not likely."

"How old are the women you date?" Arnita asked.

"In their twenties, I'll bet. Why don't you date women your age?" Kahara demanded.

"Kahara calm down," Arnita said.

"No, she had it right, most of them are in their twenties. Put it this way, I perform better sexually with younger women."

"That crap's all in your head," Kahara said.

"Of course it is. Most sex is mental. Young women give me erections—old women don't. Simple as that. I prefer a young, tight body. It feels better, smells better."

"Smells better?" Kahara said.

"Man, please. Change the subject," Keith said.

"I'm sorry, but that mixture of perfume and mature body odor is sickening." He leaned back in his seat. "I like women who smell young and fresh *under* their perfume."

Kahara gave him the middle finger. Arnita grabbed her hand and pulled it down. "Maybe the women you ran into didn't use good hygiene."

"Let me tell you something," Kahara said glaring at him. "This whole—my dick won't stay hard unless I'm with a younger female is a crock of shit."

"Kahara."

"What?"

Arnita got up and took her by the arm. "Excuse us, we're going to the *ladies'* room."

Kahara rose out of her seat. "And another thing, unlike you, my stuff will still work when I'm fifty-eight."

"Come on Kahara."

"And I won't need Viagra," she said, as Arnita led her away to the restroom.

"Can you believe that bastard?" Kahara said, once they were inside.

"I could tell you were about to take his head off. That's why I removed you from the area."

"I like women who smell young and fresh," she said, mimicking him. "See, it's men like him—old women are no less desirable than old men. In fact, if you compare it just on sexual performance—we come out ahead. My stuff will still work when I'm sixty, while many of them will be struggling just to stay hard for five minutes. But they know that. And they know that most older women, given the choice would choose a young man with a stiff dick than an old man with a limp one. So they make us seem obsolete to limit our choices. That way they can pick from a pool of younger and older woman. It takes the pressure off of them but turns us into throw-aways, and I resent that shit. We pass a certain age, we become old hags. But old men are desirable, distinguished and wise. My ass. We've been sold a bill of goods Arnita. I'ma go out there and tell that old bastard that," she said, heading for the door.

Arnita grabbed her arm. "No, cool off K. He's one old clueless man. Let it go. Let—it—go."

Kahara gave her a strained look. "I'll let it go. I'll let it go," she said.

They left the restroom a few moments later. When they returned to their seats, a petulant looking Al greeted them.

"I'm sorry if I upset you ladies," he said.

"No you're not," Kahara shot back. "You did it purposely. You need to make us feel obsolete because you feel obsolete. You and this whole sick ass society that tells women over the age of 40 that we're worthless. You have issues with aging, so you scapegoat women. You're terrified of growing old. But it happens. Get over it. Deal with it."

"Kahara," Arnita said softly, trying to quiet her.

"And stop blamin' us because your dick won't stay hard."

Keith sighed, shaking his head. "Told you to change the subject man."

Al excused himself about ten minutes later and left. Keith looked at Kahara as she sipped her drink.

"What?"

"Don't you think you were a little hard on him?"

"No. He deserved it. You thought that was bad, you should have heard what I said in the bathroom."

"Look, I'm not excusing his rudeness," Keith said. "Yes, he has a tremendous ego and very antiquated views about women, but do you ever know when to let up?"

"Keith, I did let up. After I got through telling him how I felt," Kahara said. "I've seen his type before. My uncle only messed around with twenty-year-olds too, until he had a stroke a few years ago. Now he's lookin' for a mature woman to play nursemaid."

"I hope I don't wind up like that," Sergio said, shifting his large body in his seat.

"What are you going to do when you get old Serge," Kahara asked, "pay some young blonde to wipe your ass—change your diapers?"

"If I can sell enough screenplays, yeah."

Kahara couldn't help but laugh. As she walked home from the Ramada, she thought about what Keith had said. She was less concerned about his cousin's ego than she was about what her temper might do to her budding relationship with Gary.

Chapter 14

As Kahara was jotting down the segments where she would lay backdrop music for her film she received a phonecall from Gary. She told him about her long hours at the office, the sound difficulties she was having with the film, and how she'd fallen behind schedule. Gary returned to Chicago in mid-October to help her, bringing special sound software to install on her computer.

As Kahara sat next to him, watching her film, she felt a little apprehensive being under such scrutiny, since she wrote and directed it. After the film was over she turned to him.

"So?"

He smiled at her. "I liked it," he said. "It held my interest. Some of those arguments were pretty heated." He studied her for a moment. "Did you draw from your own experiences when you created the dialogue?"

"Oh come on Gary," she said nudging him. Gary pulled her close to him and kissed her on the forehead. Kahara lifted her eyebrows, biting her bottom lip. She wondered to herself how Gary would react when he found out that she did indeed have a temper.

Gary installed the sound software he brought with him. He worked with her, helping her get the hang of the complex functions. Sitting next to him as he instructed her, she couldn't help but get a little turned on. He seemed so sure of himself and confident. He walked her through each of the special features and guided her as she worked through a few scenes. After working with him for a few hours, she felt confident she could finish fixing the remaining sound problems on her own.

Later that evening, they went to dinner at Heaven on Seven, a popular Cajun restaurant located in downtown Chicago. They dined with Gary's cousin Darren, his girlfriend Angie, and another couple, Derrick and Lisa. Kahara considered it a good sign that he was introducing her to relatives. Darren was about five years older than Gary. He was divorced with two children, and lived less than a mile south of Kahara in a new development. He and Gary could almost be mistaken as brothers. Both were tall and slim, around 6-2, Gary standing about an inch taller.

As they ate, Gary's cousin began playing devil's advocate about his cousin's budding relationship.

"Yeah, I can't remember the last time Gary dated a woman who wasn't from the South," Darren said. "This is something new to me."

"Alright man—"

"Kahara, I can't tell you the number of women I've tried to hook him up with here and—nope. Very particular. You must be something special, because this brotha doesn't do long-distance. And that whole limo thing. Ah ah." Darren leaned forward. "You didn't do no roots or nothin' on him did you?"

"Stop, Darren, don't you see you're embarrassing her," his girlfriend said.

Kahara looked away not knowing what to say.

"Seriously though Kahara, Gary's a good brotha," Darren continued. "I wouldn't trade him. But then I don't have a choice—he's blood."

"Keep steppin' in it. You gonna wind up with nobody to shoot that concert for you," Gary said.

"Ah man now, don't do me like that. Help me out Angie," Darren said, looking over at his date. "Tell him I was just kiddin'."

"Oh, now you want to backpedal. No, I'm out of it," she said.

"See now, if you had my back you'd have jumped in to defend me. See how mean she is to me? Help me out Derrick, Lisa," Darren pleaded to the other couple.

"Nope," Derrick said, cutting into his steak. "He's shooting my wedding,"

"Is he doin' it for free?"

"No, but he's giving me a good rate," Derrick said.

"Ah man. I'll get you a better cameraman."

"That's right. You better let that cameraman shoot the concert too," Gary said, leaning back in his seat, giving him a knowing smile.

"Kahara, see how mean he is to me? Does he treat you like this?" Darren said, shaking his head. He looked away. "Bastard," he said, under his breath.

"Don't mind them, Kahara," Angie said. "They go at it like this all the time."

"Gary man, you still gonna shoot that piece for me, right?"

Gary looked at him saying nothing.

"You gonna do it, right man?"

"Where's that waiter at?" Gary said, looking away.

Darren looked at Angie. "He's gonna do it. Aren't you Gary? Gary?" Darren shifted in his seat. "Gary, you know what I was thinkin' man? And this—this would be real slick too—Kahara being an indie filmmaker and all.

Why don't—why don't the two of you produce a film. Something black-themed, you know. Help the race. Give back."

Gary looked over at Kahara. "He's workin' you K, don't even listen to it."

"Why I gotta be workin' somebody? I made a suggestion. A good suggestion." He turned to his girlfriend. "Wasn't it a good suggestion, Angie?"

His girlfriend laid down her fork. "Look, I told you leave me out of this."

"See what I mean, black man don't get no support from his women. I mean woman. I'm getting me a white girl. I'ma marry a white girl."

"Go ahead. And that concert shoot won't be the only piece you don't get," Angie said, giving him a hard stare.

"Ah man, I'm blowin' up all over the place here. Look Angie, I was just kiddin' okay. I'm not gonna run off with some white woman." He leaned back smiling at Gary. "I may mess around with a few when you're not lookin'. But I won't leave you for one. You feel better now?"

"I'd feel better if you thought about what you were going to say before you opened your mouth sometime. How about that?"

"Yeah whatever," he said, leaning forward. "Gary man, I'm serious though about that film thing though. Ya'll should do it."

Gary gave him a skeptical look.

"Seriously."

Gary nodded. "It's a good idea," he said.

Kahara smiled slightly, happy that he was willing to consider working with her on a project. It made her feel their relationship could have some longevity. They left the restaurant, and Daren took them to one of his favorite nightspots. On the way there, Darren and Gary continued their spirited exchange. Kahara liked Darren and Angie, and found a certain reassurance in the fact that they seemed to have a stable relationship. The dance club was packed with people when they arrived. Kahara watched the hopeful sea of female faces, as they headed to the dance floor. As they slow danced, Gary held her close in his long arms. Kahara draped her arms around his neck, taking a deep whiff of his cologne.

"You enjoying yourself?" he asked softly into her ear.

"Oh yeah," she said sighing. She gently stroked the back of his neck with her fingers. He drew back after a moment, then kissed her on the lips. His cousin, who was dancing next to them, pushed Gary's arm.

"No kissin' in here," he said sternly.

"I got somethin' you can kiss," Gary said.

"You see how he talks to me, Angie?" Darren said. Angie shook her head and said nothing.

"Your cousin is a trip," Kahara said, as they continued to dance.

"You think he was bad tonight—you should see him at the family reunion."

Kahara was going to ask when that was, but stopped herself, not wanting Gary to think she was trying to invite herself to it. She found out later that the reunion would be held next year, toward the end of the summer. Kahara hoped she and Gary would still be going strong by then. Gary left the next day, and let her know that he would be back in town some time in November.

The following week, Kahara held a screening of the film's rough cut for the cast and crew at her apartment. Everyone had arrived by seven except the two leads,

Jasmine and Charles, who showed up thirty minutes later. As they stood in the doorway, Kahara could tell by their glum expressions that they must have just had an argument.

"I'm sorry Kahara. I would have been on time if a certain person didn't leave me waiting in the lobby for over twenty minutes," Jasmine said. Charles left her standing in the doorway and walked over to the couch, taking a seat next to Lawrence, the cameraman.

"The one time—the only time she's ready for somethin'," he said, shaking his head. "I had car trouble Kahara, that's why I couldn't get here in time."

"Like hell," Jasmine said, walking over, plopping down on the other side of Lawrence.

Charles leaned forward. "You got here, didn't you?" He leaned back in his seat. "Then shut the hell up."

Jasmine bent forward. "Don't tell me to shut up. Don't ever tell me to shut up."

Lawrence looked over at Kahara for help. She hurried over. "Hey listen, listen," she said, clapping her hands together. "Everyone, tell me your preference, and I'll order up a couple of pizzas."

After dinner, Jasmine and Charles were on good terms again. Lawrence traded places with Charles so that they could sit together. The group enjoyed the film with no further interruptions. After everyone left, Kahara relaxed on the couch, encouraged that everyone was pleased with her preliminary edit.

Gary called Kahara from Los Angeles that evening. Kahara filled him in on how the screening went, and about the drama between Charles and Jasmine.

"I don't see how they've lasted this long, if they fight the way you say they do."

Next Time

"Didn't you have any disagreements in your past relationships?" Kahara asked. She was a little concerned whether Gary was the type to cut and run at the first sign of turbulence.

"I had some, but for the most part—no. I don't have time for a lot of drama."

"Hmph, neither do I, but it happens," she said. She had hoped for a more tolerant response.

Gary filled her in on the music video shoot he was doing in L.A. He called her when he returned to Norfolk, and they discussed what they would do when he returned to Chicago.

"My cousin's invited us to a celebration at the TV station. You feel like going?" he asked.

"How about if we just stayed in this time?" she said. "We could order a pizza, rent a movie, pop some popcorn, and just snuggle, you know."

"Yeah, I know." She could feel him smiling through the phone. "Sounds like a plan. I've got a shoot that Saturday, but we should be wrapped up by six. That'll leave us plenty of time to—snuggle, as you put it," he said, his tone suggestive.

As Kahara readied for bed, she hoped Gary's idea of snuggling didn't include sex. Her sexual attraction to him was strong. At times she wondered if he would fade away if he had to wait too long, but she was firm in her resolve to be absolutely certain before allowing herself to sleep with him.

Chapter 15

Kahara's late hours at the office forced her to move the completion date from the end of November to the end of December. Once she finished the film edits, she would devote her time to concluding the screenplay for the feature-length version of her short film.

Gary arrived back in town around the middle of November. His shoot was to last two days, and he promised Kahara he'd be there Saturday evening around seven. At six-thirty, he called her to say they'd run over schedule and that she should expect him around eight. As she showered, she thought about the evening that lay before them, and smiled. This would be the first time they would be alone together for an extended period since they started dating. She looked forward to their isolation.

Smoothing scented lotion over her arms, bosom, and down her legs and thighs, she donned a soft cream-colored knit sweater and a black corduroy skirt with black tights, to keep her thick legs warm. Kahara decided to order a pizza, not yet all that secure with her cooking skills. At eight o'clock, confident that Gary would show up any minute, she sat at the dining room table, the hot pizza sitting squarely in the center. At eight-thirty, she became concerned, and at nine-fifteen, angry. Kahara sat there with her arms folded, snatching up the phone when it finally rang at nine-thirty.

"Hello," she snapped.

"Kahara, listen it's Gary. I'm sorry babe, but I'm not going to get out of here until well after midnight. We had some major problems with the equipment, and half of the footage from yesterday got erased by one of the crew members."

"Why are you just calling me? You were supposed to be here over two hours ago," she said loudly.

"Did you hear anything I just said?" Gary said, his voice betraying his impatience.

"Yes, I heard you, but I still didn't hear you answer the question."

"Look, I have to get back. I'll call you when I get done."

"When is that supposed to be?"

"When I get *done*," he said tensely.

"Whatever," she said, hanging up without waiting for him to say goodbye.

Kahara looked at the uneaten pizza and sighed hard. She got up and put the pizza in the refrigerator, too despondent to eat any of it. She undressed, and put on her nightgown and watched TV in bed. A little disjointed by their first tiff, she wasn't sure if she should be mad at him, or mad at herself for not being more understanding. Kahara dozed off, but was awakened around one in the morning by the telephone.

"Hello," she said, groggily rolling over, TV droning in the background.

"Yeah, it's Gary. Just wrapped up everything here. I'm heading over my cousin's house now. Listen, I need to talk to you about something. What time are you free tomorrow?"

"I don't know, around three."

"Alright, I'll see you then."

"Fine," she said, not sure how to take what he just said to her. She hung up, cut off the TV, and went back to sleep.

Kahara milled around her apartment the next day, a little nervous as to what Gary wanted to discuss. She had an idea though. He sounded miffed at her for being upset about their cancelled date. She made a few phone calls to friends, then watched a movie, trying to distract herself from her growing concern over the subject of the impending conversation.

Around 3:00 p.m., Gary arrived. They sat in the living room and chatted, the opening conversation polite enough, but once the pleasantries were spent, Gary got to the meat of why he came over.

"Listen," he said, "the last relationship I had ended because she didn't understand the demands of the business I'm in. I could see early on it wasn't going to work. I've been down this road enough to know how it ends."

Kahara's heart dropped. Did he come over to end it? They had barely gone out two months and he was going to end it? She interrupted him before he could finish.

"Are you telling me this to issue me a warning, or to break it off? Because—"

"Neither, I just need you to understand the nature of what I do for a living."

"If understanding means I just roll over when you do something wrong—"

"I didn't do anything wrong—"

"You didn't?"

"Not on purpose. Yeah, I should have called—"

Next Time

"You damn right you should have called—that's how you should've started out the conversation, instead of issuing a warning to me like you're getting ready to write me a ticket or something."

Gary breathed hard. "You've been on shoots before Kahara—you know how hectic things can get. It's easy to lose track of time." He paused for a moment, letting that sink in. Kahara thought about what Gary said, and realized he was right. She could have been more understanding.

"Listen," she said. "I'm sorry, you're right. Sometimes, when I'm let down, I—I don't respond that well. It's something that's been brought to my attention before, and I know I need to work on it. It's just that I really wanted to see you. I mean I really, really wanted to see you. I was all perfumed up."

"You were," he said, pulling her close, his voice softening. He stroked her cheek. "K, you were on my mind the whole day—from the moment I got there, all I was thinking was when this is over, I'ma have my arms wrapped around my girl. I'm sorry baby."

"It's alright," she said. "Listen, I wanted you to see the still photos from the shoot." Kahara planned to include some of the photos in the press packets she would send out, once her film was accepted at a festival. She went into the office. Gary followed.

He noted two large open boxes on the floor and a half-built wooden structure sitting in the middle of the room. "What's this?" he said, "It looks like half of a desk."

"It's a computer desk I ordered from OfficeMax." Kahara explained that she had tried to escape the $50 assembly fee by hiring one of the maintenance men in the building to assemble the desk. After working for four hours trying to put together the overhead hutch and special hidden compartment, he finally gave up. Kahara still paid him $25 for his effort and decided she would call OfficeMax and have them come out and assemble it. Gary listened patiently, then squatted down over the two large boxes, and pulled out the instructions. He stood up, looking over the instructions carefully, and then walked over to the partially assembled desk.

"I'll do it for you. No sense in spending $50."

"Gary no, it would take too long. You'd have to dismantle the old desk, put together the new desk—"

"And?"

"Lug the old desk out of here."

"K, I can do it. I put things together for my mother all the time. It's no big deal." He looked at her and smiled. "These are the kind of chores you supposed to let your man do."

"My man?" Kahara stood back on one leg, placing her hand on her hip. "When did you hear me say I wanted to be your woman?"

"Ok then, you can pay me $50 to put this desk together, and I can start seeing other—"

She walked over to him quickly and put her hand over his mouth before he could finish. "I'm just kiddin' baby."

Gary dismantled the old desk, and began the task of correctly assembling the new one. Kahara left and did her laundry, then returned a while later, watching him as he continued his task.

"So how's everything at work?" he asked.

"I got a promotion a few weeks ago."

"Why didn't you tell me? Congratulations. So what will you be doing?"

"More of the same," she said letting out a long sigh, "general forecasting for expenditures, revenue income, research, analysis." She trailed off after a moment.

Gary stopped working and looked up at her. "You don't like your job, do you?"

Kahara looked away for a moment and sighed. "Not at all," she said. "I like the money. It pays well and I'm good at it. But no, I'd much rather be making films full-time." Kahara explained to Gary how exhausting it was to work 10-12 hours a day, then come home and work on film projects. She told him about her desire to raise enough money to turn her short into a feature length film. This would require her to solicit investors, a task she could not perform while holding down a full-time job.

"Can you afford to quit?"

"I've got enough saved up to last a few years. But it's just—"

"You don't want to give up that paycheck."

She smiled at him. "No, I don't." His piercing gaze seemed to look right through her thoughts at times.

"I'll admit it. There were times in the beginning when I got scared," he said. "But you learn to push past that. When things got rough, it just made me more determined. And I can tell you got your head screwed on straight. Plus you're tight with your money."

"I am not."

Gary looked down at the desk then up at her. "Yes you are."

Kahara smiled, thinking back on how long it took her to decorate her apartment. "Alright, maybe about some things. I just don't want to look up ten years from now and wonder where the time went. I want to make films."

"Then you gotta quit K. When do you think you'll be ready?"

"About a year. In about a year." She looked at him as he continued working. "Don't you want to take a break? It's been two hours."

"No, I want to finish this."

Kahara went into the kitchen and brought him a tall, ice-cold glass of lemonade. As she stood there watching him work, she couldn't help but admire his ability to stay focused. She appreciated his willingness to listen as she vented her frustrations. None of the men she had dated in the past seemed to take interest in her goals. She smiled as he looked up at her a few times, giving her a curious grin.

"You're quiet. What's up?" he asked.

"Nothin', just standing here watchin' you. You're sweet, you know that?"

He gave her an embarrassed smile and continued working. An hour later her new desk was assembled and the old one gone. They sat in the living room and relaxed. Kahara showed him photos from the shoot. Gary ordered a pizza, and they watched the DVD *For Love of Ivy*, an old Sidney Poitier movie. They snuggled, kissed, and touched during the film, but Kahara did not let things get too out of hand.

Kahara called Arnita later that week to volunteer her services as a babysitter that Saturday. She tried to help out whenever she could, realizing Arnita felt more comfortable leaving her children with her than anyone else. Her babysitting efforts usually went off without any major problems. Arnita's daughter, Darlene, and her son,

Next Time

Kenny, were used to aunt Kahara, and knew they couldn't pull the same stunts with her as they did with their young babysitter CJ.

Chapter 16

At the end of November, Gary made a special trip back into town to take Kahara to see Al Green at the House of Blues, a concert venue located in downtown Chicago. Seconds before Gary's arrival, Kahara checked her outfit in the mirror and smiled. She was decked out in a tan wool mini skirt, black tights and sleek pair of tan leather boots. Gary smiled when he saw the outfit.

"You like?"

He nodded. "I like those big legs." He pulled her close and kissed her. "We better get out of here before I start bothering you," he said.

They rode to the concert with Gary's cousin, Darren, and his girlfriend Angie.

Darren looked back at Gary with a devilish grin on his face. "Kahara, you never heard Gary sing, did you?"

Kahara turned to Gary. "I didn't know you could sing."

Darren laughed. "He can't. When we were little, he would grab my mama's big spoon and pretend it was a microphone and walk around the living room croaking."

"I crooned," Gary said, grinning. He slid his arm around Kahara's shoulder and began singing Al Green's "Simply Beautiful."

Kahara winced a little. "You could use a little work on that, but—"

"Naw, no but, don't encourage him," Darren said. "The brother can't sing—period."

"Shut up D," Gary said, pulling Kahara close for a kiss.

"Hey, hey, hey, hey, none of that in my car. Gary man, can't you control yourself?"

"No," he said, rubbing Kahara's cheek gently, and kissing her again. "You forget, you got yours full-time. I'm a thousand miles away from mine."

They arrived at the concert a few minutes later. The House of Blues had only a handful of tables. The majority of the crowd stood on the large floor facing the stage. After checking their coats, they all found a spot in the middle of the crowd, which enabled them to see the entire stage. Gary stood behind Kahara, his arms wrapped around her waist.

As they swayed to the music, Kahara smiled to herself as she felt Gary's penis stiffen against her behind when she backed against him. At first, she did not realize what she was doing, but as she felt him growing harder and harder, a sense of mischief overtook her. What she had been doing by accident, she began to do on purpose.

She continued rubbing her behind against his penis until it was bone hard. Her movements were subtle enough that only he knew what she was doing. Gary squeezed her shoulders and kissed her on the side of her neck. "You gonna be in trouble when we get back to your place," he said, softly nibbling at her ear.

She reached her arm behind her, grabbing the back of his neck. They continued to sway, and she continued her slow but subtle grind. He placed his hands on the side of her hips, and began rubbing and squeezing them gently as he pressed his lips up against her ear, biting it. Darren and Angie were standing in front of them, unaware of what was going on.

During the ride back, Kahara's mind raced. She was so turned on, she was afraid she'd give in once they reached her place. They barely spoke the whole ride home, both probably thinking the same thing.

Once inside her apartment, Kahara turned on the stereo and put in her favorite jazz CD. She brought Gary a glass of cranberry juice, then sat next to him on the couch.

"The concert was nice," she said, nervously rubbing her hands against her skirt.

"Yeah it was," Gary said, taking a sip of his drink. He placed the glass on the marble cocktail table and pulled Kahara close to him. He took her chin in his hand and kissed her, inserting his tongue deep into her mouth while rubbing his hands over her breasts. Gary felt her nipples stiffen as he circled them with his fingers.

"Oooh, Gary," she moaned. He eased his hands under her sweater and unclasped her bra, feeling her full breasts for the first time. He lifted her top and began kissing them, finding her erect nipples with his tongue, licking them feverishly. Kahara rubbed his head moaning. He lay back on the couch and pulled her on top of him, then eased his hands under her skirt and inside her panties, squeezing the bare flesh of her behind. Kahara jumped a little as his fingers hungrily searched for her opening. He bit her neck and began teasing her clitoris. Kahara's head was whirling as she felt her body spinning out of control. Gary's knowing fingers teased and played with her clitoris, bringing her to the brink of orgasm. Kahara yelled out.

"Damn it, if you keep doing this, we're going to fuck."

Next Time

"That's the idea," he said, drawing slow circles around her clitoris.

"Oooh baby, stop. I can't take it," she moaned. "Please stop Gary, please."

"You don't want me to stop," he said hoarsely.

Kahara did not respond. Gary squeezed her behind with one hand while he continued stimulating her with other. Kahara squealed and moaned with delight as he brought her to a crashing orgasm. "Ooh, I want this dick!" she yelled.

"Don't worry, you're gonna get it," Gary said, unbuckling his belt and unzipping his pants.

She caught herself a moment later. "I can't—I can't do it yet—it's too soon," she said.

"I'm not going anywhere babe. It's not too soon."

Kahara was calm now, having reached orgasm. She felt a mixture of emotions—guilt, fear she'd lose him if she didn't give in. "Let me do you," she offered.

"Let's do each other," he said.

"Gary, we can't make love now, it's still too soon."

"Why you tease me at the club?" he said, ignoring her, biting her ear. Kahara bit her lip, feeling convicted. "Rubbing that big ass all up against my dick. I know you felt it. You had to."

"Baby, I'm sorry, but we—we can't do it yet. I have to be sure." Gary ignored her and began moving her body to the side. "Baby stop. Please. We can't. Not yet. Gary!" she exclaimed, as he pulled her body underneath his, easing on top of her. "It's too soon babe, it's too soon."

Gary let out a long sigh and slowly rolled off of her. "Ok, ok, ok, I got it, I got it," he said impatiently, sitting up on the couch.

Kahara sat up, smoothing her clothes down, as Gary fastened his belt buckle. "You understand don't you?" she said, looking over at him.

"Yeah. Yeah. I understand. Look, why don't we just watch some TV."

He took the remote without looking at her, and switched on the television. They watched TV in complete silence. Gary made a polite but cool exit less than a half-hour later. Kahara sensed a growing distance on his part. She realized she made a major mistake by arousing him at the concert, then turning him down once they got home.

Kahara met Sergio for lunch the next day at Cosi, a trendy sandwich shop a few blocks from where she worked. Sergio took a cab there from Columbia College, where he worked as a screenwriting instructor. Sergio had a blunt way of communicating that amused Kahara. Never one to pull punches, he always said exactly what was on his mind. She watched him grimace as she related the events of her last date with Gary.

"You're a man. What does it mean when you all get quiet when we won't give you any?"

Sergio shifted his large frame in his seat. "How long have you been seeing him?"

"Let's see… September, October, November, wow. It's been almost three months."

"Three months!" he said, loud enough for everyone in the restaurant to hear. "And he still calls you? That's too long."

"No it's not. You forget we're long-distance."

"Give the man some sex. What are you waiting for?"

"I want to be sure."

"Sure of what? You women kill me with that. I want to be sure he won't change after we have sex. *All* men change after sex. The sooner you do it, the sooner you'll find out what he's really like."

"No," she said, shaking her head. "I've been burnt too many times in the past."

"He may get tired of waiting."

"That's fine," she said, looking away.

Kahara put up a brave face in front of Sergio, but inside she was nervous about losing Gary. He seemed so distant that night, that she wondered if he would continue to pursue her, or lose patience and just let things fade away. After being burned so badly by Marshall, she just couldn't bring herself to have sex until she was certain.

There were times she was almost grateful that Marshall ignored her the way he did after their encounter. It jolted her back to reality, and made her take a long look at what she realized was reckless behavior. She understood now that she wasn't the type of woman who could lay down with a man after knowing him just one night, then get up the next day and shrug it off. She needed a slower process to determine whether the man really cared about her. And while she didn't want to lose Gary, she wasn't willing to throw away her principles in order to hold onto him.

When Kahara got home from babysitting for Arnita that Saturday evening, she was disappointed to see that she had no messages. It had now been a week since she heard from Gary. On Monday evening, while showering, she turned off the water a few times, thinking she had heard the phone ring. As she sat eating some shrimp fried rice she'd picked up from a nearby Chinese restaurant, she thought about what Sergio had told her that Monday.

Later that evening, she sat in the loveseat reading her Creative Screenwriting magazine, still hoping the phone would ring. It didn't. A sense of sadness came over her, as though something very valuable had been lost. She readied herself for bed, turned the water off again while brushing her teeth, thinking once more that she'd heard the phone ring. Kahara climbed into bed, pulling the covers close to her body, and turned on her side. A sad smile crossed her face as she fantasized about what it would be like to have Gary lying next to her. She fell asleep with that thought.

The following evening, as Kahara was making additional changes to the film, the phone rang. She walked over to the cocktail table and picked it up.

"Hello?"

"Hey Kahara what's up?" Gary said.

"What's up?" she said tersely, standing back on one leg. "You tell me."

"What's with the attitude?"

"Are you not calling because I haven't had sex with you yet?" she blurted.

"What?"

"Is that why I haven't heard from you?"

"No, I've been busy. That's why you haven't heard from me. I just got home. I've been gone for over a week in L.A. working."

"Why didn't you call me?"

"I should have babe, I'm sorry. I got tied up. What, you missed me, is that it?"

"No."

"Come on."

"Yeah," she said slowly. "Gary."

"Yeah, babe."

"Umm, I need to apologize to you for something. I got you worked up at the concert, rubbin' up against you with my behind. I knew exactly what I was doin', and it was wrong, especially when I didn't follow through with the act. I could tell you were mad when you left."

"Don't worry about it," he said. "I admit. My dick was hard as a brick when I left your place. I just have to remember to stay away from that weapon you got back there."

Kahara laughed. She was happy that he was able to joke about the incident. It reassured her that he wasn't ready to run because he was impatient about sex.

Chapter 17

During the second week of December, Gary returned to Chicago and took Kahara and her mother out for brunch. Kahara's mother Harriett was about the same height as Kahara, with the same shape, but about thirty pounds heavier. She lived on the southern tip of Hyde Park, about a half-mile away from Kahara. As they sat in the Pancake House, Kahara's mother continued to grill Gary.

"So, you've been married once before," her mother said. "Kahara's never been married."

"Mama," she said, giving her a "don't go there" look.

"What? It's true. She's very self-conscious about it."

"No she is," Kahara countered. "She thinks I should have been married with three kids by now."

"Well what are you waiting for?" her mother replied. She looked over at Gary. "I don't mean you necessarily," she added. "I just don't understand why an attractive woman like her has never found a husband."

"I'm not hunting for a husband," Kahara said flatly.

"I know a number of women in their forties who have never been married," Gary volunteered.

"I don't see why any woman would choose not to be with someone," her mother said, shifting in her seat.

"Tending to children and a husband takes time," Gary said.

"I hope you're not counting on Kahara to tend to you," she said. "She's too independent. I keep tellin' her that. You're from the South too, so I know what kind of woman you're used to." She looked at Kahara. "When you gonna make the man dinner?"

"Tonight," she said defensively. "I'm making him dinner tonight—a big dinner."

"You are?" he asked, sounding surprised.

"Sure. Sure I am. Real big dinner."

"Real big, like what?" her mother asked.

"Like chicken," Kahara said, clearing her throat. She had not planned on cooking dinner, but felt backed into a corner by her mother. "I'm making chicken, candied yams, ummm… greens, aaaand, maybe biscuits if they turn out right."

Kahara's mother shook her head at Gary. "She's not a good cook."

"Mama!"

"Well, there's no sense in getting the boy's hopes up. She cooks okay—and that's on a good day, but definitely not like the girls from the South you're probably used to," she finished.

"Thanks," Kahara said, sighing and looking away.

Gary squeezed Kahara's shoulder. "I'm sure dinner will be fine."

Her mother smiled, apparently impressed by Gary's support. "My baby is good at some things though," she said. "She's very loyal. Fights for what's hers and what she believes in—always has."

Kahara sat back in her seat and smiled, grateful that her mother finally said something nice about her. Her mother had a tendency to be critical, but Kahara tried to overlook it, realizing she was only trying to ensure that her daughter didn't make the same mistakes she did. After getting pregnant, Kahara's mother dropped out of college at the age of nineteen, and married shortly after that. Her mother and father divorced when she was just a child. Although her father more than provided for them financially, because of her mother's hostility toward him, he was seldom around. Kahara's father died a year before she graduated high school.

"You're right. She doesn't back down from a fight," Gary said.

"Oh, you found that out—I guess after two months you would," Kahara's mother said.

"Three," Gary said, looking over at Kahara, grabbing her knee from under the table.

Kahara knew he was subtly reminding her that they had been together three months with no sex.

"Boy, it's cold out there isn't it?" Kahara said, trying to change the subject.

After they finished eating, Kahara dropped her mother off and then drove Gary to his cousin Darren's house. Gary and Darren were going to the electronics show at the Arie Crown, a large Convention Center located not far from downtown Chicago.

Kahara drove to her neighborhood grocery, to shop for all the items she'd need for dinner. The brunch with her mother did nothing to boost her confidence. She imagined over the years that Gary had numerous Southern women wooing him with their cooking skills. Nervous, but anxious to please him, she set about preparing an old-fashioned Southern dinner of fried chicken, biscuits, candied yams, greens and mashed potatoes. She tasted the candied yams and winced, having added too much cinnamon and not enough sugar. After sprinkling more sugar on them, she put the yams back in the oven.

"Dammit!" she said, as she turned the fried chicken over in the skillet, only to have most of the crust fall off. She looked in at the biscuits she had attempted to make from scratch. To her delight they were turning a beautiful golden brown. "At least something's working," she said, removing them from the oven. She decided to taste one. Kahara bit into the biscuit, grimaced and spat it out. "That's awful, awful." She sighed hard, looking at the crustless chicken frying in the skillet. "This is a disaster," she said. After twenty minutes, she removed the wrinkled yams from the oven and tasted them. The added sugar did nothing to cover up the fact that she used too much cinnamon. She let out a deflated sigh. "What a joke," she said.

Five minutes later, her phone rang. It was the doorman letting her know that Gary was downstairs. "Yeah. Alright, let him in," she said, her voice giving away her irritation. "Oh he would be *early*," she growled. She rushed back to the stove to prepare the mashed potatoes. Draining off most of the water, she hurriedly added salt, butter, and milk and began beating the potatoes furiously. She realized a moment later that she hadn't drained off enough of the water. As she stirred the soupy potatoes, she heard a knock at the door. Kahara pulled it open quickly, still holding the big spoon with potato dripping from it. "Let's go out for dinner," she said.

Gary smiled, amused by her frustration. "It'll be fine K. Come on, let's eat what you made. I'm starving."

"You would be," she said, turning and heading back to the kitchen.

Kahara prepared the table as Gary watched anxiously. As she put the watery potatoes, dehydrated yams and pasty biscuits on the table, her heart sank. The only dish that turned out as expected were the greens. She placed the crustless fried chicken in the center of the table. Gary's neck jutted back a little.

"What?" Kahara asked defensively.

"Nothin' nothin'. What?" He looked down at the food. "I'll say blessing."

"You better," she said, under her breath.

Gary said the blessing and they began eating. Kahara studied his face anxiously as he tasted the food. He shifted in his seat as she continued to stare at him.

"What?" he said, looking up at her.

"How is it?"

"It's fine."

"It is?" she said, looking at him in disbelief.

"It's okay." He poked his fork into the dry chicken.

"Just okay?"

"I don't know, what do you want me to say?"

Kahara got up from her seat and walked over next to him. "I'm just thinking about all those women who've cooked for you in the past."

"Is that what this is?" he said, grabbing her by the waist and pulling her close to him. "The food is okay. I appreciate the effort more than anything."

"Thanks, baby."

"Now go sit down and eat. You're making me nervous."

Kahara smiled and took her seat. She was pleased that although he wouldn't lie and tell her the meal was good, he was kind enough to be tactful. After finishing dinner, they sat in the living room and watched the DVD *Love Jones*. Kahara snuggled next to him.

"You know, that was sweet what you did today," he said, holding her close. "I know you had to have spent all afternoon making that for me. You're somethin' special," he said, kissing her forehead. She took his hand and squeezed it. "You ever wear that t-shirt I gave you?" he asked.

She looked up at him. "Not yet. I'm saving it for a special occasion."

"Special occasion?"

Kahara looked up at him and smiled.

"Oooh, okay, okay. I got it," he said, rubbing her shoulder. Gary stared ahead at the TV. "So when can I expect to see you in it?" he asked softly.

"Pretty soon."

"Hmmm," he said, smiling, nodding his head.

"Not this soon," she said quickly.

"Ah, go on. Put it on. You know you wanna," he said grinning.

Around five-thirty the next morning, Kahara went out to the living room to watch Gary sleep. He looked so peaceful resting there on the couch. She woke him a few moments later, gently kissing him on the forehead.

"We better get going if I'm going to get you to the airport on time," she said, stroking his hair. Gary got up and readied himself. Kahara drove him to Midway airport, about a twenty-minute ride from her home.

Kahara and Gary did not see each other during Christmas. She spent the holiday with her mother, and Gary with his son, who he flew in from California. He sent Kahara flowers and a gold necklace for Christmas, and a card with a Crate and Barrel gift certificate for her mother. Kahara sent him a pair of slacks and two shirts, and a pair of gold earrings for his mother. Gary phoned Kahara Christmas morning and later that evening.

The day after Christmas, Kahara and her mother went furniture shopping. Her mother, inspired by her daughter's redecorating, was looking for a new sofa and loveseat.

"So you think this boy will marry you?" her mother blurted out as they rode the escalator up.

Kahara looked around, embarrassed that someone might have heard her. "Mama! I don't know," she said. "I'm not thinking that far ahead."

"Well why not? Girl, do you ever intend to have children?"

"Not at forty going on forty-one."

They idled through the sofa section. Her mother spotted a dark brown leather sofa and plopped down on it. Kahara scrunched up her nose. She hated dark colors.

"You like earth tones don't you?" Kahara asked.

"Your aunt had Yolanda at forty-three," her mother reminded her.

Kahara sighed, hoping they could move off of that subject. "Yeah Mama, but she already had two other children by then. You remember what happened to Aunt Jessie. I'm not going through that." Kahara's aunt waited until she was over forty to start her family. Both her children were stillborn. She stopped trying after that. "It's too late for me Mama."

"You always bring up Jessie," her mother said. "Her body wasn't strong enough to have children, that's why she lost them. Nothing to do with her age. I don't think you want to have kids."

Next Time

"My eggs are too old. I don't want to talk about it anymore Mama."

Her mother got up from the couch and they continued browsing.

"Look at how thick you are on the bottom," she said, patting her rear end.

"Mama! Stop it!"

"You can have kids till you're fifty girl. What are you worried about?"

"Can we just drop this?"

"What about him? Don't you think he wants to have any more kids?"

Kahara spotted a cream-colored couch much like her own. She went over and sat in it. "Now this is what you need right here. Why don't you get this, Mama—it'll brighten your place up."

"I don't like cream. So you don't think he wants to have any more children?"

Kahara let her head drop back. "Oh boy," she said sighing. "It hasn't come up—we've only been together three months—come on, give me a break," she said, getting up off the couch.

"You're too independent Kahara, you know men don't like that," her mother said, following her. "Especially men from the South."

Kahara looked back at her.

"They like nice quiet girls—girls who know how to cook and take care of their men. You're anything but quiet, and you have a bad temper."

"I do not," she shot back. "And so what if I do," Kahara said, folding her arms.

"Have you slept with him yet?"

"Mama we're not *even* going to go there."

"But Ka—"

"End of conversation. Na—ah. No. This is where I draw the line. Here, let's check out some of these other sofas." Kahara continued into the next section and left her mother standing with her mouth open. Mother followed daughter. Kahara withstood the remainder of the grilling her mother gave her. At the end of their shopping trip, no decision had been made on a sofa or a loveseat.

Chapter 18

News Year's Eve fell on a Saturday that year. Gary came back into Chicago that week to do a shoot. Kahara saw him briefly that Tuesday. He stayed at the hotel with the rest of the crew for the first few days. He planned to spend Friday and Saturday with her, then leave for Norfolk late Sunday, New Year's Day. His shoot finished on time for a change. At Kahara's behest, they had made plans to go to a jazz club that evening. She always enjoyed the ritual of preparing herself for her dates with Gary. She took an extra-long bubble bath, splashed herself with her sexiest cologne, and lotioned up before putting on her outfit. Kahara was smoothing down her long-sleeved, black knit mini-dress in the mirror when Gary arrived. His eyes lit up when he saw the dress.

"Ummm, come here," he said, pulling her into his arms for a kiss.

"You act like you missed somebody," she said, looking up at him.

"Maybe, maybe," he said, grinning slightly.

Kahara grabbed her coat and they left. She drove for about a half-hour and found a parking spot a few blocks away from the club. As they walked, Kahara dropped back a little and watched Gary as he walked ahead of her. She loved his gait, the way his long legs flowed as he walked. "Like liquid," she said to herself. He looked back at her and slowed his stroll so she could catch up with him.

"What are you doing?"

"Watchin' you walk," she said slyly.

Gary gave her a confused smile, as though uncertain where all the attention was coming from. Once inside, they found a small, secluded, cozy booth tucked away in the corner. Kahara had picked the intimate getaway. The club was quaint and dimly lit, with small red candles on each table. Gary smiled as the saxophonist played "In My Solitude."

"I figured you'd like traditional," she said.

"This is one of my favorites," Gary said, folding his arms leaning back in his seat. He looked at her for a few moments saying nothing, and then broke his silence. "You know, your skin glows under this candlelight."

"Does it," she returned.

"Yes it does. It's beautiful."

They continued listening to the music, barely saying a word. Kahara eased her foot out of her ankle boot and began nudging Gary's pant leg with her toes. He looked at her and smiled as her foot eased higher.

"What's up?" he said, touching her knee softly from under the table.

"I'ma come over there and sit next to you so I can mess with you," she said, giving him a wicked smile.

"No, stay there," he said, easing his hand up the inside of her thigh.

Kahara sat back in her seat and closed her eyes; grateful the club was so dark. His hand slid further up.

"Damn, girl you got some big legs," he said, squeezing her thigh as his hand inched up closer and closer, finally touching her entrance. He let the tip of his finger sit there for a moment, lightly teasing the tip of her clit. Kahara felt her panties becoming creamy.

"Damn, you're wet. I can feel you through your stockings." he said, gently stroking at the material.

She blushed, and then looked up at him. "Your fault."

He circled her clit with his finger.

"Stop it, Gary," she whispered.

"Why, you getting ready to come?" he said softly.

"You keep it up, yeah." Kahara straightened up after a moment. "You keep messin' with me I'ma come over there."

Gary leaned back in his seat. "So come on over then," he said softly, patting the area next to him. Kahara got up and moved to his side of the booth, sliding in next to him. He gave her a shy smile and draped his long arm around her shoulder. He kissed her on the cheek, then on the lips. The waitress walked up at that moment.

"Would you all like something to drink?"

"Yeah, I'll have a glass of burgundy," Gary said, straightening up a little. "K, what'll you have?" he asked.

Kahara looked up at the waitress, a dreamy expression on her face. "Some cranberry juice," she said. The woman left.

Gary looked down at her, grinning. "You look like you're high."

Kahara stared up at him, a serene smile on her face. "You shouldn't be messin' with me here." She leaned in close to him and began stroking the fabric of his shirt. She watched as the flame from the candle danced in the creases of the fabric. "You look nice in maroon," she said. She began playing with the buttons of his shirt, unbuttoning three of them, and kissing him on the chest. The waitress came back with their drinks, and Kahara, still immersed in his chest, barely looked up. Gary gave the waitress an embarrassed smile, reached in his pocket with his free hand, and pulled out his wallet. He removed his arm from around Kahara's shoulder and paid the waitress. After he put his wallet back in his pocket, Kahara took his arm and put it back around her shoulder, snuggling closer to him and undoing the fourth button. She breathed in deep getting a good whiff of his cologne. It made her head swim.

"Oooh, let's go back home," she sighed, laying her cheek against his chest.

Gary looked at her, as though reading her mind. "Now?"

She nodded without looking up. They left a moment later. Kahara was so anxious to get inside, she parked her car crooked in her garage space, something that was a no-no in her building complex. They walked hurriedly to the elevator. Kahara fumbled with her keys, trying unsuccessfully to open the door. Gary took them from her and unlocked it, taking her by the hand and leading her inside. He pulled her close.

"You sure?" he asked.

She took his hand and moved it to the bottom of her dress.

"Pull it up," she said.

Gary did as she asked, and pulled her dress up, revealing a red t-shirt underneath—the one he had given her when they were in Virginia. The one she said she'd wear when they made love. He took Kahara by the hand again and led her into the bedroom.

As they lay there after their lovemaking session, Kahara felt a rush of emotions. This had been the first time in her life she made a man wait this long before having sex.

She liked the feeling of control it gave her. Now she was feeling the same uncertainty she always did after sex. Suppose it didn't work? Most long-distance affairs didn't. How would she know if he started seeing someone else? She decided to push all that out of her mind and settle in the moment. Curled up in each other's arms, they slept until the morning.

Kahara awoke at around nine and prepared Gary a huge breakfast of pancakes, bacon, hash browns and scrambled eggs, which she served him in bed. They had another lovemaking session, then watched TV in bed until noon.

After showering and getting dressed, Kahara showed Gary the final cut of her film, *The Best Thing*. He helped her tweak a few remaining sound problems, then reviewed the more complex functions of the software he had installed for her.

They left, then went downtown to take in a show and do some shopping. Gary purchased a sheer red nightgown for Kahara from Victoria's Secret. He took her to the Hyatt Hotel in downtown Chicago, where most of the crew was staying. The majority of the crew had left, but a few had decided to stay in town and spend New Year's in Chicago. Kahara waited in the lobby while Gary went up to talk to one of the crew members. He came down ten minutes later.

"I got us a room," Gary said, bending over to pick up their packages.

"How'd you do that?" she said, getting up.

"One of the guys that was going to stay for the weekend had to leave unexpectedly, so I got his room."

Kahara followed Gary as he headed to the elevator. Her eyes lit up when she saw the room. It was a large suite with a king-sized bed. A forty-inch TV sat in a dark mahogany wall unit. Gary went to the bathroom while Kahara put their packages in the closet.

"I'm going to need to buy some toiletries," she said.

"We can stop off at a drug store on the way back from dinner," Gary called from the bathroom.

Kahara opened the pink Victoria's Secret bag and removed the sheer red teddy Gary had bought for her. She held it up smiling, and then laid it gently on the bed.

"See you later," she said, patting it.

She walked over to the window to check out the spectacular view of Lake Michigan.

"This is beautiful," she said, after pulling back the heavy, dark green drape.

"Yes it is," Gary said, walking up behind her, stroking the sides of her hips. "Can't wait to see all of it again."

Kahara turned and draped her arms around Gary's shoulders. "Happy New Year baby," she said, kissing him.

They left for Water Tower Place, an elegant mall built right across the street from the original Water Tower, one of the few structures left standing after the Chicago Fire. They had an early dinner across the street at the Cheesecake Factory, a restaurant in the bowels of the historic John Hancock building, a black steel-and-girder skyscraper which sat adjacent to Water Tower Place.

Gary looked at her grinning, as they finished their meal. He leaned back, stretching out his long legs. The waiter cleared away their dinner dishes, and then brought them their desserts. Gary ordered chocolate mousse and Kahara ordered a triple chocolate cake. "Let me have some of your mousse," she said. Gary dipped his spoon into the pudding and reached over, placing it against her lips. She opened her mouth slowly and wrapped her lips around it. "It's good," she said, after swallowing. "You want some of my cake?"

"Later," Gary said. "Take it back to the room with us so I can eat it off of you," he added, giving her a wicked grin.

The waiter walked up just as Gary finished his statement. "Will there be anything else?" he asked trying not to laugh.

"Yeah, I'll take an extra order of that triple chocolate cake," Gary said, clearing his throat.

"Aaaand some chocolate mousse," Kahara said smiling.

The waiter laughed softly as he walked off.

"What are you going to do with the chocolate mousse?"

"Same thing you're gonna do with the cake," she said.

After finishing their desserts, they headed back to their hotel room. Kahara put the mousse in the tiny refrigerator and they left for the New Year's Eve celebration given in the ballroom of the hotel. They partied with about six other crew members that remained. At midnight, they lifted their champagne glasses and toasted in the New Year. They took a seat at one of the empty tables and watched as the crowd began dancing again.

Gary looked at Kahara and smiled. "You want to know what I like most about you?" he said, leaning back in his chair.

"My cooking."

"Hell no," he said, shaking his head laughing. "You're not a pushover." He looked at her and grinned. "You stand your ground. I admit, it gets on my nerves sometimes, but it makes you sexy as hell to me."

She smiled and took his hand. "I love your ambition and your confidence," she said. "It's what first attracted me to you."

"I love you K."

"That's nice," she returned, winking at him. "I love you too."

They danced and celebrated with the group for about an hour, then excused themselves, anxious to bring in the New Year in a more intimate way. Kahara moved close to Gary as they rode up on the elevator. "You want me to wear the red teddy," she said, unbuttoning his shirt, kissing him on the chest. He pulled her close, kissing her deeply on the mouth. A couple got on the elevator with them, and Gary was forced to stop. He rebuttoned his shirt. When they reached their floor, Gary walked hurriedly, with Kahara scampering behind him.

"If I can find the key," he said. Kahara could feel the nervous energy in his voice. He fumbled a little with the key, dropping it. She bent down, picked it up and unlocked the door.

"I want to take a shower," she said, once they were inside.

"Yeah, you better," he returned.

"Ok, that's strike one," she called.

He joined her a moment later. They emerged from the shower dripping. Gary squeezed her full bottom and kissed her. "Ride in the new year on all this big ass," he said hoarsely. They scurried into the room and fell onto the bed. Gary climbed on top of her.

"Wait, wait, wait, I gotta put on the gown," she said, reaching over for it.

Gary rolled over on his back and watched as she put it on. She went to the refrigerator and took out the chocolate mousse.

"Bring the cake too," Gary said, motioning over to the table.

Kahara scooped up the bag with the cake in it and crawled into bed.

"Lie on your back," he commanded softly.

Kahara did as she was told. Gary removed the cake from the bag and sat it next to her. He lifted the sheer gown up and smeared a portion of the cake on her stomach. Kahara jumped a little. Gary buried his face in her stomach and began licking and sucking the cake off. He moved the gown up further, taking another portion of the cake and massaging it slowly against her breasts. Kahara moaned as he sucked the chocolate off of her nipples, making his way down her stomach toward her mid-section. She grabbed his head as he went lower and lower, finally reaching her clitoris. He dabbed a piece of cake on the tip of her clit, quickly licking it off. Kahara jumped and squirmed as he continued to lick. He pulled the hairs back, fully exposing it.

"Oooh," she said, barely able to take it.

He turned his tongue into a vibrator and brought her to a crashing orgasm. Kahara sighed.

"Thank you," she said breathlessly, looking up at the ceiling. She turned on her side and reached for the container of chocolate mousse, as he lay down next to her. She sat up and knelt next to him. "Payback time," she said, grinning. She opened the container and scooped a huge gob of mousse into her hand, smearing it on his stomach, then his genitals. "Don't want to miss a spot," she said, spreading it over each of his balls. She kissed his stomach as she licked off the mousse, working her way down to his penis. Massaging his balls with her hand, she put her mouth over the length of his penis and began sucking hungrily. Gary's moans could be heard above the noisy sucking sound Kahara made as she slurped and slurped his penis like a popsicle. She alternated teasing the tip of it with her tongue, then covering the head with her mouth, sucking and swirling, over and over, bringing him to the brink of orgasm. He pulled her up.

"Sit on my dick before I come," he rasped. She pulled out a rubber and quickly applied it, then positioning herself over him, lowered her body until she felt the full length of his curved manhood. She humped up and down, joyfully, wildly, laughing with delight as she gyrated and grinded herself to a monstrous orgasm. He came a moment later, pulling her down hard as his juice spurted out in waves of moist ecstasy. She fell over on her side afterwards, exhausted. Gary peeled the rubber off and dropped it on the floor. He draped his long arm around her and they fell asleep. When Kahara awoke that morning, she looked over at Gary, who was lying next to her with a sheepish grin on his face.

"You hungry?"

"Yeah, you want to go get something," she said, pulling back the cover.

"Naw, naw, lay there. I'll order it. What do you want?"

Kahara stretched out on her stomach. "Let's see, umm pancakes—buttermilk pancakes, hash browns and a ranch omelet. Oh, and a chocolate shake."

Gary smiled as he picked up the phone. "You got quite an appetite," he said, patting her bottom. "You not going to blow up on me are you?"

Next Time

She rolled over onto her back and looked up at him, smiling. "Never."

He called in their order. Kahara got up, brushed her teeth, and jumped in the shower. Gary came in a few moments later and began brushing his teeth. Kahara peeked out at his naked body and smiled. As he finished, she handed him the soap.

He stepped into the shower with her, sudsed up the bar then placed both hands over her breasts. He smoothed the lava over her nipples, teasing them until they became erect. She took the bar, soaped up her hands, and then began massaging his already erect penis.

"You got the hardest dick. What do you eat—this thing is so rigid it's scary," she said, as she continued to squeeze it.

"What do I eat?" he said, slipping his fingers between her legs, sudsing up her bush until it became frothing white. He turned her body towards the water and let it run against her mid-section until all the suds washed away.

"I'ma show you what I eat that keeps my dick so hard," he said, slowly dropping to his knees. He separated her hairs and began to lick viciously at her clit. She held his head in order to keep her balance. His tongue swirled and flicked. In, around, down, up, out, in again, everywhere. He gripped her butt, and just as he was sensing her orgasm, he slowed his fierce licks to a crawl. Her body jerked and jumped as she came.

"Ooh I can't take it. Fuck me!" she said.

They hurried out of the shower and onto the bed. Gary pulled out a rubber just as a knock came at the door.

"Oh shit," she said, looking up at him, "the food."

"Just a minute," Gary hollered, reaching for his robe. Kahara ran back in the bathroom to get hers.

Gary paid the attendant as Kahara exited the bathroom. After the attendant left, they let their robes drop to the floor and fell back onto the bed. Kahara put the rubber over his stiff penis then got on all fours. He grabbed her buttocks with both hands and thrust deep inside her. She moaned and groaned, turning and grinding her hips against each of his thrusts.

"I like all this ass," he said, kneading it with his hands as he thrust in and out of her.

"You better, it's yours," she returned.

He reached a shattering climax and they crumpled onto the bed afterwards. Kahara got up after a minute, remembering the food.

She removed the stainless steel cover and placed her hand on the pancakes. "They're still warm," she said, smiling down at Gary, who was stretched out on his back. She buttered a piece of his toast.

"Open," she said, holding it over him.

He took her hand and guided it into his mouth. He sat up, and they finished breakfast.

Chapter 19

"Ummh! I have never been fucked so well in my life!" Kahara said softly to Jackie the next day, as they sat in the break room having lunch.

"Better than Marshall?"

"Oh please, hell yes!" Kahara looked around at the three people sitting on the other side of the room and then leaned forward. "His dick is like steel. I'm serious—through the whole act! You know, no turning soft in the middle of making love, then getting a little hard maybe just before he comes."

"The 'now you feel it, now you don't' dick," Jackie said, shaking her head.

"I don't know, it must be his diet or that county air—somethin'. It's so strange. I always pictured Gary as the conservative, straight-laced type, but not in bed."

"About time you gave the brother some."

Kahara shoved Jackie's arm. "Oh listen to you—the main one saying wait, wait, wait!"

"I said, don't do it the first night—I didn't say make him wait a year."

"Three-and-a-half months is not a year."

"No, but you have a special situation here. He *knows* about your previous encounter. It's only natural for him to measure what he had to go through against the brother before him. Don't think he won't. Gary may not say anything to you now—but it will come up, trust me. Could be next week, next month, or next year, but it *will* come up. And the question's going to be—why'd I have to wait, when that other brother didn't?"

"He's not that petty."

"Honey, men are just like women when it comes to that—more so because they have to factor size into the deal. He'll be thinking—did she give him some because his dick was bigger than mine?"

"Oh please, Jackie. Men don't think like that."

"Okay, just don't say I didn't warn you when you find the subject creeping into the conversation. He'll ease it in sooner or later. You'll see."

Kahara brushed off Jackie's ominous warning. As she rode the train home though, she remembered back to the conversation she had with Gary at the festival. He stated then that he did not like women who put themselves out there. Kahara had certainly done that with her escapade with Marshall. It did strike her as curious that he never mentioned his name since they started dating. She shrugged it off however, grateful that he hadn't brought Marshall up. She pulled out her script, which was nearly completed, and began reading through it.

On Wednesday, Kahara had lunch with Sergio, and discussed with him the chances of her film, *The Best Thing*, being accepted into the Chicago Black Visions Film Festival held at Columbia College. The festival would take place in late August. Sergio was the lead organizer of the event. She had sent him a copy of the final cut a few weeks prior to their luncheon.

"I liked it," he said. "And I'm no big fan of romance. Oh yeah—thanks for not making the black man the villain. We take a vote around the end of May. You had the screening for the cast and crew yet?"

"We screened the rough cut months ago, but I'm having them over again to view the final version tomorrow."

"Good, do me a favor."

Kahara gave him a suspicious look. "What?"

"Hook me up with Jasmine."

"Sergio! Aren't you seeing somebody?"

"Yeah. So what?"

"Dog, dog, all men are dogs."

"Just because—just because I drive one car, doesn't mean I can't get inside another."

"She's taken, Sergio."

"Who, that Charles guy?"

"Yeah, that Charles guy," she said, mimicking him.

"That's okay, Tell him I'll share. Just give me one shot. One shot."

"You're a sick man you know that?" She took a sip of her drink. "Did you ever have luck with your screenplay?"

"Still waiting to hear something from my lousy agent. I need to fire that guy." He got up. "Look, I gotta go. What time is the screening?"

"Seven o'clock and you're *not* invited."

"Yeah, okay. Give Jasmine my number and tell her to call me." He walked away before she could respond. Kahara laughed and shook her head as she finished her lunch. Sergio was a different sort. He had a gruff exterior, which put some people off. Kahara knew he used his caustic manner and his size to force situations to his favor. Sometimes it worked for him, and sometimes it didn't. But that didn't stop him. She admired his tenacity.

When she got home that evening, she continued writing the expanded version of her short film. It was nice to be able to get away from the tedium of film editing. Now she could do what she loved most—write. She would often wake up early during the week and write before going to work.

On Thursday evening, she had fish, chicken, spaghetti, rolls and an assortment of vegetables catered for the cast and the crew for the screening of the final cut of her film. They had just finished dinner, and Kahara was preparing to show the film when she heard a knock at the door. She looked through the peephole and breathed hard, opening the door just a few inches. "How did you get past the doorman? I told you that you weren't invited," she hissed.

"Yeah, I know," Sergio said, pushing the door open, handing her his coat as he walked in.

He spotted Charles and Jasmine sitting on the couch with another cast member and walked over to them.

"Hi, I'm Sergio, coordinator of the Black Visions Film Festival," he said, heaving his chest a little. He shook Charles' hand, then took Jasmine's hand gently in his. "I've seen all your films. I'm a huge fan," he gushed.

Jasmine smiled. Charles looked at Sergio as though sizing him up.

"Okay, move over, move over," Sergio said, motioning quickly to Jasmine.

Kahara walked up to him holding a folding chair. "There's not enough room there for your large frame Sergio. Why don't you sit your—on this nice chair." She unfolded the chair hard and sat it down firmly.

"Nah, that's okay. I'll sit here," he said quickly, trying to unassumingly wedge himself in the space next to Jasmine. Charles and the other cast member exchanged glances and moved over, trying to accommodate him.

"Why don't you sit there man, there's more room," Charles challenged.

"Nah, this is fine," he said.

Kahara walked toward the kitchen. "Sergio, can you come here for a minute please?" she said sweetly.

"What? What do you want?"

"Sergio!" she yelled loudly from within the kitchen.

Sergio sighed hard and pushed himself up off the couch. The others adjusted their positions after he got up.

"You are going to have to leave," she said, as he walked in.

"Why, I just got here."

"Look, this screening is for the cast and the crew. If you're going to stay, you're going to sit on that chair. You here me?"

"Yeah, alright," he said, scowling as he walked out. Sergio took his seat on the hard chair. Charles put his arm around Jasmine and pulled her close. Kahara sat next to Jasmine, keeping watch over Sergio until the screening was over.

Before leaving, Sergio shook hands with everyone, lingering a few moments longer than necessary while shaking Jasmine's hand. Charles sat patiently; obviously unintimidated by the extra attention Sergio was paying Jasmine. Sergio left shortly after that.

Kahara expressed her gratitude to the crew and the cast for their hard work. They praised her editing skills, and the look of the final product. She discussed with them which film festivals she planned to submit the film to.

Chapter 20

Gary flew Kahara out to see him toward the end of January. February looked promising. Kahara was elated at first to hear that Gary would be in Chicago most of the month filming events relating to Black History Month. It was the first time during their relationship that he was in the city for such an extended period of time. But to her disappointment, Gary was so busy, she seldom saw him.

Although understanding at first, Kahara began to feel taken for granted when almost three weeks passed and the only time she saw him was to drop him off at the airport.

"Thanks for taking me out Valentines Day," she said sullenly looking over at him.

"I worked Valentines Day, what are you talking about?" he said, looking down at his watch.

"Yeah, I know you worked. That's all you did."

"K, I called you Valentines Day and I sent you flowers. What's up? You trying to start a fight right before I leave?"

Kahara said nothing, trying to maintain control of her famous temper. Gary got out of the car and removed his things from the trunk. He set the luggage down on the curb next to the driver's side and looked in the window at her.

"March should be better," he said, a little too nonchalantly for her.

"I can tell it really breaks you up that we hardly saw each other at all this month," she said, at that point almost wanting to spark an argument with him.

"Couldn't be helped K," he said, ignoring her tone. He gave her a peck on the cheek. "I'll call you," he said. He collected his luggage and headed inside.

"When?" she called to him, but he didn't hear her.

The month of March didn't bring the improvement Gary promised. He was supposed to come in town on his birthday, but had to cancel a few days before because of a shooting engagement. In the weeks that followed, he and Kahara began to have run-ins centered on last-minute visit cancellations and a series of missed phone calls. Frustrated, she called him one evening to discuss it.

"Hey babe."

"Listen Gary, I need to—"

"Wait, hold on. I got another call." He clicked over before she could continue.

Kahara held on, her anger building. A minute-and-a-half later, he clicked back.

"Sorry babe."

"Gary I—"

"Listen, listen, listen," he said. "I'm gonna have to call you back. I got a guy on hold I've been trying to get business with for over two months. What is it, seven-thirty your time—I'll call you back by eight. Promise." Gary hung up before she could respond. Kahara struggled to keep her temper in check while she waited for him to call her back. It was after eleven-thirty when her phone rang.

"Hello," she snapped.

"Kahara?"

"Who else?"

"I was beginning to think I had the wrong number the way you snapped off."

"It's eleven-thirty Gary."

"I know."

"You told me you'd call me back three-and-a-half hours ago."

"Look Kahara, I'm sorry but I had a client—"

"It's always a client. Every time you fail to do something, it's conveniently because of a client."

"Kahara I have a *business* to run. I don't have a nine-to-five job like you do."

"Gary—"

"My income and stability begins and ends with *me* and my ability to attract and maintain clients."

"Listen I—"

"My ability to do that is what allows me to fly you out to see me. Remember that the next time you want to go off about a missed phone call."

"Don't ask me to be grateful because you forgot to call."

"I didn't forget. I couldn't."

"You weren't on the phone with a client for three hours. Don't lie."

"No, I wasn't on the phone with a client for three hours. I was on the phone with potential clients for three hours. Listen, I don't want to keep going over this."

"Neither do I. Look, I have to go to work tomorrow. Bye."

She hung up the phone without waiting for a response. She sat there afterwards staring at the phone, wondering what Gary was thinking of her abrupt end to their conversation. Tired of being placed second, tired of Gary's many excuses, and tired of being the long-suffering, understanding mate that got taken for granted. Kahara knew what she did was rude, but was too angry to care at that point.

That weekend, Kahara, Sergio, Keith and Arnita attended a panel discussion on the role of blacks in cinema, given by the Independent Filmmakers Association. After the event, they went to the reception. Kahara and Arnita began chatting by the appetizers.

"You see that guy over there in the cardigan?" Arnita asked.

"Yeah."

"He gave me his card. He's looking for a black western screenplay. I'm going to introduce Sergio to him if he ever stops talking to Miss Thing over there." Arnita tapped her straw in her drink. Looking over at the far side of the room, she spotted a man eyeing Kahara. "Oh buddy," she said softly, nudging Kahara.

Kahara took a few hors d'oeuvres and put them on her plate.

"What?"

Arnita motioned toward the man in the corner. "He's been staring at you for the past ten minutes."

"Oh yeah, that's just great. Where was he before I got involved with Gary? Never fails, it always shows up when you're not looking for it."

"You gonna call Gary back and apologize?"

"For what?"

"For hanging up on him."

"I told you already, I didn't hang up on him. He completed his statement, so I ended the conversation. I said bye."

"Did you hear him say goodbye?"

"There wasn't time. I was in a hurry."

"Kahara."

"Oh alright," she growled. "I'll call him." She folded her arms. "I hate being the one making the first move."

Arnita spotted Sergio heading for the men's room. "Sergio!" she said, motioning to him.

He walked over to her. "What? I gotta take a piss."

"I want to introduce you to Mr. Coleman. He's looking for screenplays."

"Can he wait till I take a piss?"

"Go ahead Sergio," she said, shoving him away.

Sergio walked away mumbling.

Arnita shook her head. "I wonder about that boy sometime."

"What are you two cackling about now?" Keith asked as he joined them.

"How gullible you men are to a pretty face," Kahara said.

"Oh, her," Keith said, looking at the woman. "Nothin' upstairs."

Sergio walked up to them a moment later. "Okay, what is it?"

"Come with me," she said, grabbing his arm and leading him over to Mr. Coleman.

Not less than two minutes later, Sergio left Arnita with Mr. Coleman and rejoined Kahara and Keith.

"What are you doin' back?" Kahara asked.

"What? I got his number."

Kahara shook her head. "Men."

"What I do?" Sergio asked.

"You spend fifteen minutes with the hoodrat, and two minutes with someone who could actually option your script."

"Are you kidding? I met that guy before. He's got no juice. She stands a better chance of getting it optioned than he does. Not to mention her other skills," he said smiling at her. "So I put getting laid over a huge maybe. So what?"

Kahara motioned to Arnita, who was across the room talking to Mr. Coleman.

"Who says she's a hoodrat anyway?" Sergio continued.

"Look at her," Keith said, motioning towards her.

Sergio looked at the scantily clad woman. "Okay, so what if she is. What's your point?"

"If all you want is a hooker, why don't you just go on Western avenue?"

"Because I got lucky here."

"Oh boy, here we go," Kahara said.

Arnita returned, and she and Kahara refereed as Sergio and Keith got into another one of their famous disputes. The group left a few minutes later, and went to a nearby restaurant for dinner. They discussed the move of the Virginia Beach Black Film Festival from the third week in April to the middle of July. It was part of a huge restructuring of all of the black indie film festivals. The Virginia Beach Black Film Festival, one of the largest and well-known in the country, agreed to move up its date to avoid scheduling conflicts with other, smaller festivals. Kahara was happy to hear about the date change, as it would make scheduling time off from work easier.

When she got home that evening, she phoned Gary. Unable to reach him, she left a message on his answering machine. It hurt her pride to do it, but she apologized for hanging up on him. The old insecurities Kahara thought she had conquered began to resurface after not hearing from him that evening. She began wondering if Gary was tired of the long-distance relationship and wanted out. As the third day came to an end, she thought of calling him a number of times but stopped herself. Gone were the days of Marshall—that desperate, clingy, insecure, needy little girl. Kahara was not about to go back to that old place, even if it meant she had to be alone. She cried herself to sleep that night. At about midnight, the phone rang.

"Hello," she said groggily.

"Hey, it's Gary."

"Who? What time is it?"

She looked at the display on her clock radio. It was 12:01 a.m.

Kahara sat up in her bed, glad to hear his voice but angry at the same time. "You call me three days later at midnight?"

"I didn't realize it was this late. I've been working twelve-hour days for the last two days."

"You don't call me up at midnight on a weeknight Gary, you *know* I have to work tomorrow. I called you *three* days ago. You got some damn nerve."

"Look, if you don't want to talk—"

"No I *don't* want to talk—not now," Kahara said.

"We can't seem to get on the same page about anything lately."

"Meaning?"

"Meaning we don't seem to get along too well lately."

"You don't want this to work." Kahara said tensely.

"Listen, when I don't think things are working, I don't have a problem saying it, okay? Look, I'll call you tomorrow."

Kahara rolled over after she hung up. Her anger was replaced with uncertainty. After calling her back three days after she called him, Gary seemed more annoyed than apologetic. He didn't volunteer what time he would call her, and she was too proud to ask. Kahara stared up at the ceiling, thinking back on how their relationship had evolved from being so passionate to so strained. She smiled wistfully, thinking back to the first time they made love, and their stay at the Hyatt Hotel New Year's Eve. January couldn't have been more perfect, but things cooled off considerably in February and March. Was there someone else? The thought of that never crossed her mind until now. How else to explain the chasm that seemed to have developed between them?

The next day was taxing. Kahara had to work late to catch up on a backlog. After getting home, she checked her answering machine hoping for a message, but to her disappointment, there were none. After dinner, she curled up in her favorite chair and listened to jazz, knees pulled up to her chest with her arms wrapped around them. The phone rang a few moments later. Kahara's heart leaped.

"Hello?" she said anxiously.

"Yeah, it's Sergio. Listen, I got tickets to that new Tilman movie that's opening this weekend. They're screening it Thursday night. You wanna come?"

"Yeah, yeah, sure Serg. That's great."

"What's wrong?" he said abruptly.

"Nothin', why?"

"I don't know, you sound tense. What, you two break up?"

"No," she said, frowning. She hated how her emotions were so transparent. "Did that contact Keith gave you work out?"

"No, that fell through. I gotta move to L.A. Nothin's happening here. Let me get off so I can call Keith."

He hung up before Kahara could say goodbye. Kahara laughed softly to herself. Sergio was not one for pleasantries. She sighed hard, thinking about Gary, and leaned back in her chair, frowning. The phone rang again a few moments later.

"Hello," she said.

"Yeah, it's Gary," he said. His voice sounded disengaged.

Kahara's stomach tightened as she waited to hear him give her the send-off. "So, what did you want to talk about?" she said.

"I'm gonna be honest with you, I'm tired of all the arguing."

"You mean you don't like admitting when you're wrong."

"Don't put words in my mouth Kahara."

"Well, what do you want me to say, Gary?"

"Nothin' for a change." He paused for a moment. "Stop ambushing me every time I make a mistake."

His statement caught Kahara off guard. "Ambush? Is that how you feel, like I ambush you?"

"Kahara, you're fine as long as everything is going your way. But the minute somethin' unexpected happens, you turn. Take the last fight we had—okay, yeah, I should have called when I said I was going to call you but—"

"Instead of three-and-a-half hours later."

Gary sighed. "See what I mean? You never know when to let up."

Kahara thought for a moment about the weekly grilling sessions her mother put her through. For the first time, she realized that she was doing to Gary the same thing her mother did to her—not letting up, being too exacting. The thought that she was like her mother scared her and sobered her for a moment.

"Okay," she said, softening. "I see your point. I get intense sometime. But it's not just me. You use your job as an excuse sometimes and that's not right. And you know you should have called me back sooner."

"Fair enough," he said. "I apologize. That's somethin' I need to work on."

"Gary," she said, pausing, afraid to ask what had been on her mind since February.

"What babe," he said.

It had been so long since she heard him call her that. "Are you getting tired of me?"

"I'm not tired of you—I'm tired of arguing. We just got some stuff we need to work through, that's all."

"I miss you," Kahara said, reaching behind her head for the throw pillow. She hugged it close to her body.

"Miss you too, babe."

At the end of March, Gary flew her out to visit him for the weekend. They went for long drives and talked. Gary's mother was out of town, but Gary took her to visit some of his cousins in Norfolk. They took in a movie, and spent the remainder of the weekend making love, only coming up for air that Sunday to take a walk before Gary dropped her off at the airport.

He came back on the twentieth of April to work on a three-day shoot with Darren. It had been almost a month since they had seen each other. Gary spent the night at Kahara's, and departed at five o'clock the next morning. Around 6:40 a.m. the phone rang.

"Hello?"

"Yeah, put Gary on the phone."

"Who is this?" Kahara said, propping herself up on one elbow.

"Theresa. Who is this?"

"Kahara. How do you call someone's home and not know who you're talking to?"

"Gary mentioned something about a K something—I couldn't recall the name," she said dismissively.

First strike. Kahara sat up on the bed rubbing her eyes. "Well, what did you want with Gary at six o'clock in the morning?"

"Don't get nervous. What was it, Ka–?"

"Ha–ra. Kahara," she said.

"Whatever. Listen, Gary works for me. I'm a client. I thought he might have mentioned me to you."

"He may have mentioned a T somethin'. I don't know, I don't remember the rest," Kahara returned.

"Touché. Well when he gets back in—he is coming back there tonight?"

"Of course," she said flatly.

"Well, aren't you lucky. Listen Korea, it's very important that I get a hold of him, and he isn't picking up his cell. If he calls you, tell him to get in touch with me—ASAP."

She hung up before Kahara could respond. Kahara looked at the phone as though it were Theresa, then hung up. She looked at her clock. Who did this woman think she was anyway calling so early? "Put Gary on the phone," she mimicked. Kahara punched her pillow and went back to sleep.

When Gary got in that evening, Kahara barely let him in the door before barreling into him. "Who the hell is Theresa, and why did you give her my number?"

"Can I get in the door first?"

Kahara walked back in the living room, as Gary closed the door. He took off his jacket and draped it over the chair.

"Now, what was your question?" he said, walking toward her.

"Theresa. Who is she, and why did you give that witch my number?"

"I didn't think it would matter. She's a client."

"She's a very rude-assed client."

"Well, since you don't work for her that shouldn't concern you, should it?" he said a little crisply.

"Yeah it should, when she calls my house at the crack of dawn. She has your cell number. Tell her to use it."

"K we've been over this before. You can't get jealous whenever a female client—"

"It's Kahara—and that's another thing—tell her to pronounce my name correctly—it's not that difficult."

"I'll make it a point. Look, I've had a long day. I'm tired, I'm hungry, and I really don't want to deal with this now."

"Who the hell does she think she is anyway?" Kahara said, folding her arms. "Being woke out of a sound sleep by some self-important, demanding bitch."

"I think you need to look in the mirror on that one," he mumbled.

"Excuse me? Was that your roundabout way of calling me a bitch? I know you didn't just go there. I know you didn't just—"

She stopped short as Gary grabbed his jacket off of the chair and headed for the door.

"Where are you going? You just got here. Gary, don't leave while we're in the middle of a—"

"Fight? No thanks. Not in the mood," he said, putting on his jacket.

Kahara stepped in front of the door.

"Kahara, get away from the door," Gary said sternly. Kahara reluctantly stepped aside.

Gary opened the door. "Give you a chance to cool off. I'll be at Darren's," he said, as he walked out.

Kahara slammed the door behind him and stood there fuming. "Bitch better not call here again," she said, walking fast into her bedroom. She looked down at the bed, and the new sheets she had put on it for what she hoped would be their lovemaking session that night. Kahara sighed hard. She warmed up the dinner she had prepared for her and Gary, and thought back over their argument as she ate supper alone.

Gary came over the next day. He gave her a solemn greeting as he walked in. After hanging up his coat, he sat on the couch, Kahara sitting opposite him in the loveseat she usually camped out in to read and unwind. He looked at her, his sad eyes showing his fatigue. Kahara wasn't sure if that fatigue was from work, her, or a mixture of both.

"How did the shoot go today?" she asked, trying to make light conversation.

"Alright," Gary said, rubbing the back of his neck and sitting further back against the couch. He seemed to relax a little. Kahara didn't give him much time to unwind before barreling into him again.

"I don't like you leaving in the middle of a fight," she blurted.

"I told you I would talk to her but you wouldn't let up. I don't think this is about her calling you early anyway, I think this is about you being jealous."

Kahara unfolded her arms, got up off the chair, and went over and stood by the window. She searched back through the conversation they had the night before and realized Gary was partially right. She turned back toward him.

"Did you talk to her?"

"Yes I did. Come here."

She looked at him apprehensively. "What do you want?"

"Come here," he said, patting the side of his thigh.

She walked over to him. He took her hand and pulled her into his lap. "Listen. I told her not to call you so early anymore. As a matter of fact, I'll tell her to just call me instead. If I don't pick up, she can just leave a message. Can we put this one away now?"

"Yeah, alright," Kahara said, pulling at his shirt.

"Think we can go for at least one week without an argument?"

"You make it sound like I like to argue."

"You do," he said softly, kissing her on the forehead. "Let's have some makeup sex."

She turned around and straddled his lap. "You just want me for my body," she said, grinning.

"Why else?" he said smiling.

The following evening, Gary was taking Kahara to dinner then to a nine o'clock set to hear Rene Marie, her favorite contemporary jazz vocalist. Gary called at six to let her know that things had gotten backed up on the shoot. He assured her though, that they'd still be able to make the concert. It was after eight forty-five when he called again to let her know that the shoot had been extended, and that he would not be able to attend. Kahara sat in her living room fuming as she spoke to him on the phone.

"You had to know before now. It's almost nine o'clock Gary."

"Things came up Kahara."

"You should have called me earlier. I am so sick of this."

"Sick of what? If I could've gotten away earlier, I would have. Look, I can't talk now. If you can make it down here I can give you the ticket, and you can call Darren up on his cell phone and hook up with them. They're already there."

"But I wanted to go with you."

"Look, Kahara, I can't go back and forth with this, I'm in the middle of a crisis here and I don't have long to talk. Do you or don't you want the ticket?"

"No, I'll stay home," she mumbled.

"You just gotta make this difficult. Look, I'll try to come by when I finish."

"Whatever," she said, hanging up.

She sat in her loveseat still fuming. She understood that shoots run over, but still felt he should have called her sooner. Their relationship seemed on a constant seesaw. They'd have small periods of peace topped off by arguments, usually related to his job.

At 12:00 a.m., her phone rang. The doorman let her know that Gary had arrived. Kahara got up out of bed to answer the door. "Nice of you to call before coming over," she said, as she opened the door a few minutes later.

"I told you I'd try to make it by. What is it with you?" Gary said, giving her a cross look as he walked in. He turned to her as she closed the door. "Listen, I need to explain something to you—*again*. When I'm on a shoot—my focus is there—nowhere else."

"You could have called."

"I called you to tell you the shoot was going to run over."

"That was six o'clock Gary."

"That was the only break I got. I can't just drop the camera to make a phone call."

"You're going to stand there and tell me you were stuck behind a camera for three hours? Come on Gary."

He sighed, rubbing the back of his neck. "I did not say I was behind a camera for three hours."

"Yes you did. You just said you couldn't drop the camera to make a call. I heard you."

"Look, it's too late for this Kahara. I'm behind the camera, I'm adjusting a monitor, I'm fixin' a light and, no, in the middle of all that, I could not stop to make a call."

"Twenty seconds? You didn't have twenty seconds to make a phone call? You didn't have twenty seconds to let me know you weren't going to be able to make it? Twenty seconds?"

"I said I was busy. I couldn't get away. Listen, I don't have time for this," he said, walking toward the door. "I've got a six-thirty flight tomorrow morning. I'm gone."

"You mean you don't want to stay here? Again." she said, folding her arms.

"I've worked sixteen hours—I'm tired and I don't want to argue. I'm going to go to my cousin's house so I can get at least two hours of sleep." Gary opened the door and walked out.

"I don't give a damn what you do," she said, slamming the door behind him.

Kahara leaned against the door for a few moments, tears rolling down her face. Why was it so hard for them to get along? As usual, she mentally rolled back through her own behavior, looking for ways she could have helped avert the conflict. Was she too demanding? Was she still acting like her mother? She returned to bed frustrated. Kahara tossed and turned all night, unable to sleep. Gary did not call her that evening, and she refused to call him. He did call the following evening. As they discussed the event that led to their dispute, Gary tried to get her to understand his frustration with her temper.

"Yes, I was wrong *again* for standing you up. I offered you the ticket—late, but I did offer it. You turned it down, then you snapped off at me before I could even get in the door. And after working sixteen hours, I'm sorry, I wasn't in the mood for it."

Kahara sighed. "I guess I could have come and gotten the ticket from you," she said. "It just always seems to be something that gets in the way."

"When can you get some time off?" he said.

"What?"

"In two weeks, my calendar should be clear. The whole week."

"You want me to spend the week with you?"

"Yeah. I'll finally get a chance to take you by my mom's, and my son's flyin' in that weekend, so you'll get a chance to meet him. And no shoots. Promise."

Kahara was elated. As she readied for bed that night, she thought about her pending trip. She had been to Norfolk to see him, but never for more than two days, and his visits to her never lasted more than a few days. This would be their first extended time together.

Kahara found out a week before her visit to see Gary, that her film, *The Best Thing*, had been accepted at the Los Angeles Black Film Festival, which was scheduled to be held the second week in June. Gary assured her that nothing would stand in the way of his attending. He offered to convert her film from digital format to Beta, a festival requirement.

Kahara obtained media contact names, then prepared and mailed out press packets. Each packet contained a synopsis of the film, photographs from the shoot, a list of cast and crew, and the date, time and location of the screening. She phoned Craig Adams, the journalist from the *Los Angeles Central*. Kahara was grateful that she had taped the interviews for him at the Virginia Beach festival the previous year, before seeking any help from him. He promised to do an article profiling her film once he received it. She mailed him a copy the next day.

A few days before her flight Sergio called. "Conference Jasmine in, I'll hold," he demanded.

"You sure will, because I'm not going to. Sergio, I told you already, she's taken."

"Alright, well your film was accepted at the Black Visions fest. Now will you call her?"

"No, I won't call her. I tell you who I *will* call. Sondra, to let her know what a dog she has for a lover."

"Women."

He hung up a few moments later. Kahara was always amused by Sergio's brashness. He was relentless when he wanted something, a trait she admired, but one that frustrated her at times. She was elated however, to hear Sergio's good news. She had recently received notice that the New York Urban Works festival had also accepted her piece. Black Visions was held in mid-August and Urban Works the weekend before Labor Day.

Chapter 21

When she arrived at Norfolk International Airport, she used her calling card and phoned her mother. After that, she called Gary and found out that his shoot had run over schedule. As she sat waiting for him to pick her up, she worked on smoothing over her feelings of irritation. She brought the final version of her film, which she copied from her computer to a digital tape, to give to Gary so he could convert it to Beta. She benefited from his skills, so she had to squelch the temptation to complain when what he did for a living inconvenienced her.

When Gary arrived over an hour later apologizing, she remained calm. He seemed a little shocked, since his lack of timeliness and last-minute cancellations had been the subject of some of their fiercest debates. Gary took her luggage, and they headed for the shuttle which would drop them off at the parking lot.

"See, if you had a cell phone I could have let you know I was going to be late."

"I knew that when you didn't show up," she said, as she walked next to him. "Besides, I have a cell phone."

"You have a company cell phone."

"Yeah."

"But you only use it for work."

"Exactly. That's all I'm allowed to use it for."

"So, why don't you buy a separate cell phone?"

"Because I have one."
"You have another cell phone?"
"No I have one cell phone."
"A company cell phone."
"Exactly."
"We're going in circles here. Why don't you have a separate cell phone?"
"Because I already have one. That'd be stupid to have two."
"You don't want to own a cell phone for non-work purposes."
"No I don't, or I would have bought one. Why do we keep going over this? What are you sayin' Gary, I should *buy* a cell phone so you can feel better about being late or standing me up? I should spend $50 a month for that?"
"Here we go," he said, sighing. "I was hoping we could at least get home first before having a fight."
"I'm not fighting. But if you think I'm going to buy a cell phone so you can feel better about not being time-conscious, it's not going to happen."
"Was that a dig?"
"A slight one," she said, remembering her pledge to lighten up while on vacation. They boarded the shuttle. Gary expressed skepticism over her reason for not using her work cell phone. "Okay," she said, "I'll be honest, I don't like the idea of being accessible 24 hours a day. It's enough I have to be accessible for work. If I open up the work phone, that means people feel entitled to reach me wherever I am, whenever it suits them. And sometimes I just don't want to be reached. Like now. People can reach me at work. When I get home I check my messages. When I'm out I check my messages. That's enough access."
"I just realized something. You're touched."

"Yeah," she shrugged, as they exited the shuttle. "Whatever. I just know too many people who say they can't live without their cell phone." She shook her head. "I refuse to ever be that dependent on anything."

"I still think you're touched."

"Yeah, but you like it."

When they reached his car, Gary loaded up her luggage, then drove her to his mother's house. His parents divorced when he was thirteen. His father lived in Philadelphia. His mother lived in Suffolk, Virginia, which was about an hour's drive from the city of Norfolk, where Gary lived.

"You nervous?" he asked, as they pulled up in front of her house.

"Why? What did you tell her about me?"

Gary got out of the car, saying nothing. Kahara got out and followed him.

"What did you tell her about me?" she asked again.

Gary smiled, still saying nothing as they walked up to the door. His mother lived in a large, red brick home. She opened the door and smiled upon seeing Kahara. She was big-boned but not heavy, thick from the waist down like Kahara, but about four inches shorter.

"What did he tell you about me," Kahara blurted before Gary could introduce her.

"Mama—Kahara. Kahara, this is my mother, Katie." Gary said, reaching out and giving her a big hug. She invited them in.

Katie laughed a little. "What did he tell me? Well, Gary said you had a temper," she said, as she sat down.

Kahara nudged Gary. "Why'd you tell her that?" she whispered to him.

"Because it's true," he whispered back.

The three sat on the couch and talked for a bit, then headed to the car. Gary was taking them out to dinner. Kahara sat in the back seat behind Gary, his mother sat next to him.

"Have you two had a fight yet?" his mother asked.

Kahara looked at the back of Gary's head, wanting to poke it.

"Not yet," she said.

Gary looked back at her. "Almost. She just got here though, give it time. We average about one explosion per week."

"Explosion! Excuse me?" Kahara leaned forward. "Mrs. Mount, it's not like that at all. I don't have a temper—I'm a very reasonable person."

"Oh, you don't have to tell me honey—I *know* what's eatin' my son. Believe me, I clearly understand."

"Ma."

"See, he knows what I'm about to tell you—"

"Ma!"

"And he knows no matter how angry he gets, I'm still gonna say it."

Kahara smiled, wanting to hear more. "What?"

His mother turned around and looked at Kahara. "He's spoiled."

"Spoiled?"

"Spoiled rotten," she said, turning back around. "My son is no different than most successful black men today. These women nowadays are so desperate to have a man, they'll do anything—anything to keep one. My son's not in debt. He ain't got sixty kids by different babies' mamas. He's a catch, and he knows it."

"Ma," he said, sounding embarrassed.

"I ain't sayin' it went to your head."

Kahara looked at the back of Gary's head. "Looks like it from back here," Kahara said. "I get it now."

"You get what?" Gary asked.

"Nothin'. Tell you later."

Gary looked over at his mother. "See what you started?" They arrived at the restaurant a few minutes later and were seated. The waiter returned to their table a few moments later. Gary and his mother put in their orders. Kahara still had her head buried in the menu when the waiter got to her.

"Babe, he's ready for you," Gary said, pinching her side gently.

She squeezed his hand. "Okay, okay, okay. Let's see, umm... I'd like some turkey, yams, dressing—and please put the gravy on the dressing as well, cranberry sauce, cornbread and mustard greens. Oooh yeah, and some macaroni and cheese—from the edge I like it burnt." She handed the waiter the menu.

Gary looked at her and shook his head. "Sure that's all?"

"Oh and a slice of sweet potato pie. I'll have that to go," she said. The waiter took their menus and left.

"So," Kahara said, leaning forward, touching his mother's arm, "tell me a little more about these women who've spoiled your son."

Gary shot his mother a look.

Katie shrugged. "I'ma tell her, since she asked," she said. "Let's see, the last one he brought by—what was her name. Oh yeah, Cynthia. Now she was a good cook." His mother looked at Gary. "She wanted to marry you so bad."

Gary shrugged.

"You should have seen how that child fell apart when he broke up with her. Calling him at all hours, parking in front of his house. She even came over my house tryin' to get me to change his mind. I told her honey, no sense talkin' to me about it. When he's through, he's through."

"Hmph," Kahara said, looking at him. She wondered if he would be that cold if he broke things off with her. "Tell me some more," she said.

"I'll tell you the worst, was that lunatic that came running over my house claiming Gary had got her pregnant." Kahara looked at Gary, then back at his mother. "Oh yeah, we had a real time with her. She kept coming by too, until the baby was born. The judge made him pay child support until the blood test came back. Gary paid it, but went him one better, and ordered a DNA test. Haven't heard from her since. But that was years ago. The ones he's been with since then haven't given him any trouble. Anything he said they went along with. I don't know how he did it."

Kahara placed her elbows on the table, and rested her chin in her clasped hands. "Yeah Gary, tell us, how did you do it?" she said.

"I didn't do anything."

"You have to understand," Katie continued, "women from the South are a little different. And then, it could be just the women he ran into."

"I got a feeling it's the women he ran into," Kahara said, casting a knowing stare at Gary.

Gary returned her stare with an almost smug look. Kahara wondered if Gary had, as his mother said, been spoiled. Too spoiled. So much so that a strong-willed woman, like herself, would be too much for him. Why did he tell his mother she had a temper? Was Gary joking, or was her temper a real issue for him? Kahara decided she'd take these issues up with him when they were alone. Famished from the long plane ride and the wait at the airport, Kahara tore into her meal.

They returned to his mother's house afterwards. Gary took Kahara around the walkway to the north side of the house. Winding around the cobblestone red brick path, leading down to the rear of the house, was a spacious and wonderfully manicured flower and vegetable garden. Two giant weeping willows framed the end of the garden, between which sat a white stone bench. The majestic weeping willows could be seen from the family room, which was located in the rear of the house.

They entered through the back and walked around toward the front of the large dwelling. Kahara fell in love with Katie's home, and imagined what it must have been like to grow up in such a spacious environment. She appreciated his mother's frankness. The warmth and strength she generated made Kahara feel completely at ease.

Gary took her upstairs and showed her his old room, and the room that once belonged to his sister. His old bicycle stood in the corner, and various athletic awards lined his old dresser. His sister's room was decorated in pastel pink with a pink lace, checkered bedspread. A small vanity sat in the corner. They walked back downstairs to the living room. Kahara went over to the fireplace and studied the pictures of Gary's family which lined the mantel.

"Is this you as a little boy?" Kahara asked, smiling.

"Yeah," Gary said, walking up behind her, placing his hand around her waist.

"Are there any more?" she asked, turning to his mother.

"Ah baby, I got a bunch more," Katie said, getting up from the couch, heading toward the closet.

Next Time

Gary scoffed a little as his mother pulled out the family photo albums. Kahara sat on the couch next to his mother, and they began looking through photos. As the two women chatted, Gary sat in a chair near the corner of the living room leafing through a magazine. Kahara smiled as she looked at pictures of Gary and his sister as children.

"Look at those big sad eyes," Kahara said, looking over at Gary. She picked up a picture of him standing by a backyard fence with a stick in his hand. "Oh, he is so cute here. How old is he?"

"Five," his mother said. "He was a skinny little thing. Still is," Katie said, looking over at her son, smiling.

Gary shrugged, not looking up from his magazine.

"He's ten in this one," his mother said, holding up an eight-by-ten picture of him in suit and tie.

His mother showed her more pictures of Gary with cousins and other relatives.

"Mrs. Mount, can I ask a favor of you?" Kahara asked. "Would it be alright if I took some of these and made copies of them?" Kahara looked over at Gary. "You all have those Kodak machines that copy pictures right?"

"Ahh, no," Gary said, shifting in his seat. "You don't want to make copies of those."

"You don't want me to?" Kahara said. "Come on Gary, I want to frame one. Please?" She winked at him. "I'll treat you like the girls from the South."

"Be careful what you promise," he said, getting up. "I'll take you up on it." He walked over to them. "Exactly which pictures are you talking about?"

She held up three pictures of him during various stages of his childhood. He took one of them from her.

"Ah, no, not this one," he said, wincing as he looked at the one with him holding a stick.

213

"Come on, you look so sweet and vulnerable there," she said, taking the picture from him. "Let me make a copy."

"If it's okay with her, it's alright with me," he said, looking at his mother.

"Yeah baby, as long as you bring them back," Katie said.

"Oooh, I want this one too," she said, holding up another one, this one of Gary and his sister on their tricycles.

Gary took the pictures from her. "Ma, where your envelopes at?"

"Look in the second drawer in my desk, there should be a few big brown ones. You can put them in there."

Gary walked over to her desk.

"Oh, what's this one here," Kahara said, holding up yet another picture. "What is that on the floor with him?"

Gary shook his head as he looked through the drawer. He found a large brown envelope and put the pictures in, then went back to his corner. His mother took the picture from her.

"Ohhh honey, I gotta tell you the story behind this one. That's Tricky Tommy Turtle on the floor with him," she said laughing. "This child. I swear, we were sorry we ever bought that thing for him. It was supposed to roll around on the floor when you turned it on. But the switch didn't work, unless you banged the thing on the back a few times. We wanted to take it back but Gary begged us not to, insisting he could fix it. He used to bang that thing like he was beating a drum—nearly broke it a few times. He'd lug it around with him everywhere. I mean everywhere—even after it broke!" Katie began laughing. "My poor baby. He got so mad when we finally threw it out. Cried oh—wouldn't speak to us for a week."

Kahara looked over at Gary. "Oooh, that's so sweet," she said. Gary looked at her and shook his head. Kahara got up and walked over to him. "My baaaby," she said, bending over to tweak his cheek. Gary held his hand up to stop her.

"Alright, alright, that's enough. You ready to go?" Gary announced, having hit his limit.

"No, I'm just getting started," Kahara said, walking back to the couch. "Tell me, what was he like as a child?" she asked, sitting down next to his mother. "Did he get along well with his sister?"

"Oh yeah, but they argued, you know—fought like cats and dogs, but you know kids are gonna fight like that. But he took care of his baby sister—wouldn't let nobody hurt her. They were close—still are." Katie shook her head smiling. "She's in California now."

"Tryin to get you to move there," Gary said, getting up, walking over to his mother.

"Boy, don't start with me," his mother said, raising her hand and shaking her head. "I told you more than once, *this* is my home. This will be my home as long as I'm breathing." Katie turned to Kahara. "He seems to think I'll fall apart if he moves there. I know how to get on a plane. I'm grown—I raised you," she said, looking at him.

"You don't want to move—fine," he said shrugging.

Katie softened, seeing her son's disappointed expression. "I know you want to make sure I'm okay, and I love you for it. But go on and do what you gotta do baby." She turned to Kahara. "You gonna move out there with him?"

Kahara looked shocked. "Me—no—no. I—I live in Chicago. We never—he needs to move there for his business."

"Well, what about you? Aren't you into film?"

"Yes, I am but I'm not—"

"Ma, come on," Gary said.

"Oh well, let me shut up then. I just figured it would make sense—you both into film. You said you two may work on something together. Let me just mind my own business."

Gary bent over and kissed her. "That's impossible. Listen I'ma get something to drink. You want something Ma? Kahara?"

"Naw baby, I'm fine," his mother said.

"Yeah, some water please," Kahara replied.

Gary rubbed Kahara's shoulder on the way out as though sensing her embarrassment. The exchange left Kahara feeling a little off-kilter. While the idea of living with Gary was something she had thought about to herself, it embarrassed her that his mother shoved the idea out in the open the way she did. Gary's response was what she expected. He remained neutral. Kahara knew it was too soon to even discuss it as a possibility, especially in light of the fact that the two of them were still adjusting to each other's temperaments and idiosyncrasies. Not to mention their frequent arguing. She looked over at his mother and gave her an embarrassed smile.

"Boy, it's so much warmer here than in Chicago," she said, trying to make light conversation.

His mother took her arm and pulled her close. "I'ma tell you somethin'," she said softly. "I'm glad he's got somebody like you. That's my son, and I love him, but those other girls he had were no good for him. They were too weak. And a woman who's too nice to a man can do more damage than a mean one. I ain't sayin' you are, it's just I can tell from the way he spoke of you that you stand up for yourself." She patted Kahara's hand as Gary walked back in with a glass of water. "Keep it up," Katie said, winking at her son's girlfriend.

He handed Kahara the water.

"Thanks," she said, taking the glass from him.

"I hate to break up this little party, but we're gonna have to be going. I'll bring her back by before she leaves."

"When do you leave, baby?"

Kahara finished her water, then stood up. "I've got the whole week, I leave Sunday," she told Gary's mother. "So we got some time." She bent over and gave Katie a hug and a kiss on the cheek. "It was really nice meeting you. I really enjoyed myself and I can't wait to come back."

Gary's mother stood up and gave him a hug. "You take care of this girl," she said, squeezing her hand. "I like her spirit."

Gary gave his mother a hug and a kiss. "Love you Ma."

"Love you too baby. Ya'll be careful."

As they walked back toward the car, Gary looked over at Kahara.

"What?" she said, sounding slightly annoyed.

"Well, go ahead."

"Go ahead and what?"

"Get it out of your system," Gary said, opening the door for her.

Kahara held the top of the car door with her hand, not getting in.

"Get what out of my system, Gary?"

"I knew it," he said, walking around to his side. "Whenever you use my name like that it means you're mad."

"I'm not mad Gary." Kahara slid in and pulled the door shut out of Gary's hand as he was about to close it.

Gary laughed softly as he walked around to his side, got in and turned the ignition.

"I just don't see why you had to tell her I like to argue."

Gary shook his head knowingly and sighed. "I didn't tell her you like to argue, I said you had a temper."

"Same thing," she said, folding her arms.

"No it isn't. And I wish she hadn't—"

"And I don't have a temper."

Gary pulled off and headed to his house, saying nothing. Kahara looked over at him after a moment, noting his silence.

"I *don't* have a temper."

He stared ahead, still saying nothing.

"Do you think I have a temper? Because I don't."

Gary shrugged. "You like to challenge."

"Is that the same thing as liking to argue?" she asked.

"No, it isn't. But you do have a tendency to turn a tiny dispute into a large argument."

"Oh, okay," she said, nodding. "So you're saying I like to argue *and* I have a temper."

"What I'm saying, Kahara, is that when you get wound up, you go on a rant."

"Go on a—"

"*And*," he interrupted, "you don't know when to let up."

"You make it seem like we argue all the time. We've been okay lately."

"Until the next explosion."

"Explosion? See there's that word again." They went back and forth on the issue nearly all the way home.

Kahara reached in her purse and began searching through it frantically. "I know what the real issue is," she said, as she pulled out a piece of gum. "You want some?"

"Yeah," he smiled. "Oh, you mean gum. Naw, no thanks," he shook his head.

"Like your mother said, you're spoiled."

Gary sighed. "I knew you'd jump all over—"

"You're spoiled. You got all these weak-assed, desperate, phony-assed women who want a man so bad they won't open their mouths when something's wrong. Well, I don't pretend. If something bothers me, I say it. And that's not going to change."

"See what I mean? Always ready to throw a punch."

"Oh, come on," she said, shifting away from him looking out the window.

"You always turn away like that when you're afraid you're wrong."

"And I'm getting sick of this pseudo-psychoanalysis, because I can play Freud too. Why would you involve yourself with women who don't question you?"

"I didn't do it purposely, it just happened. Most of the women before you just didn't raise a lot of issues."

"So, what'd they do? Suck your dick on cue, then ask you how you liked your steak?"

He laughed. "You sound jealous."

"Of what? Weak-assed, simple-minded women? Not in the least."

"I wouldn't call them weak or simple." He pulled up and parked in front of the house.

Kahara got out. "I would."

Gary pulled her luggage from the trunk and walked toward the front door. Kahara followed him. Gary lived on a quiet, tree-lined street. His house, like most on the block, was a mid-sized, four-bedroom, two-bath, red brick Georgian. The front yard was small with neatly trimmed bushes along the walkway.

Gary looked back at her and smiled suggestively. "I've already had dinner."

"So?"

He pulled out his keys when they reached the front door. "So, what was it you said all my ex-lovers did." He opened the door and she followed him inside. "They cooked me a steak and…?" he said prompting her.

She rolled her eyes at him.

"Give me some head," Gary said, as he closed the door behind them.

"You *must* be insane," Kahara said, shoving his arm.

He turned toward her and pressed her up against the wall, kissing her deeply on the mouth.

"Listen," he said softly, as he stroked her cheek. "I like who I'm with or I wouldn't be with her. Don't be so insecure."

"Insecure—"

He kissed her again before she could protest. Kahara's body weakened as he pressed up against her. It had been almost a month since they had been intimate, and she was in no mood to fight him now. Gary moved back after kissing her and headed toward the bedroom with her suitcase. "Now get in this room and give me some head."

"You!" she said, running up behind him. They spent the next two hours making up for lost time. Exhausted from the long day, and their lovemaking session, Kahara began to drift off to sleep.

"Listen," Gary said slowly, nudging her a bit. "I know I said there'd be no shoots but—"

Kahara woke up immediately upon hearing this. "Don't tell me. Gary, you promised."

"I know babe. Listen, it's only a half-day. Tell you what. Why don't you come with me? We'll take in a movie or somethin' afterwards."

"You'll be too tired."

"No I won't. Look, it'll be fun. You'll get to meet one of my biggest clients and—" he stopped short before finishing his statement.

"What?"

"Nothin', on second thought, why don't you spend the morning with my mother. I'll pick you up."

"Wait a minute. Is Theresa the client you're workin' for tomorrow?"

"Yeah," Gary sighed, as though he knew what was coming.

"Did she know you had other plans—plans with me?"

"She knew I was on vacation and yeah, I mentioned you to her. It's a two-day summit. She only needs me part of the day tomorrow. The camera operator she had lined up can't get there until one o'clock. Look, it's only a half-day. I told her she's got me until 1:00 p.m., then I'm out. I mean it."

"I want to come," she said defiantly.

"Kahara—"

"I—want—to—come. I'll be okay. I won't make a scene."

"Okay, but we have to be there by 7:00 a.m."

"Oh brother," Kahara said, turning over, punching her pillow, imagining it was Theresa's face.

Kahara dragged herself out of bed at six in the morning to accompany Gary on the shoot. She watched as he loaded up his large white van with lighting equipment, light stands and other necessities. She helped load up items that weren't heavy.

"Babe, you don't have to do that. I got it," Gary said, smiling as she handed him a light stand.

"No, I want to help," she said. "I won't even charge you—I mean her."

"Kahara."

"What? I wasn't going to say anything bad about her. I'm tryin' to help."

When Kahara and Gary arrived at the university, Gary introduced Kahara to Theresa Graves. She was a little shorter than Kahara, with a trim and perfect hourglass figure, honey-colored skin, long brown hair and shapely legs. Her eyes were piercing, almost black, with a slight oriental slant. She was dressed in a tailored, cream-colored suit. Theresa had been hired to produce a videotape segment of the Educational Summit, sponsored by Norfolk University.

Theresa seemed a little on edge as she led them to the room where the interviews of various black scholars would take place. She draped her stylish jacket over an empty chair, then left for a moment while Gary and one of the staff members went out to his truck to unload equipment. Kahara did her best to be gracious toward Theresa, but she was decidedly chilly.

Kahara wasn't sure if it was because Theresa was miffed Gary brought her along, or whether Theresa was just born a bitch. She brushed past Kahara a couple of times without excusing herself. Kahara bit her tongue, not wanting to spoil Gary's client rapport, but after a while, her patience began to wear thin.

"You're going to have to move over there, sweetheart. You're still in the way," Theresa said, as she passed again.

Kahara sauntered to the other side of the room. "That makes two of us."

Gary looked back at Kahara and gave her an admonishing look. Around twelve forty-five, Kahara got up, ready to ask Gary how much longer they'd be, when Theresa walked by again.

"Sweetie, you're going to have to really try to stay out the way. I mean, I understand he's your boyfriend and all, but we have business to take care of here."

"You have a very nasty disposition. You could use a good colonic. You know that?"

"Excuse me. What did you say?"

"Never mind, probably wouldn't help," Kahara mumbled as she walked away. Gary looked at her, sighing and shaking his head. Kahara knew she would hear about this later on, but really didn't care. She walked slowly back to her hard chair in the corner and sat there for another twenty minutes until the shoot was over.

As they were finishing up, Kahara saw Theresa pull Gary over to the side to talk to him. From the angle that she was viewing them, it appeared that Theresa's body was touching Gary's. Kahara jumped up out of her seat, walked over quickly, and stood next to Gary. It was at that point that she realized Theresa's body wasn't in contact with Gary's. Feeling a need to mark her territory, though, she stayed at his side until Theresa left. Ms. Graves returned a few moments later with an itinerary for another shoot that would take place in a few weeks.

"I'll give you a call in about a week," Theresa said to him before turning to Kahara. "Nice meeting you face-to-face," Theresa said stiffly.

Kahara tried to keep from rolling her eyes at Theresa, but couldn't help it. "Whatever," she mumbled, turning away.

Gary and the staff member loaded his equipment, and Gary and Kahara left. The ride back was chilly. Gary hardly said a word. About ten minutes in he began to talk.

"Answer me a question?"

"Yeah?" Kahara said, braced for what was about to come.

"Why did you find it necessary to be so rude to her?"

"Answer me one," she shot back. "Why do your clients find it necessary to rub up against you?"

"She wasn't rubbing up against me, Kahara, and why were you standing guard over me? The woman is ten years older than me."

"And I'm four, so what's six more?"

"I can't have you on shoots with me if you're gonna act like this."

"She was rude to me, Gary. Snotty bitch. I don't like her, and I don't like her standing close to you like that. What the hell was that all about? Is that how you get clients?"

Gary pulled over and stopped the van. "What the hell is that supposed to mean?"

"Just what I said."

"You know, you got a bad habit of blurting out shit before you think. I don't sleep with my clients, if that's what you're asking."

"I don't like her."

"You gotta get off this jealousy thing, Kahara, or this isn't going to work. Do women approach me on shoots?

Yeah. Do clients throw hints and try to sleep with me on occasion? Yes. The same way men you work with may try to hit on you. But you can't fall apart every time someone doesn't take an instant liking to you."

"You don't understand," Kahara said, looking out the window. She wanted to explain to him that she didn't expect Theresa to become her best friend, but at the same time, she didn't expect her to be so nasty either. She wanted to tell him this, but figured he'd just dismiss her complaints as jealousy. So she held it in.

"Do you trust me?"

"Yeah," she said unenthusiastically, still looking out the window.

"Do you think I'd say no if a customer tried to step up to me?"

Kahara looked over at him. "Why are you askin' me this?"

"You don't think I'd say no, do you?"

Kahara said nothing.

"I'll be honest with you, back in the day, if an attractive woman came to me like that—I'd have hit it, yeah. But it's not that serious anymore. You gotta trust me K."

"Alright," she said sighing. "It seems like all we do is fight lately."

"That's not all we do," he said, starting the van. "At least that's not all we're gonna do today." He looked over at her grinning.

"After we eat," she said.

"I'm gonna take you to my uncle's place. He lives a few miles from my mother. My aunt promised me some honey-baked chicken, biscuits, and macaroni and cheese burnt around the edges like you like it," Gary said, smiling at her, "and homemade peach cobbler."

Gary's uncle owned an auto repair shop in Suffolk. It was one of the few black-owned businesses left there. Gary stopped off at his house so that they could freshen up. They showered, changed, then headed to his uncle's house, which was about a one-hour drive from Gary's. They entered the winding, tree-lined driveway, which was set back from the country road. Kahara looked in awe at the large, white, two-story home. As they got out the car, she ran up onto the huge porch, which wrapped completely around the house.

"I didn't know we lived like this," she said, turning back to Gary, who seemed touched by her amazement.

He walked slowly up the porch stairs. "I plan to retire out here," he said, as he walked up to the front door.

"You mean after you make your millions in L.A. Hell, this would be worth retiring to early," she said, leaning over the porch railing, dangling her arms.

She ran around the far side of the porch as Gary knocked on the door. His uncle answered.

"Oooh, it has a balcony upstairs!" Kahara yelled, running back to the front.

Gary smiled, a bit embarrassed, as his uncle looked on. "This is the nut I told you about," he said, as they entered the house.

"Who you callin' a nut," she said, jostling his arm as they walked into the living room.

Gary introduced her to his uncle Vince. His aunt Eunice emerged from the kitchen to greet them. Vince and Eunice had three children; one son away at college, another that lived out of state, and a nineteen-year-old daughter Tonya, who was sitting on the couch. They all ate dinner, and afterwards Gary grabbed a blanket from his van and took Kahara out to view the large bean field adjacent to his uncle's home. As they sat in the middle of the field, Kahara rested her head against Gary's lap and let out a long sigh.

"It's so peaceful out here," she said, stretching her arms up toward the sky.

"I come out here a lot to unwind when I've had a hectic day," he said, stroking her hair. They could hear the cicadas in the distance. "You about ready to head back to my place?"

"Can't we stay a little longer? This is so beautiful."

"Let's spend the night," he said, rubbing her shoulders.

"Naw we don't have anything."

"Anything—what's anything?" he said, teasing her.

"You know," she said, blushing a little.

"We can pick that up at the drugstore. Come on," he said, getting up. Kahara followed him to the van. They drove to a small convenience store a few miles away. Gary purchased some rubbers and toiletries for both of them. They returned to his uncle's farm, put their things in a guest room upstairs, and then snuck back out into the field with the blanket. They stayed out watching the sun set. As it became dark, Gary went to his van and got two more blankets. He draped one over her body, and the other around his shoulders, then stood over her unbuckling his pants. "You ever done it in a bean field before?"

Kahara looked up at him and smiled. She wrapped her hands around the back of his legs and pulled herself up onto her knees. His uncle's house was far off in the distance. With no one around for miles, she let go of the self-conscious feeling she would normally have, out in the open making love. In the city, she would never have even thought of doing anything like this. But out in the country air she felt so safe, it just seemed like the natural thing to do. Easing her hands up the front of his legs, she caressed his penis through his pants. She stroked the khaki material with her fingers and pressed her head against his groin, nuzzling it lovingly before unzipping his trousers. Gary placed his hands on top of her head, as his pants fell to the ground. She pulled down his boxers and began kissing his thighs, slowly making her way toward his penis.

"That's my baby," Gary encouraged, as he rubbed her head.

She licked the tip of his penis without touching it, and then took the whole thing into her mouth, giving him one long, good suck. Her fingertips gently teased his balls as she continued to suck his engorged rod.

"Lay down," she commanded softly, looking up at him.

Gary did as instructed lying on his back with his hands behind his head. She pulled the extra cover over her head, and went to work completing her task. She pulled at the hairs around his balls, licking them gently, taking each ball in her mouth, and wrapping her tongue around it as she sucked it. After pleasuring his balls, she moved back to his penis, which was sticking straight out, ready to shoot.

"I'ma see if you come harder out in this country air," she said, taking the entire organ into her mouth, sucking the full length of it. Gary moaned as he held her head with his hands.

"Suck it—just like that," he whispered.

"I know how you like it baby, don't worry," she said, taking it out momentarily to tease the tip of it with her finger. "Love the way your dick feels," she said, rubbing her nose against it before swallowing it again. She continued sucking until he came, swallowing every drop. "That's love baby," she said. "I haven't swallowed in years." Kahara stretched out on her back, her task completed.

Gary rolled over on top of her, sliding her skirt up and her panties down. He squeezed her thighs with his knowing fingers, then eased his hands gently between her legs, teasing her clitoris with the tip of his finger until she was good and wet. Gary positioned his head near her entrance, his nose lightly touching the tip of her clit. He nuzzled it playfully as she squirmed in anticipation, taking one long circle around her button. His tongued flicked and licked quickly, like a human vibrator, before slowing down to a vicious crawl. He spread her legs farther and farther apart as he teased her clit with slow licks then lightening flicks. Her hands found the top of his head, squeezing it in gratitude.

"Ooooh, you got this pussy," she moaned. She came a moment later. "Gary fuck me!" she yelled.

He pulled out the rubber, tore it open, applied it quickly, and buried his long rod inside of her. She grabbed his back as he rode her. "Damn this is some good dick," she said, letting loose.

As they lay there afterwards, covered with the blanket looking up at the sky, Kahara felt completely at peace. She reached for Gary's hand, squeezing it. He rolled over and stroked her cheek gently. "How long you been in love with this guy?"

She looked at him and smiled. "I don't know. A few minutes. How about you?" she asked. "When did you know?"

"That day you made me that terrible dinner."

"What? It wasn't that bad."

"Yes it was, but that's not the point. It was the fact that you went through the trouble to do it."

He rested his head in her lap. Kahara scratched his head lightly.

"My cooking's improved since then," she said a little smugly.

"Some," he returned.

"Some?"

"Some." He looked up at her. "That's not why I'm with you K."

She smiled down at him.

"I'm still amazed at how long you made me wait."

"Really," she said, getting a little nervous thinking back to how soon she let Marshall have sex with her, and Jackie's warning about this topic.

"Yeah. I have *never* waited that long to have sex with a woman."

"Oh," she said, not knowing how to respond.

Kahara became afraid that he would suddenly bring up Marshall and ask how long she made him wait. She wondered if he knew they had sex. She knew Gary probably assumed that they fooled around—but did he make the next assumption that they had been intimate? He had never mentioned anything about Marshall, much to her relief. Lying back, with Gary's head still in her lap, she fell into a peaceful sleep.

Gary woke her after a half-hour, and they snuck inside the back door and headed to the small guest room upstairs. As Kahara lay in the tiny twin bed next to Gary, she listened to the country sounds and smiled, hearing the crickets. She looked around the quaint little room with its antique dresser that sat in the corner. A small, old TV rested on top of it, and a large family picture of his aunt, uncle and their three children hung on the wall over the TV.

Kahara got up, went to the window, opened it wide, and knelt down, the long flowered curtains blowing against her face. Propping her elbows on the ledge, she rested her head in her hands and listened again to the crickets chirping as the warm breeze blew against her face. It was so peaceful there.

"What you doin' babe?" Gary said, waking up.

"Oh, I'm just enjoying this," she said, still looking out the window. She got up and climbed back into bed with him, sensing he wanted her near. He hugged her close and kissed her. She fell asleep in his arms.

They awoke the next morning from a restful sleep and enjoyed a huge breakfast of scrambled eggs with salmon, homemade waffles, sausage and grits. Kahara ate until she was about to bust. Her visit so far had been enjoyable, save for the episode with Theresa. She felt very at home there with his aunt and uncle, and felt a certain bond with Gary's mother. Gary took her for a long walk in the thicket. They hiked up a path then walked along the train tracks, the hot sun beating down on them.

"So you like this sort of thing, huh?" he asked.

"Yeah, this is great. My mother's the same way—she'll walk for miles and miles whenever we visit my uncle Johnny in North Carolina."

"Walkin' helps me clear my head. I usually go for a walk after we've had one of our big fights," Gary said. He looked over at her. "You're something else sometimes, you know that?" He pulled her body close to his. "But you still my girl."

"You ain't so bad either, Country."

"I ain't the one staying up a half-hour listening to crickets," he said, smiling.

As they continued walking, they discussed the project his cousin had suggested, over dinner, months ago. They batted around a few ideas, including one Kahara had about quizzing men on relationship issues. As the conversation progressed, Kahara could hear the apprehension in Gary's voice. She decided now would be a good time to put it out into the air.

"Listen, I'll be honest. The idea of working with you scares me," she said.

"Scares you."

"What if we start arguing and can't agree on an approach? I mean, what if we simply can't work together?"

"If we can't work together, what are we doin' together?"

"Gary—"

"If what we have isn't strong enough to withstand that, then it probably won't last anyway."

She looked away from him, sighing. "You got a lot of faith in us I see."

"You're the one who said you were scared."

"At least I'm honest about it. You sound just as hesitant as I do, but you just won't admit it."

"Look, to avoid yet another argument, let's do this—"

"It's not me starting it this time," she fired back.

"I didn't say you were; would you let me finish a statement? Alright, look. Why don't we hold off until we've been together a year-and-a-half, then bring up the topic again."

"A year-and-a-half. Why that long?"

"You just said you were scared."

"Okay, fine. I got no problem with that." She reached out and took his hand. "Bighead," she said, under her breath.

"Thanks," he said smiling, pulling her close to him as they walked.

"I wasn't talking about that head, but you're welcome," she returned, nudging his side.

The next day she, Gary, and another couple he knew took a trip to Busch Gardens. Wednesday hit an unexpected snag. Gary's friend and business associate, Phil, was hired as the photographer to shoot an awards luncheon given that week. The client decided he wanted the event videotaped as well as photographed, so Phil asked Gary if he could do the job. Gary discussed it with Kahara and told her if she didn't want him to go, he'd tell Phil to find someone else.

"I'm not going to stand in the way of you and your work," Kahara said, sighing as they sat in his living room listening to jazz. "Go ahead."

"You can come if you want. I'll only be a few hours."

Kahara got up and walked over to the stereo to look at some of the CDs stacked in the cabinet. "Will Theresa be there?"

Gary sighed. "No, she won't."

"Then I don't need to be there," she said, opening the CD player to insert a Billie Holiday disc she had chosen.

Gary got up and walked over to her. "My woman doesn't trust me."

Kahara slid her arms around his neck. "I trust you. I don't trust her."

The next day around 9:00 a.m., Gary dropped Kahara off at his mother's, then went to meet Phil. Kahara sat in the living room watching TV, as Mrs. Mount talked on the phone in the kitchen. Gary's mother came out of the kitchen about twenty minutes later.

"Gary got called at the last minute, did he?" his mother asked.

"Umm hmm," Kahara nodded.

"I know my son. He's very ambitious. Sometimes too ambitious. I tell him that all the time, but he's hardheaded, and doesn't listen to me. But you. You may not know it, but you got influence over him. He's got it for you, girl. That's my baby, I know him. I've seen him shrug off girls before, but not you. He's stuck it out with you—even when you make him mad. But like I told you already, he's spoiled. He bats those sad eyes and the girls just melt. Just stand your ground. I know you're doing it already. He told me. But don't stop—don't roll over."

Kahara smiled. "I won't," she said. Gary's mother took her to the mall for a shopping trip. Kahara saw a beautiful sterling silver watch that she wanted to buy, but the $450 price tag made her decide against purchasing it. She and Mrs. Mount had a late lunch, then returned home. When they arrived at 3:00 p.m., Gary was waiting in the living room.

"You kidnapped my girl," he said to his mother, as they walked in.

"Somebody had to—you were too busy," his mother returned.

"Ma, don't start. I'ma hear enough from her after we leave."

"You sure will," Kahara said, heading for the bathroom.

They left shortly after she returned.

"I get points for this, right," she said, as they walked toward the van.

"Points?"

"Yeah. I get points for being so understanding and not making an issue out of it, and for not going off. Even though you weren't supposed to be working at all when I came to visit you. *At all.*"

"K," he said sighing. He opened the door of the van and she got in.

"No, I'm not going to say anything else about it. I just want you to remember this the next time you want to say I don't understand the business you're in."

"Alright, fair enough," he said, closing the door.

He took her to Virginia Beach for a walk along the ocean, then out to dinner. Two days before her departure, she and Gary went to pick up his son, Calvin, from the airport. After getting him, they headed to Gary's mother's house. Gary's son had a caramel complexion like his father, and his father's tall, thin build. He also had Gary's deep, sad eyes. During the drive, Gary began to quiz his son.

"So, how are you doing in math these days?"

"Okay. Had a test last week."

"Oh yeah, what did you get?"

"B-minus."

"Let's see about pullin' the dash off of that B next time," Gary said.

"I don't like math."

"And?"

"And I don't like it."

"Why?"

Calvin shifted in his seat.

"Because you're not good at it?" Gary asked.

"I don't know. Maybe."

"I'ma talk to your mother and see what we can do about getting you a tutor to help you through those rough spots," he said, looking over at his son. "That sound good to you?"

"Yeah," Calvin replied. "When you movin' to L.A.?"

"About a year," he said. "Tryin' to convince your grandma, but she ain't budging. Why, you miss me?"

His son looked out the window, apparently uncomfortable admitting what his father could sense. "It's no big deal, I was just askin'." He paused for a moment. "Yeah, a little."

"About a year. You'll be datin' around then, and you won't even want to be bothered with me."

"Datin' now," his son mumbled.

"Glad we had that talk then," Gary said.

"Come on, not with her in the car."

"I ain't said what the talk was about. You the one said you was datin'. That's all I was gonna say on it."

"Good," Calvin said, under his breath.

Sitting behind them, Kahara smiled as she listened to their exchange. She admired Gary's directness, and his troubleshooting skills. Kahara could tell by the way he spoke to Calvin that he cared deeply for his son.

They picked up Gary's mother, and then headed over to his uncle's. They all ate dinner, after which Gary, Calvin and his uncle went for a walk. Kahara stayed behind with Gary's aunt Eunice, her daughter Tonya, and Gary's mother. She helped them clear away the dishes, and sat talking with them in the living room afterwards.

Gary's mother looked over at Kahara and smiled. "Gary's got a real firecracker this time," she said.

"Really," Eunice said. "That's good. That's what he needs."

Kahara blushed.

"I'll bet they get married," his mother continued.

Kahara looked away, not sure what to say. Tonya gave her a reassuring smile.

"They make a sweet couple," Eunice said. "You should have seen them yesterday. They must have stayed out in

Vince's field half the night." She leaned forward a grin on her face. "What was ya'll doin' in that bean field all night like that? Messin' around?"

Kahara's breath got short. A look of embarrassment rushed over her face. "Oh, we weren't doin' anything—just watchin' the sunset. That's all."

Gary's mother and aunt exchanged knowing glances. "Yeah, they'll get married," Eunice said.

Kahara heard laughter outside, then stood up quickly when she recognized Gary's voice.

"I'm gonna go out," she said, heading quickly for the door.

Eunice and Katie smiled, nodding to each other. Kahara went out and joined the men. Gary, his uncle, and his son were in the huge backyard playing softball. Gary was up to bat. Calvin was far back in the field and his uncle was pitcher. Kahara smiled as she watched Gary standing there, holding the bat with his baseball cap turned backwards.

"You look like you could be on someone's team," she yelled.

"I'm gonna knock this one out," he said.

She stood there with her hand on her hip, watching him adjust his position as his uncle pitched. Gary cracked the ball on the first hit. Kahara cheered for him as he ran across the makeshift bases. "That's my baby," she yelled.

His son raced back in the field to catch the ball, missing by one foot. He scooped it up and threw it to his uncle.

"Come on, Calvin," his uncle said. "Show Kahara how far you can hit the ball. See if you can top your dad."

"No way," Gary said, smiling. He rubbed his son's head as he walked forward to pick up the bat. Gary went out into the field and waited, as his uncle pitched the ball to Calvin. A swing and a miss. Kahara retrieved the ball.

"I'ma throw a curve atcha this time," his uncle Vince said, gearing up. Calvin swung and missed a second time. Gary looked at him.

"Don't freeze up," he yelled. "Relax. You can do it."

Vince pitched another curve ball, and Calvin hit it far out into the field, past his father. A broad smile spread across Gary's face.

"That's *my* boy," the proud father said, as he went after the ball.

"Good hit," Kahara called. Calvin smiled as he rounded the bases.

"Why don't you hit one," Vince said to Kahara.

Kahara took the bat from Calvin and took a stance similar to Gary's.

"Let me pitch to her," Gary said, walking toward his uncle.

His uncle handed over the mitt and the ball, and Calvin stood behind Kahara to catch her misses.

"Throw me a curve. I want to see if I can hit it," she said to him.

"I got a curve for you, all right," he said, grinning.

"Keep it clean ya'll—youngster present."

"Where's your mind? I was talkin' about the ball," Gary said.

"Yeah, that's what I'm talkin' about," his uncle said, laughing.

Kahara stood firm, swung twice and missed twice, as Gary threw to her.

"Okay, I'ma throw you an easy one," he said.

"No!" she said, digging the bat into the ground. "Throw it the way you normally would. I want to see if I can hit it."

"Alright," he said. He threw her another curve and she missed.

"Throw one more."

"That's three strikes."

"Throw one more anyway," she said. Gary threw another and she managed to hit a ground ball. Kahara leaped up in the air. "I did it. I did it!" she yelled, as she raced for first base.

"My girl," Gary said, clapping.

Gary's uncle smiled, and Calvin went to retrieve the ball. They played a little more, then relaxed on the porch.

Kahara looked over at Calvin. "So, how many girlfriends you got, young man?"

"Pray you never get a jealous one like this," Gary remarked, grinning at Kahara. "Very jealous. *Very* jealous."

"Don't flatter yourself," Kahara said, turning her attention back to Calvin. "So, what's her name?"

"I don't really have one yet—not official. You know I see people—but nobody's nailed me yet," he said, brushing the dirt off his slacks.

"That's fine, you're young," she said. "Now, when you get real old like your daddy, you'll probably want to settle down with one woman. When you get real old like him." She nudged Calvin. "Real, real old—you know, like him."

Calvin laughed a little. "She's a trip," he said to Gary.

"One way," Gary said.

"One way where?" she challenged.

"Inside joke," Gary said. "Man-boy talk."

"You mean old man—very, very, old man."

"You got more than four years on this old man so I wouldn't press it," he said. "What'd it take you? Six swings just to hit the ball?"

"Oh, shut up," she said, leaning over, pulling at the flap of his cap.

Eunice, Katie and Tonya joined them after a while, and they all sat around the porch talking. A little over an hour later, Gary and Kahara dropped his mother off at home, then left for his house. The next day, Gary took Kahara and Calvin to visit Hampton University, Gary's alma mater. They returned to Katie's house that evening. Gary sat in his favorite dark green recliner, while Kahara and Calvin sat on the couch with Gary's mother. Calvin was drawing an action hero on his sketchpad.

"That's good," Kahara said, looking over his shoulder. "You thinking about being an artist?"

"Graphic artist," Calvin said. "I'm going to be a graphic artist."

"Listen," she said, "show me what you can do with a K and a J. I'm looking for something unique to use on my website. I need a new logo."

He sketched her initials on his pad, then handed it to her.

Kahara smiled. "I like that. I really like that," she said. She got up and went to show it to Gary. He took the pad and viewed his son's work. "Looks good," he said, nodding. "Calvin won an award last year at his school for Best Art Design."

She walked back to the couch and handed Calvin the pad. He tore off the sheet and gave it to her.

"I can work this up on the computer and email the design to you," Calvin said.

Next Time

"Yeah, that'd be great," she said, sitting back down. She wrote her email address on his pad.

"He's going to be famous someday," his grandmother said, hugging Calvin, kissing him on the cheek.

"Grandma, come on," he said, pulling away a little.

"I'll bet if I was Teesha you wouldn't pull away," Katie said.

"That's different," he said, fighting a smile.

Kahara smiled. "Just like his father," she said, looking at Gary. They stayed a little while longer, then Gary took them home.

Gary and Calvin dropped Kahara off at the airport the next day. Kahara was sad to see her week-long trip end. As Gary waited with her, he noticed the furrowed look on her face. He pulled her close as though sensing her sadness. "I'll get a copy of your film to you by next week," he said, hugging her.

She hugged Calvin. "Thanks for the logo," she said.

Kahara gave Gary a kiss, then hurried off to her gate. While people like Sergio and her mother expressed skepticism over her relationship, they didn't understand their dynamic. Kahara could hole up for days talking to no one, totally engrossed in her work. Gary understood that. Just as she understood when he would go into three or four-day editing sessions and ask not to be disturbed for a week. They understood each other's unique rhythms and intermittent needs for isolation. The only area they still needed work on was adjusting to each other's temperaments.

Chapter 22

The Los Angeles Black Film Festival was held in mid-June. During the preceding weeks, Kahara mailed out press packets and copies of her film to various newspapers, made follow-up calls, and was pleased to learn that two papers would be running articles about her film. Gary kept his word and converted the digital version of her film to Beta. Kahara called Gary after viewing it to thank him, then shipped it to the festival site the following day. Jasmine and Charles were the only cast members able to attend the fest. Kahara paid their plane fare, and agreed to pick up the hotel bill for the four nights they'd be there. Everyone would all share a suite.

They took the ten o'clock flight out to L.A. Wednesday night. Kahara sat in the row behind Jasmine and Charles. She fell asleep as soon as the plane took off, but was awakened an hour later by the sound of angry voices.

"Dammit, would you let me sleep?" Charles said angrily. "We can talk about it when we get to the hotel." Charles turned his body completely away from Jasmine.

Kahara leaned forward. "Jas. Jas, let it go. Please. Wait till we get to the hotel."

Jasmine's body stiffened as she mumbled something else to Charles then became quiet. Kahara sighed and tried to go back to sleep.

The couple argued from the time they got off the plane until they reached the Orchid Hotel, the site of the festival. Kahara watched almost in fascination as the two made up while waiting to be checked in. Now on good terms, they decided to get their own room. Kahara agreed to pay for half the hotel fee, just grateful not to have to share the same room with them. Gary was due to arrive Friday, the day before the film screening. Kahara awoke late Thursday morning and rushed into the bathroom, hurrying to get ready before Craig's arrival. He was treating them all to breakfast. Craig had written a flattering article on her film, *The Best Thing*, in the *Los Angeles Central* newspaper. A minute after she started to shower, Kahara heard a knock at the door. She jumped out, grabbed her robe and answered it.

"Give me five minutes, I was just showering," she said to Craig, closing the door behind him. She hurried back into the bathroom before he could respond. Kahara was in the shower no more than two minutes, when she heard a knock at the bathroom door.

"Kahara, Gary's on the phone," Craig said. She heard him talking to Gary. "She's in the shower man. You want to—"

"I'll be right out!" Kahara yelled. She wished he hadn't said she was in the shower. It made things awkward. She jumped out of the tub, quickly put on her robe, and came out. Craig handed her the phone with a smirk on his face. Although he never expressed it to her directly, there were times when Kahara wondered if Craig might have been interested in her.

"Hey baby, how you doin'?" she said, shooting a mean glance at Craig.

"Everything okay there?" he asked.

"Yeah, yeah, everything's fine. I was just getting ready. We're going to check out a few films, then there's a reception this evening."

"Who answered the phone?"

"Oh, that was Craig—you know, the journalist from the *Los Angeles Central*."

Gary said nothing.

"The one that did the article."

Gary was still quiet. "He going to the reception with you?"

Kahara paused. "Yeah, yeah, he is. Well, we're all going. You know Jasmine and Charles, me and Craig." She cringed a little, hoping it didn't sound like a double date. "What—what time do you get in tomorrow?"

"Around noon."

"Tell him if he needs a lift I can pick him up," Craig said.

"Tell the brother I got that covered," Gary said, apparently hearing him through the phone.

Kahara shook her head at Craig. "He's okay, but he said thanks anyway." Kahara had picked up some tension in Gary's voice that concerned her. If only Craig hadn't said, "shower." Kahara wondered how she would feel if she were to call up Gary's hotel room, and Theresa answered, telling her Gary was in the shower.

"Look I'ma cut out. I'll see you tomorrow," Gary said.

"I'll call you when I get back from the reception," Kahara said, sensing he needed some reassurance.

"You don't have to check in. I'm secure in my talents. Just take care of yourself, smile and network, smile and network. Alright?"

Kahara smiled. "Alright." She paused for a moment. "Gary."

"Yeah K."

"I love you."

"I love you too babe. See you tomorrow."

She hung up the phone and turned around to face Craig, who had a big grin on his face.

Kahara hit him on the arm. "Why'd you tell him I was in the shower!"

"Because you were."

"I'm just glad he's so secure," she said, grabbing her clothes. "You're no help."

"You want a cheerleader? Okay, I'll be your cheerleader. But if the brother has problems with you removing dirt from your body, that should tell you something."

Kahara shook her head and went back into the bathroom to get dressed. When they arrived at Jasmine's room, Jasmine opened the door only slightly, still dressed in her nightgown.

"You're not going?" Kahara asked.

"We're going to stay in," Jasmine said, giving her an embarrassed smile.

Craig gave Kahara a knowing look.

"You're still attending the reception this evening?" Kahara said.

Jasmine looked back at Charles smiling. "Hopefully."

"Alright, well, I guess we'll see you there," Kahara said.

Jasmine closed the door, and Kahara and Craig left.

"Looks like a blooming romance," he said, as they got on the elevator.

"Strange romance," she said. Kahara filled Craig in on the Jasmine-Charles soap opera on the way down.

"You ever thought about doing a reality show around them?" Craig commented. "You could follow them around with a camera."

"No thanks," Kahara said.

They registered, had breakfast at the International House of Pancakes, then headed to the Orchid Theatre, which was adjacent to the hotel. They watched a series of shorts, as well as one feature-length film. One film told the story of a man trying to decide between an Afro-centric artist and an aloof executive. Another was a drama about a boy on a quest to find the father he never knew. After the films, Kahara and Craig returned to the hotel to attend a town hall meeting on the State of Black Cinema.

"People complain that there are no good black films out here, but there are," Kahara said, as they left the meeting.

"If more of us would get up off our asses and come to a few festivals, we'd find them," Craig said.

"Everybody can't attend festivals, Craig, and what happens to these films once the festival is over?"

"You can find some of them on the web, at Blockbuster."

"That's still too limited. There needs to be something broader—something that will reach a larger audience."

"You got any ideas?"

"Yeah, but I haven't pieced it all together yet."

They had dinner, then met Charles and Jasmine at the reception, which was being held at the hotel. Craig introduced them to others from the press and a few black dignitaries from the Los Angeles and Oakland area. Kahara had four hundred four by five pluggers printed up. One side of the plugger contained the title of the film, a silhouette

Next Time

picture of Jasmine and Charles, each looking in opposite directions. On the other side was a brief description of the film, and the date, time and location of the screening.

    She passed out the pluggers and introduced Charles and Jasmine to other filmmakers and festival attendees. The attractive couple, poised and on their best behavior, charmed everyone they met. Kahara, relieved at not having to babysit, networked with as many people as she could. An attractive filmmaker from Detroit, Michigan, introduced himself to her, gave her his card and suggested they have breakfast together the following morning. Kahara demurely refused the tall, well-built man, letting him know her significant other would be in town the next day. As Kahara lay in bed, she couldn't help but wonder to herself why she hadn't met anyone like the filmmaker from Detroit when she wasn't involved.

    The following morning, Kahara went to pick up Jasmine and Charles. Craig was attempting to take them all to breakfast again. As she walked down the hall toward their room, she heard loud voices. The door swung open. Charles rushed past her without saying a word. When Kahara reached the doorway, Jasmine was standing there in a lavender nightgown, tears streaming down her face.

"Jas, are you okay?"

Jasmine walked towards the window, wiping her eyes. "Yeah."

Kahara entered the room, not sure what to say to her. "Do you want to talk about it?" she offered.

"No."

Kahara sighed. "Alright then, look, I'll stop by later." Kahara was long passed the point of losing patience with their dramatic episodes.

Craig was waiting in the lobby when Kahara arrived a few minutes later.

"Where's Bonnie and Clyde?" he asked.

Kahara gave him a knowing look. "If they're not boning, they're fighting," she said.

Craig laughed as they headed for the car. They had breakfast, attended a workshop, then went back to the Orchid Hotel to meet Gary, who had just arrived.

"Well, I guess this is where I take my leave," Craig said, as the three of them all stood in the lobby. "I've got a function to attend." He turned to Gary. "I was just fillin' in until you got here." Craig looked at Kahara then back at Gary. "Well not fillin' in all the way—just a stand-in, you know."

"I got you brother, you don't have to clean it up," Gary said, smiling his usual confident smile. It was apparent to Kahara that Gary did not feel the least bit intimidated by Craig. "Thanks for keeping my lady company and looking out for her," he said. "I appreciate it." Ever the professional, Gary extended his hand to Craig.

They stood in the lobby chatting for a few more minutes, then Craig left. Kahara and Gary dropped off his luggage in her room, then went downstairs to get something to eat. The lobby was teeming with festival attendees. Gary helped Kahara pass out pluggers.

Later that evening, she and Gary went to get Jasmine and Charles for a cocktail reception being held in one of the hotel banquet rooms. Kahara felt her body tense up as she and Gary headed for their room. As they stood in front of the door, only the TV could be heard. Kahara knocked softly. Jasmine opened the door, smiling. Both she and

Charles were dressed and ready to leave. Kahara looked at them in disbelief and then introduced them to Gary. A few moments later, the two couples left for the reception.

Kahara marveled at how professionally Jasmine and Charles handled themselves as they networked with the others. She did note that Jasmine seemed a little tense as she sat watching a woman who seemed to take an acute interest in Charles. At one point, he was in the corner for over thirty minutes talking with the woman, while Jasmine sat at the opposite end of the room with a sour look on her face.

As they prepared for bed, Kahara found herself becoming more and more apprehensive about the screening. Kahara spooned against Gary's body, her back facing him. "You're nervous," he said, squeezing her almost rigid shoulder.

"No. What makes you think that?" she said, trying to un-tense her body.

"Come on K," he said, rubbing her back gently.

She sighed. "Yeah, a little."

"Why?"

Kahara explained to him that she was a little anxious about whether Jas and Charles would have another argument and not show up. She was also concerned about the type of questions that might come from the audience during the post-film Q&A session. Gary suggested that she focus on the questions the audience would ask instead of worrying about Jas and Charles, whose behavior she could not control. He spent the next half-hour throwing a series of tough questions at her as a sort of rehearsal. He covered everything from her casting choices, to subject matter and dialogue. He even asked about the bad language used in the film.

"What's with all the cursing?" he said. "Couldn't you have gotten your point across without all the profanity?"

"Yes there was cursing—that's the way I wrote it—so that's the way I filmed it."

"You might want to soften that a little," Gary said. "You want one more?"

Kahara turned around and kissed him on the cheek. "No, I'm fine now. Thanks baby."

"You sure you're ready?" he said, tickling her a little.

She squirmed, trying to get away. "Gary, stop! Look now, I bet you're just as ticklish as me." She tried to poke at him in between tickles, but Gary caught her hands before she could get to his rib cage. He continued tickling her mercilessly. Kahara fidgeted, trying to get away.

"You give up?" he asked.

"Okay, okay, okay, yeah. I give up. I give up!" He stopped and Kahara caught her breath. "You make me sick sometimes, you know that," she said, smiling at him. She turned back around and spooned her body against his again. Gary held her close.

"I can't tell you how much all the help you've given me has meant. The software, the lessons, converting the film for me, and then these questions." She let out a long sigh. "It just feels so good having you here."

He kissed her gently on the shoulder. "You gonna make me proud tomorrow."

She paused for a moment. "Gary."

"Yeah K."

"I love you."

"I love you too babe."

Charles and Jasmine were arguing when Gary and Kahara arrived the next morning, so they left without them.

"They're no doubt fighting about that woman who was flirting with Charles last night," Kahara said, as they boarded the elevator.

"If they are, she needs to get a grip," Gary said.

They had breakfast in the restaurant at the hotel, then headed to the theatre. Kahara's screening would take place at eleven. Gary brought along a hand-held camcorder to tape the Q&A. On their way inside the packed theatre, they noticed Jasmine and Charles in the corner of the lobby arguing.

A few minutes later, Kahara saw Jasmine and Charles walking to the front of the theatre. Kahara's film was wedged between a film about a woman rebuilding her life after a brutal breakup, and another, about a man who plots revenge against his cheating wife.

During the screening, she reached for Gary's hand. He put his arm around her, and she leaned her head on his shoulder. Kahara was touched by the audience's reaction to her film. She noticed women wiping their eyes at the point where Jas and Charles come together one final time toward the end. She felt her film more than held its own against the other two entries.

Kahara asked Jas and Charles to join her on stage during Q&A. Gary moved to the front and began taping. She felt at ease and in control as she stood fielding questions. The film received numerous compliments. None of the questions asked were as confrontational as the ones Gary had hurled at her. But toward the end, one man delivered a zinger, berating her for some of the bad language used in the film. Kahara took a deep breath before answering, grateful that this was one of the questions Gary had prepped her for. "I appreciate your input sir, and I'm sorry if you were offended, but I believe in shooting straight from the hip, so from time to time my stories will contain colorful language. I intended no disrespect to my audience though, and again, I'm sorry if you were offended."

"Well I was."

"And that's your right. Just like it's my right as a filmmaker to tell my story, the way I think it should be told. And I won't edit it down. I would not be true to my art if I did."

Kahara smiled, surprised as some in the audience began to applaud her answer. The woman who had taken a special interest in Charles was there. She introduced her credentials to the audience. Her name was Carlotta Taylor, a well-known independent filmmaker based in New York. She praised his performance and asked a few questions about his past work. She raised her hand again toward the end of the session.

"Young man, I know I've said it before, but I'm just so completely impressed, I have to say it again. You have *exceptional* talent. Exceptional. And as I said to you last night, I'm not going to stop asking, until you agree to star in my next film. We begin shooting in October. This would be an excellent reel to add to your resume. The shoot should last about six weeks, and I guarantee you, you'll get a taste of New York you won't soon forget."

Jasmine gave the woman a cold stare. Kahara believed the woman's motives were legitimate, until her last statement. What exactly was she guaranteeing him a taste of? Charles smiled, and rubbed the back of his neck, obviously embarrassed by the special attention he was receiving. "Thank you," he said, clearing his throat. "We can talk more about it later." Kahara glanced over at Jasmine, whose body looked as rigid as a board.

Next Time

After Q&A, Kahara and the other filmmakers made their way toward the back of the theatre. Kahara shook hands with audience members, passed out business cards, and exchanged cards with other filmmakers. Craig gave her a big hug and snapped a picture of her.

Gary stood in the background as different men, including the attractive man from Detroit, came up and hugged or shook hands with her. The consummate professional, Gary remained composed and supportive, never showing a twinge of jealousy. Kahara chided herself for not being as mature, and hoped that she would return the favor and behave as professionally, the next time she had the misfortune of being around Theresa.

One of the last people to approach her was a distributor from Showtime, who discussed the possibility of purchasing her film, so that it could air during Black History Month. Since her next step was to try to get financing to expand her short into a feature length film, having her project air on Showtime would give her the ammunition she needed when meeting with potential investors. She rushed up to Gary, who was waiting in the back of the theatre, and showed him the gentleman's card, and gave him the good news.

They proceeded to the lobby to tell Charles and Jasmine. When they got there, they saw Jasmine, Charles and the filmmaker from New York in the corner, engaged in a heated discussion. Jasmine was standing an inch away from the woman.

"I don't see where any of this concerns you," the woman said.

"First last night, and now today. Stop bothering him. He's not interested—"

"Listen," Charles said, interrupting Jasmine.

"I've had enough of this shit, no *you* listen. She wants to fuck, she's not trying to make a film."

The woman looked as though she had just been stung in the face by a wasp.

Charles grabbed Jasmine by the arm. "Excuse us," he said, his voice tense.

The three stood watching as he led her quickly out of the theatre. Gary and Kahara walked outside a few moments later to find them. They were nowhere in sight.

"They must have gone back to their room," Kahara said. She sighed. "Well, at least we made it through Q&A."

Gary looked at her and shook his head. They left and had lunch at a small Chinese café three blocks from the festival. As they ate, Kahara studied Gary curiously.

"What?" he said, dipping his fork into his rice. "You got a question. What is it?"

"You can always tell can't you?" she said, smiling at him. She leaned back in her seat. "How come you never get jealous?"

"Jealous? Jealous of what?"

"All those men coming up to me."

"You *want* me to get jealous?"

Kahara sat and thought for a moment. "Yeah," she said softly, smiling to herself. "Yeah. I do."

"You want me to get jealous and *show* it?"

"Well—"

"Or do you want to know if I *feel* jealous, but just don't say anything?"

She shook her head. "Yeah, yeah, that's it." It amazed her sometimes how Gary could burrow to the core of what she was feeling and verbalize it better than she could.

"Do I like seeing other men run up on you? Of course not. But if I stood there looking mad or worse, went off like Jas, that could kill an opportunity for you."

Kahara thought about Theresa. She wasn't so sure if she wanted Gary to be jealous because it would be flattering to her, or because him acting jealous would give her clearance to set Theresa straight in the event they had another run-in.

"I can't see you snapping off like your girl did today," he said, smiling slightly. Kahara looked away. He studied her uncertain expression. "You'd never do that, right?"

Kahara began picturing a scenario where she would go completely off on Theresa, and then smiled to herself. It would almost be worth the risk, just for the satisfaction. "Yeah, yeah, right. No way," she lied.

"Your girl's got some issues," Gary said.

"I can't totally fault Jas for this one," Kahara said. "That woman cornered Charles for over a half-hour last night, then drooling all over him during Q&A. It was sickening."

Gary shook his head. "That happens. Like I said before, she needs to get a grip. I'd have cut that loose a long time ago if I were him. Man, if you *ever* pulled something like that on me—"

"What?"

Gary gave her a cold stare.

"You'd end it?"

"I'd have to. K, my clients—"

"Pay your bills. Yeah, I know. I know. If I hear that one more time."

"Fifty percent of my business is through referrals. Turning off one client could cost me five."

"So you'd just end it. Cold—just like that."

"If the circumstances warranted it, yeah. Like that little sideshow your girl put on. Hell yeah. I'd be out."

Kahara sized him up for a moment. She thought back to what his mother said about how much he liked her and then smiled. "I don't believe you," she said. "You couldn't be that brutal if you tried."

Gary shook his head, saying nothing, and continued eating. Kahara wondered if he meant what he said. She poured some soy sauce on her egg roll. "You know, the more I think about the film, the more I wish I had ended it differently—you know, let them stay together."

"Why? The ending was fine."

"I'll be honest. When I wrote the script, I didn't have a lot of faith in relationships." Kahara studied him for a moment. "But I feel differently now."

"People can love each other and it still not work. It happens," he said, shrugging.

"Well, don't be so cavalier about it."

"I'm not talking about us," he said.

"You aren't? You sure?"

"Sure I'm sure."

"Do you think we'll work out?"

"Do you?"

"Yeah," she said, a little defensively. "Don't you?"

"I hope it does."

"You hope. That's the best I can get is 'I hope'?" She took a sip of her drink. "I could see if we were like Jas and Charles."

"We are."

"No, we're not that bad. Come on now. We go at it, but not like that."

"Not in public."

Next Time

"Not yet," she said, nudging him. She relaxed slightly, seeing him smile for the first time during their conversation. Kahara leaned back in her seat, stretching her legs out in front of her. "The hard part's over. Now I can relax and enjoy myself. Maybe give you some later, if you don't piss me off," she said, under her breath.

"If I piss you off, I'll still get some," he said, grabbing her leg from under the table.

"Oh yeah?" she said, shoving his hand off her leg. "You just think you got this all wrapped up, don't you? I'm not one of them weak-assed chicks you're used to dealing with."

"Could've fooled me," he said.

"Ohhhh okay. Okay," she said, shaking her head. "We'll see tonight."

"I won't even have to ask," he said, giving her a confident stare.

"You're a cocky somethin'. I see now, I need to bring you down a notch."

They went over the film schedule, and picked out three films they wanted to see. After the Q&A, Kahara went down and introduced herself to each filmmaker and exchanged cards. She and Gary attended a small reception later that night, then headed upstairs. Gary went to their room while Kahara went to check on Charles and Jasmine. They were both in their room, but the atmosphere was icy.

"How are they?" Gary asked, as she came inside.

"Barely speaking, but they'll probably be doing what we're about to do soon."

"Oh yeah?" he said, pulling her to him. "And just what might that be?"

"What we do best, other than fight," she said, smiling.

He eased her back toward the bed. "Told you I wouldn't have to ask."

Kahara won an award for Best Short Film at the awards ceremony. Gary taped her acceptance speech. Craig, who also attended, let Kahara know that he would run a follow-up column about the fest, and would mention that her film won an award.

They returned to the hotel, then headed to LAX. Kahara and Gary said their goodbyes, then Kahara headed for her gate.

Charles and Jasmine got into another argument while waiting for the flight. Jasmine spat out a few choice words, then walked off. Kahara who was seated across from the couple, got up and took a seat next to Charles.

"What's going on with you two?" she asked. "Why do you fight so much?" She caught herself as she made the statement, thinking about herself and Gary.

"We can't go one week—one week without a major fight, and it's always over some bullshit," he said.

"How long have you two been together?"

"Over a year."

"And you fight like this every week? Why do you put up with it?"

He sighed. "I love her. Why else?"

Kahara stared at him almost in disbelief. Most men she had known were ready to cut and run after the first few disagreements. Even Gary seemed to have a low tolerance for arguing.

"You must love her bad to go through all this," she said. Kahara realized she had been all wrong about Charles. Initially thinking Charles had hit it and wanted to dump Jasmine, Kahara now saw that he was as hopelessly hooked as Jas was. After a few moments, Jasmine returned. Charles got up and the couple went for a walk. About twenty minutes later, they returned, apparently reconciled. Kahara shook her head and laughed softly to herself.

    The flight home was quiet. Watching Jasmine and Charles together made Kahara feel a little wistful for Gary's company. Her birthday was in less than two weeks, but Gary would be in L.A. working. Gary planned to fly in the weekend after Kahara's birthday and take her out to celebrate, while in town to help Darren with a shoot.

Chapter 23

It was 6:00 a.m. Thursday morning when the phone rang. Kahara's arm felt like lead as she reached over to grab it. She cradled the receiver next to her ear.

"Hello," she said, her eyes still closed.

Gary began singing "Happy Birthday."

"Boy, you and my mother need some serious voice lessons," she said, pulling herself up. Gary began another verse. "Okay, okay baby. I got it. You can stop now." Kahara rolled over and smiled. "I wish you were here. Can't wait to see you Friday."

Gary stopped abruptly and cleared his throat. "Listen K, I got some bad news. I'm not going to be able to get in town this weekend like I thought."

"What happened?"

"The shoot Darren had lined up got cancelled."

"Well, you can still come, right?"

"Well, no. I've got to stay in Norfolk to do another shoot."

Kahara's voice became tense. "Another shoot for who?"

Gary hesitated before continuing. "Theresa needs me to do a shoot for the NAACP gala this weekend."

"You wake me out of a sound sleep to tell me one, you're not coming, and two, it's because of her."

"It couldn't be helped Kahara."

"So, you weren't coming in town to celebrate my birthday, you were just coming here to work."

"No. Well, both. Yeah, I was coming to do both."

"No, if you were coming to do both you'd *be* here this weekend."

"The job fell through Kahara. Something else opened up."

"Something else, or her?"

"Not again." Gary sighed hard. "I'm not in the mood to listen to another one of your rants."

"Not in the mood? You cancel the trip because of her, then say you're not in the mood to discuss it?"

"What for? We'll just go around in circles like we always do."

"All she has to do—"

"Kahara–

"All this bitch has to do is snap her fingers and you—"

"Look, I don't have the patience for this shit anymore. Why don't we just cut through the bullshit okay? Either get over the fact that I have female clients, or find somebody else. Simple as that."

His words stunned her. Kahara sat there unable to respond. She bit her lip and breathed hard. "Go to hell Gary," she said, slamming down the phone.

Tears welled up in her eyes. She pulled the top sheet off and got up out of bed, pacing the floor, trying to process what had just happened. One minute he's singing "Happy Birthday," the next he's telling her to find somebody else. How could he turn so cold so abruptly, or had this been building up all along? Kahara wiped her eyes and slowly got ready for work. As she walked to the train station, she heard a noise behind her. She turned around and there walking not three feet from her was Gary.

"What? How did you—what are you doing here?"

He walked up to her and gave her a long hug. "How could you think I wouldn't be here?" he said, as he let go of her. He put his arm around her shoulder as they continued walking.

Kahara stopped suddenly. "No, no. I've got three weeks of vacation and seven sick days. I'm going home." They changed direction, and began walking back to her apartment building. When they reached the lobby, the doorman stopped her.

"I've got something for you," he said smiling. He went to the back room, returned with two dozen yellow roses, and handed them to Kahara.

Kahara cradled the flowers in her arms and reached up and hugged Gary. "You are so sweet," she said. When they got inside her apartment, she phoned her manager letting him know that she would not be in.

Kahara took her flowers into the kitchen. She reached into her cupboard and pulled out a large crystal vase which was given to her years ago by her aunt Jessie. After filling the vase up with water, Kahara began gently placing each rose inside, one by one. When she got halfway through the second dozen, she noticed something metallic wrapped around one of the stems. She delicately removed the item. Kahara's face lit up in surprise. "Gary!" she called.

He walked into the kitchen smiling. "What?"

She turned to him holding up the sleek sterling silver watch.

"How did you know?" she asked.

"Mama told me how much you liked it, that day you two went shopping at the mall," he said.

He walked up to her and put the watch on her wrist. Kahara lowered her head, wiping her eyes. He took the tip of her chin in his finger and lifted it up.

"What's the matter, baby?" he said, kissing her forehead.

"Nothing," she said. "I'm just—nothin'."

He took the vase and they walked into the living room. Kahara held her wrist up, admiring her present. She took her birthday flowers from him and placed them delicately onto the marble cocktail table. Gary came behind her and slid his arms around her waist. "Had you going for a minute there didn't I?" he said, kissing the back of her neck.

She turned around and gave him a hug. "Yeah, you did," she said. "You knew just what to say, and who to use as a blocker." Her tone softened. "I'm sorry I told you to go to hell."

He pulled her close and held her. "Don't worry about it," he said, stroking her hair.

They went in her bedroom and made love. Gary took her out to breakfast, then they went to the grocery store to pick up some items for her mother, who was home sick with a cold. When Kahara and Gary arrived at her mother's apartment, Mrs. Jenkins sang an off-key "Happy Birthday," and promised a cake when she got better.

Kahara made her mother lunch. Her mother's illness made her more subdued. She didn't subject her daughter to the usual grilling session. After visiting with her mother, they went for a walk on the beach. Kahara looked over at Gary. "You know what I'd like to do," she said, as they walked along. "I'd like to find a way to promote black independent films, so that people who don't attend festivals can know about them."

"You mean you want to become a distributor?"

"Well, most indie filmmakers distribute their own films. What I'd like to do is market the films to a broader audience—reach people where they live. You know, maybe something web-based."

"Well, if they put together a two-minute clip of their film it could be uploaded to the web."

"Yeah, that sounds good. Upload it to the web. The next step would be to reach out to black organizations and churches. Tell them to preview the films on the website then order them."

"Then you're talkin' distribution too."

"I don't want to get into distribution. I just want people to know about the films—they can order them directly from the filmmakers."

"But if you start out with a small inventory of films you could do the distribution yourself and charge a fee."

"That's a thought," she said. She took his hand. "Remember when I interviewed you over a year ago, and you talked about owning a company the size of Dreamworks?"

"You remembered that, huh?"

"I told you nine months ago, I catch everything."

He put his arm around her. "You mean, put my idea and your idea together."

She smiled. "I like the fact that you can read my mind sometimes," she said.

Later that evening Kahara and Gary met Sergio, Arnita and Keith at Café Florin, a popular Italian restaurant in Hyde Park. Darren and Angie joined them twenty minutes later. Kahara introduced everyone and they ordered their meals.

Next Time

"Kahara, I just want to start this out by saying I had nothing to do with Gary's little scheme to trick you," Darren said, leaning forward. "It was all his idea. Pretty good one, though," he added, grinning.

Kahara let the group know that her film had not been accepted at the Virginia Beach Black Film Festival which would take place in two weeks. She did, however, give them the good news that Showtime confirmed they'd be buying her film to air during Black History month next year. Her lawyer would work out the details, allowing her to retain rights so that she could expand the short into a full-length feature. The attorney would also try to negotiate a deal to obtain funding from Showtime.

The following evening, Kahara sat on her couch looking over the brochure for the Virginia Beach Black Film Festival. In less than two weeks, she and Gary would attend the fest. Although her film had not been accepted, she still wanted to attend, since it was one of the largest and most popular black festivals in the country. She also wanted to take the screenwriter's course she passed on the year before. Keith and Sergio would also be attending the fest.

Kahara knew Marshall would be there, since he said he never missed a year since its inception. She hadn't spoken to Marshall since last year's event, and never tried to make contact with him again after emailing and calling him. The idea of running into him while with Gary was something Kahara did not want to deal with. Since making the comment to Kahara about Marshall feeling her up, months before they became involved, Gary never mentioned his name again. Embarrassed by the thought that Gary may know that Marshall had sex with her then dumped her, she had never brought up his name. It was almost as though the two of them had an unspoken agreement not to mention Marshall.

She wasn't concerned about how Marshall would respond to seeing her with Gary. The thought of having Gary to rub in Marshall's face actually brought her an enormous sense of triumph. But the questions that might arise in Gary's mind, after seeing Marshall, troubled her.

Gary arrived at around nine o'clock that evening, exhausted from an all-day shoot. As Kahara warmed up his dinner, she thought again about the uncomfortable prospect of running into Marshall at the festival. All the festival seminars took place at the Avenda Hotel, so there would be no way of avoiding him there. Besides, each night there was an after-hours party. Another awkward scenario. Gary had already made reservations at the Avenda, the same hotel where Marshall usually stayed. The thought of being on the same elevator with both of them made her so uncomfortable that she considered trying to convince Gary to switch hotels.

After Gary finished dinner, they settled in and began watching TV. Kahara, sitting next to Gary on the couch, noticed the sullen mood he was in when he had arrived had not changed.

"Alright Country," she said teasingly, nudging him, trying to lift his spirits.

Gary looked over at her crossly. "Who you callin' Country?"

"You," she challenged, unnerved by his tone.

Gary shifted in his seat. "Tell you what," he said. "I'll bet we so-called country brothers treat sisters a hell of a lot better than the brothers up here."

Next Time

She folded her arms thinking back to Marshall. "I wouldn't go that far," she said. "I've had men from the North treat me very well, and I've had men from the South act—" She stopped herself before finishing the sentence, not wanting to give Gary a segway to question her about Marshall. But it was too late, the door was already opened.

"How many men have you had from the South?" he questioned.

Oh boy, she thought. "One," she said sullenly.

"It wasn't that brother from the festival last year?"

"Yeah it was him."

"Well, you're talking about one guy. Where was he from anyway?"

Kahara sighed. "Birmingham."

"I don't know any brothers from Birmingham, but you got dogs everywhere. And maybe I'm being presumptuous assuming that's what he was, since you never told me what happened between the two of you."

Oh no, Kahara thought. *Don't go there. Please don't go there.* She unwrapped herself from him, got up and sat in the loveseat opposite the couch to brace herself for the questions she was certain were coming.

Gary looked at her curiously. "What did happen anyway? You knew him before you came to the fest, right?"

"Ahhhhhhh no," she said, folding her arms and leaning forward.

"You didn't?"

"No."

"You didn't know him before you came to the fest?"

"I said no."

"You met him when, Tuesday, Wednesday?"

"Wednesday."

"Really, and you let him dance with you like that? Hmph."

"What's the 'hmph' mean?"

"I don't know, it just seemed a little strange. Wednesday and Thursday night you two were all over each other on the dance floor. I'll be honest with you, I heard a few of the guys jokin' about it. I won't tell you what they said."

"Please don't."

"I didn't see you that Friday night, was that when—"

"Yeah," she interrupted, not wanting him to say it.

"That's strange, because when I saw you two that Saturday, you weren't dancing close anymore. You were three feet apart from each other."

"So?"

"You looked kind of lost, so I just assumed, well. Hmph."

"There it is again. Why do you keep doing that?" she said, becoming annoyed.

"I don't know, it just seems like you would have waited to get to know him better, huh?"

"Yeah, yeah, I probably should have done that," she said, curtly, not wanting to go any further with it.

"So why didn't you?"

Kahara looked at him. "What do you mean why didn't I?"

"Why didn't you wait?"

"I went with the feeling, okay?"

"Went with a feeling?" He looked at her as though she were speaking a foreign language. "Why would you let a brotha like that even get that close to you? Feelin' you up like you were in some porn video."

"Look Gary, can we—"

"Is that what you normally do?"

Next Time

"Is that what I normally do? Is that what I normally do? NO, I don't normally travel to different states letting men feel all over me and then have sex with me. But if I did, so what? Don't judge me."

"I'm not judging, I'm just trying to understand. There I am breakin' my neck tryin to get your attention, and the whole time you wringin' your hands over some dog who could have gave a damn less about you."

"And how would you know that?"

"I saw you following him around the party Saturday, Kahara. And I saw you leave—alone. I talked to you earlier that night. Remember? I could tell by the expression on your face. You two were barely together, so I assumed the brother must have hit and run."

"That's a pretty big conclusion to leap to," she said sarcastically.

"Not ten minutes after you left, he left with his arm wrapped around some woman's waist."

"Was she wearing a red sequined dress?"

"Yeah, yeah I think she was. How'd you know?"

"Never mind."

"Someone said that brother comes every year with the same agenda."

Kahara became angrier by the minute. She felt made a fool of by Marshall and picked apart by Gary. "What difference does it make? What, are you jealous?" she asked, getting up, walking to the window. Kahara pulled at the blinds and looked out.

"No, I just don't understand what a brother has to do to get your attention. I guess maybe if I had shoved my tongue down your throat the first time we danced, you'd have given me some the first night too."

"I didn't give him some the first night."

"Second, third. What's two days?" he said, getting up. "I waited over three months—*three* months, and this brother waits two days. Two days. What was that about?"

"Why is this coming up now? What are you worried about? You scared I'm going to see him and jump into bed with him again?" She walked over toward him. "I—don't—want—him. Got it?"

"You don't have to convince me."

"I must, or we wouldn't be on this so long," she said.

"Why are you so angry?"

"He hurt me Gary."

"How could he? You only knew him two days."

The statement nearly knocked Kahara back into her chair. She sat down, motionless, trying to fight back the tears that were welling up in her eyes. She bit her lip. "That whole thing with Marshall was the most embarrassing, degrading—I'm not proud of what I did, and I hate him for treating me like a piece of toilet paper he wiped his ass with. I've already beat myself up about it. I'll be damned if I'm going to sit here and let you rub my face in it some more. This bullshit."

She got up and walked hurriedly into the bedroom, slamming the door behind her. She fell onto the bed, crying, feeling used and discarded by Marshall and ripped apart by Gary. Self- recrimination crept over her. If only she had continued on, instead of attempting to talk to Derrick Johnson, she would never have felt the need to cover up her embarrassment by asking Marshall to dance. None of it would have ever happened. She'd have gone to breakfast with Gary the next day, become involved with him, and avoided all the hurt and pain she went through after Marshall dumped her.

A few moments later Kahara heard a knock at the door. Gary walked in slowly and sat on the bed beside her. He touched her back gently with his hand.

"I'm sorry, Kahara," he said softly. "I had no right to beat up on you like that."

Kahara pulled herself up on the bed and looked at him. "It bothered you that I had sex with him so soon."

"A little. Especially after I waited so long."

She swallowed. "It makes me nervous." She stopped and paused. "It makes me nervous having to talk about my past because I haven't—I haven't made such good decisions, and I have had sex too soon—way too soon. After Marshall—that burned so bad that I—I said I'd never let a man get in that quick again. Then I made you wait and I thought, if he finds out I didn't do that with everybody, he'll think I'm a hypocrite."

Gary pressed his finger to her lips stopping her. "Shhhh. You don't have to explain your actions to me. I've made mistakes. That's the past Kahara. Leave it there." He touched her shoulder gently, and then pulled her into his arms. "I'm sorry baby. I'm sorry," he said. He sat there holding her close, saying nothing.

She got up a few moments later undressed, and put on her gown. Gary disrobed and slipped on his pajama bottoms. Kahara always felt embarrassed after they had a fight, not knowing how to bridge over to be friends again. It always perplexed her how they could have such great times together, yet have such intense fights. Most of her relationships never withstood this number of disagreements. The men would get fed up and end it.

They climbed back into bed, careful not to bump into each other. Kahara lay on one side of the bed and Gary on the other, the two of them seemingly afraid to touch each other now that their clothes were off.

After a few moments, Gary eased over to her side and put his arm around her waist. She backed against him, feeling his penis stiffen against her, then turned around facing him.

He took her face in his hand, kissing her gently on the cheek and mouth, continuing down to her chest and finally resting his lips against her nipple. He teased and licked it through the gown, then eased the straps over her shoulders, pulling it down to expose her breasts. He cupped them both in his hands and began licking the tips of each nipple. Kahara felt like electrical bolts were shooting through her. She became so aroused that she couldn't wait to feel his stiffness inside of her.

She reached over to the nightstand, grabbed a rubber, and tore open the wrapper. Reaching inside his pajama bottoms, she pulled out his penis, applied the rubber, and then turned over on her back. Gary mounted her, grabbing her by the leg and moving her panties over as he pushed his way inside her wet warmth. She held onto the bed railing for dear life, as he rode her—in and out—in and out, until they both climaxed.

They lay in each other's arms afterwards saying nothing, which was their usual routine after make-up sex. No rehashing the situation. Once the fight was over, it was over—time to move on. As they were lying there, Kahara felt almost elated at the prospect of being in the same hotel as Marshall, now that the cloud of Gary's questioning was lifted. With everything out in the open now, Kahara no longer felt a need to avoid Marshall and was almost looking forward to seeing the expression on his face when he saw her with Gary. No one-night stand this time—no being pushed off to the side to be ignored afterwards. No, not this year. The festival couldn't come soon enough for her now.

Chapter 24

Kahara rushed around doing last-minute packing Wednesday morning, something she'd put off, due to her long hours at the office. By the time she finished, she realized there was no way to make it to the airport, and through security, in time for her flight.

She called the airline and found out that the next available flight would not arrive in Norfolk until six o'clock. That would still give her enough time to get to the hotel and change for the festival gala and opening night feature. It was of utmost importance to her that she arrive in time for the opening night ceremonies, especially after finding out from Gary that Theresa would be in attendance. The idea of that woman attending the gala with Gary was more than she could stomach.

After arriving at the airport two hours early, Kahara found out that her flight was delayed an hour and a half. This would put her in the Norfolk airport at about seven-thirty, which meant she probably wouldn't reach the hotel until after eight-thirty, well after the start of the gala. She sat on the plane with her arms folded, fuming. Angry with herself for being careless enough to miss that first flight, which would have put her there by twelve-thirty, she was hoping this turn of events wouldn't set the tone for the rest of her vacation. Kahara had looked forward to this for too long. Being able to return with Gary on her arm was like peeling a scab off of an old deep wound.

After waiting for her luggage, Kahara didn't arrive at the hotel until almost nine o'clock. She phoned her mother, then called Gary on his cell, but got no answer. He was no doubt already at the opening night party, which was held at the same club where she met him and Marshall the previous year. To her relief, he had left word with the attendant, and she got her key without a hassle. She missed the gala and the opening movie, but at least could enjoy the party with Gary. Once in the room, she unpacked the dress she'd wear that evening. Kahara spotted Gary's sunglasses on the dresser. She walked over and stroked them, thinking of him in some cool, loose-fitting tan shirt and slacks and smiled. She glanced over to the bed and saw a woman's jacket.

"Don't tell me," she said, approaching the bed, picking up the cream-colored jacket. Kahara realized it was probably Theresa's, since she was attending the festival. "That witch," she said out loud.

She smelled the fabric to see what type of cologne Theresa was wearing. The scent was light at first, then piercing and rather exotic. Kahara thought that her own fruity smelling lemon splash paled in comparison to Theresa's elegant fragrance. And what was her jacket doing on their bed? Kahara didn't think anything happened between them, but felt Theresa left the jacket there purposely, just to get under her skin.

She didn't bother to unpack anything, but jumped into the shower. Afterward, Kahara decided to wear the same black-and-white dress she wore to the festival party the year before. It was her own quiet way of reworking history—taking the sting out of what happened to her the previous year. Kahara wasn't sure how she was going to get in to the opening night party, since she arrived too late to register. But that was something she'd work out once she got there.

When she arrived at the club, the party was well under way. Crowds of non-festival attendees were gathered outside trying to finagle their way in, as usual. Kahara steered past them to the gatekeeper. Kahara showed him her festival confirmation email and her drivers license, and after a few minutes of back and forth, he finally let her in, seeing she wasn't going to leave until he did so. As she strolled in, she looked at her watch. It was a little after ten o'clock.

The club was teeming with smartly dressed men and women. Large palm trees towered over the front of the club, which itself was a large outdoor patio. Toward the back was a huge, sunken dance floor. Kahara walked up to the second level. She stood by the railing surveying the crowd looking for Gary.

She walked around to the other side and stood. As she scanned the excited crush of people, she spotted a woman with long hair, wearing a cream-colored dress, the same shade as the jacket on the hotel bed. It was Theresa, beaming as she danced with her tall, handsome partner. Kahara's expression turned sour, as she stood there unseen by Gary, scrutinizing Theresa's every movement. Theresa swirled and twirled and then feigned losing her balance a few times, so Gary could gallantly catch her before she fell. "She must have rehearsed this," Kahara said, under her breath.

Her first impulse was to rush forward and break up the party, but she decided instead to use this opportunity to see just how this woman acted around her man when she thought she wasn't being watched. Kahara had caught the resentful glances Theresa gave her when she was on the shoot with Gary months ago—every nuance, every snide remark, every dismissive gesture. And now was the perfect opportunity to dissect Theresa's body language.

From a distance, Gary looked composed and cool as usual, no shifty glances, no looking over his shoulder to see if he was being watched. He looked like a man dancing with an attractive woman who was not his. The lady, on the other hand, seemed self-conscious—her movements a bit too busy, as though she were trying to pretend she was at ease when she really wasn't. Theresa had the nervous presence of a woman with a plan. As she turned around, frequently giving Gary numerous chances to catch a glimpse of her well-rounded behind, Kahara studied with piqued interest. She watched as Theresa shimmied and moved her rear end ever so suggestively. Kahara watched as she grabbed Gary's arm, frequently pulling him close to speak into his ear, and she watched, as she mischievously poked his shoulder. She had her routine almost down pat. She spun around again, as Gary looked on in amusement.

"Back into him and I'ma snatch your ass," Kahara said softly, as she stood there with arms folded. "Any part of your ass touches his groin, it's over, bitch," she mumbled to herself.

Unamused by Theresa's continuing antics, Kahara decided it was time to break up the party. She made her way to the dance floor and edged up behind Gary, tapping him lightly on the shoulder. He turned around, a grin spreading across his face when he saw her.

"Finally," he said. He gave her a hug, as Theresa stood still for a moment, watching. "You just get here?"

"No, I've been here for over an hour, watching you," she said, staring intently at him to see if he flinched. He didn't.

"It's too bad you had to miss the opening movie and the reception," he said, as they began swaying to the music. He motioned to Theresa. "You remember Theresa?"

"Sure," Kahara said, mustering up the phoniest smile she could.

"Hello Katari," Theresa said coolly.

"That's Kahara," she said, correcting her.

"What dear—I didn't hear you?" she said.

"Ka-*ha-ra*," Gary repeated to her loudly.

"Umm hmm," Theresa said, nodding dismissively.

Kahara hoped that when the song ended, Theresa would excuse herself, but she didn't budge. After the third number, Kahara began to get angry. Why didn't she just leave? She peeked around Gary's shoulder as they danced.

"Theresa, I take it you're here *alone*."

"No. I flew in with some friends," Theresa said a little tersely.

"Let's get something to eat," Gary said, interrupting their exchange. "You haven't eaten yet, have you K?"

"No I haven't, and I am very, *very*, hungry," she said earnestly, hoping Theresa had already eaten.

The three of them made their way to the exit. Kahara spotted Derrick Johnson in the same spot he was in last year when she saw him. No sign of Marshall. Gary hailed a cab and they all got in, as he wedged himself between the two women. Theresa leaned her head back.

"Whew, I'm developing a headache," Theresa said.

Who gives a damn, Kahara thought, looking up in the air rolling her eyes.

"Must have been the loud music," Gary said.

"Yeah, and all that spinning around you were doin'. I saw you almost fall a few times," Kahara said sarcastically.

Theresa did not respond.

"So Kaharry, Gary tells me you had a little film play at the Los Angeles Festival."

"It's Kaha*ra*, and yes I did."

"I just don't get this whole indie filmmaker thing. No one I know has ever been successful at it. I mean, I'm not knocking what you do."

Oh yes you are, Kahara thought. *Witch.*

"But you people make all these films. They appear in festivals, then that's it. What do you have to show for it?"

"She has a great piece of work to show for it," Gary said proudly.

"Yeah, but that's all." Theresa chuckled. "All you really wind up with at the end of it all is an expensive home video. I mean really, name me one independent filmmaker that's made it."

"I will," Kahara said confidently.

Theresa smirked. "You hope. What's this thing about anyway?"

"The *thing* is about a relationship that doesn't work," Kahara said coolly.

"Where'd you get that idea from?" Theresa asked. "Or is it autobiographical?" she added, under her breath but loud enough for Kahara to hear her.

You are in rare form tonight, Kahara thought to herself. "You know, to be honest, I get my story ideas from many sources. As a matter of fact," she said, with a glint of mischief in her eyes, "as a matter of fact, I recently got an idea to do a story about an entrepreneur—a successful, lonely, brittle, abrasive, desperate, I mean desperate woman, who tries repeatedly to steal a man away from his loyal, caring, trusting, affectionate, voluptuous, sensuous—extremely sensuous girlfriend." She leaned over and looked Theresa directly in the eye. "She fails miserably. Yep, I'm going to get to work on that as soon as I get back. Just as soon as I get back," she said, leaning back triumphantly.

"*The Best Thing* is an excellent film," Gary said, trying to ease the tension. "Kahara did a great job. I'm very proud of her," he said, squeezing Kahara's shoulder.

Kahara stared ahead glaring. Theresa did not respond. When they reached the Avenda Hotel, Theresa opened the door to get out. Kahara was a little disappointed that she was staying at the same hotel they were.

"You two go on. Gary and I dined earlier, so I really shouldn't eat again. Gotta watch these hips," Theresa said, smoothing her dress down over her creamy slender thighs.

Two strikes. She had to let Kahara know she had dinner with Gary, and then verbally call attention to her svelte figure—something she had been doing all night on the dance floor.

"Listen Gary, I'll be by tomorrow to pick up my jacket. I forgot it."

"Yeah, I found it lying on *our* bed when I got to the hotel," Kahara said wryly, looking straight ahead, arms folded.

Gary gave Theresa an understanding smile. "I'll get it to you tomorrow," he said.

As the cab pulled out of the driveway, Kahara couldn't help but smile to herself. *Good riddance,* she thought as she sat back in her seat.

"Driver, wait a minute," Gary said, before turning to Kahara. "Listen, before we leave, you know there's a nice romantic restaurant inside the hotel."

"Is that where you and Theresa ate?" she snapped.

"Don't start. I told you she was going to be here."

"I know, but did you two eat there?"

He turned to her and smiled. "We ate at a restaurant called The President."

That was the same restaurant she and Marshall had breakfast at the year before. "Okay then, let's eat here at the hotel," she said.

Gary paid the cab driver and they got out.

"Why was her jacket on our bed?"

Gary looked over at her as they walked into the lobby. "It was humid out and she took it off and left it there."

"On purpose," Kahara said knowingly.

Theresa spotted the two of them. "You're eating here?" she asked, as she walked up to them. "Well then in that case, maybe I'll join you. I would like to get some dessert, and I heard they have a cheesecake to die for here," she said, looking at Gary, then at Kahara. "Do you mind?"

Kahara swallowed hard.

"No, sure you can join us," Gary said, looking at Kahara and nodding. Kahara gave him a cold stare. They headed for the restaurant with Kahara trailing behind the two of them with a grimace etched on her face. Gary looked back and motioned for her, holding out his hand. She reluctantly put her hand into his as they walked inside. Gary was right, the atmosphere was definitely romantic. The establishment was dimly lit, with long, lace tablecloths draping the small, cozy tables. Calypso music played softly in the background.

Kahara looked over at Theresa and gave her a chilly smile. Theresa looked away.

You bitch, she thought.

"You can have anything you want, as long as you pay for it," Gary said, peering over his menu, grinning at Kahara.

Kahara fought the urge to snap about Theresa paying for her own meal. "If I pay for dinner, you get no dessert," she snapped.

"I'ma get dessert," Gary said, giving her a devilish grin.

Kahara wanted Theresa gone. She suffered through the meal, trying her best to remain cordial, and not allow the conversation to degenerate into polite insults the way it did in the cab. To her relief, Theresa ordered cheesecake, ate it, then left.

"Now what was that about me not getting any dessert," Gary said, grabbing Kahara's thigh from under the table and squeezing it. Kahara jumped, caught off guard.

"Stop it, I'm a lady," she said indignantly.

"Since when?"

"Oh that's low. That's real low. You know she likes you," she said, looking at him to see his reaction.

"Who?"

"That pig."

Gary laughed. "Don't call her that. She likes the work I do for her, okay?"

"Oh come on, Gary, don't tell me you can't see it?"

"People may want a lot of things. I don't shit where I eat." He grabbed her thigh again and leaned back in his seat. "Besides, I'm taken," he said, grinning at her. "And she knows it."

Kahara smiled. She decided not to let Theresa take up any more of their time. She looked around at the scattered couples and leaned back.

"What's wrong with your cell? I tried calling you earlier."

"You're gonna laugh. After all that preaching I did to you about getting one."

"You left it at home?"

"Yep, it's sitting on the dresser."

Kahara sat back and smiled. "So, did you scare up any new business yet?" she asked.

"There's this brother that has a comedy troupe he's trying to get exposure for. They're going to be performing in L.A. in a few weeks, and we're supposed to meet with him on Saturday to discuss me handling the entire production—the lighting, shooting, editing the whole piece. You plan on doing any networking while you're here?"

"Nope. Not a bit," she quipped, leaning back in her seat. "After the stress of the L.A. festival, Jas and Charles, I just want to relax. Check out some films, do some shopping, walk on the beach."

"Tell you what, I'll meet you after your screenwriting class tomorrow," Gary said. "We can go get something to eat, check out a few films, take a long walk along the beach, and if you're lucky I'll let you get some," he said.

"If *I'm* lucky!" she reached across and shoved his shoulder, just as the waiter brought them their desserts.

"Man, you can just give the check to her." Gary grinned. "You know how these old broads are—just grateful to have some company."

"He's an escaped mental patient. Don't listen to him," Kahara said.

The waiter smiled as he cleared away the dishes. They ordered dessert. Kahara ordered a chocolate mousse to go. Gary looked at her curiously as the waiter left. "I want one to take upstairs," she explained.

"What are you going to do with it?"

Kahara leaned back, smiling mischievously. "You act right, you'll see. Remember New Year's?"

Gary grinned and leaned back in his seat. The waiter returned with their order. They ate dessert and headed to their room. While Gary was in the bathroom, Kahara grabbed Theresa's jacket off the bed and flung it toward the chair, missing it by an inch. She let it lay on the floor for a moment, scampering to get it when Gary came out of the bathroom.

"I'm going to hang this up for her," Kahara said, snatching it up off the floor and scurrying toward the closet. "There we go," she said, lining it up perfectly on the hanger and smoothing the material down with her hands.

Gary shook his head, seeing through her act, but made no comment. "Listen I'ma take a shower." He looked at the mousse sitting on the table and smiled. Kahara took the ice bucket and headed out the door, returning a moment later. Gary undressed while Kahara wedged the chocolate mousse into the bucket. He went into the bathroom and she joined him after removing her clothes. They teased at each other in the shower but fatigue began to overtake them. After showering, they slipped under the covers, hugged and kissed for a minute, then fell asleep.

Kahara awoke a little before Gary. They lay in bed, looking out the terrace at the ocean. "It's beautiful," she said, as the breeze from the terrace blew in on them. Kahara looked over at Gary, who looked relaxed and serene.

Gary got up a few minutes later, put on his robe, and stuck something in his pocket. He opened the terrace door and beckoned her to come out with him. Kahara scampered anxiously out of bed, grabbing her robe, and wrapping it around her, before stepping out on the terrace with him. Gary sat in the lounge chair as Kahara leaned against the railing, absorbing the view. He pulled the rubber out of his pocket and put it on. He reached up and pulled her by the waist from behind into his lap.

"Oooh," she said, as she sat down feeling his stiffness. She lifted her hips up and pulled up her robe, as he adjusted his position. She eased down on top of him, inching her way down over his penis. She exhaled. "Oooh shit, this feels good first thing in the morning," she moaned, as she came down on it completely. He guided her hips as she slid up and down on it. Gary slapped the side of her hips as she wiggled up and down on his rod. She looked out over the ocean, the moist morning breeze blowing in her face. "I could wake up like this everyday," she groaned, as they both neared climax.

They came back in afterwards and Kahara went into the bathroom to take a shower. Gary ordered room service and they had breakfast together. They both laughed about the forgotten chocolate mousse still sitting in the ice bucket. After breakfast, Kahara readied herself for her class.

"I'll see you later, baby," she said, kissing him on the cheek. "If I'm late, I'll be locked out." She registered, then went to class with a huge smile on her face wondering if any of her classmates had done the same thing she did before going to class. The class worked in groups, rewriting a portion of a bad script. Each group was assigned a scene and was instructed to focus on a specific aspect, such as dialogue, action sequences, etc.

Gary was waiting for Kahara outside of class as he had promised.

"Let's get something to eat," he said.

Kahara looped her arm through Gary's, and they headed for the lobby. As they were on their way out, they ran into Theresa and two friends of hers. Kahara's jovial mood immediately went sour. She was praying Gary wouldn't invite them out to lunch.

Theresa introduced her friends, mispronouncing Kahara's name yet again. At this point, Kahara didn't even bother correcting her, understanding the slight was intentional. Kahara took pleasure in catching Theresa's eyes lingering on her arm, which was gently entwined in Gary's.

"Kahaira, Gary tells me you're taking a screenwriter's—what is it?" she asked, turning to Gary.

"Workshop," he said.

"I thought you were already a writer. What's wrong, aren't you sure of yourself?"

"I'll tell you what I am sure of," Kahara said, letting go of Gary's arm, stepping in close to her.

Gary took her gently by the hand. "Well, we better get going, we got a full day ahead of us," he said, interrupting Kahara before she could tell Theresa off. "Chuck man, it was good to finally meet you. I'll see you tomorrow around ten."

"A pleasure," Chuck said. "I can explain more of the details then."

"Cynthia, Theresa, I'll see you both tomorrow."

Kahara shook hands with Cynthia and Chuck. "It was nice meeting you both. Goodbye. Bye Tissue," Kahara said, biting her lip and trying not to laugh as they left.

"By the way dear," Theresa called to Kahara. "It's Theresa, not Tissue."

"I know it is, and my name is Ka–ha–ra, not that other mess you called me," Kahara fired back, as she and Gary continued walking.

"She's a witch," Kahara said to Gary as they headed outside. "She's got one more time. One more time to mispronounce my name and—"

"So where should we eat?" Gary interrupted, trying to change the subject.

Kahara looked at him. He gave her such a perplexed and helpless look that she couldn't help but laugh. She realized Gary was in an awkward position, not wanting to offend either of them, so she decided not to raise the subject of Theresa again for the remainder of the fest.

They settled on a quaint outdoor café for lunch, then walked over to the theatre to see a few films, one of them a horror/vampire thriller, and another a black sci-fi film. As she sat in the theatre curled up next to Gary, Kahara couldn't help but think back to last year when she was there with Marshall. Last year she just felt grateful to be there with a man, regardless of her feelings for him. But being there this year, with someone she loved, helped put all that in perspective. She was happier, much stronger emotionally, and felt more secure than she had in a long time.

After leaving the theatre, Kahara and Gary decided to do some shopping.

"See what I mean," she said, as they walked along. "Where else can you find a black vampire film—that isn't slapstick and black science fiction? Excellent films. Excellent. There's got to be some way to get these films out to the general public."

He pulled her close. "Looks like somebody's found their calling."

They stopped off at the same little boutique where Kahara had shopped last year. Gary picked out a peach-colored lace teddy for her.

"This is what I want for breakfast tomorrow," he said, looking down at the gown.

Kahara could only blush as the sales attendant smiled, hearing his statement. Gary purchased it for her, and they continued shopping.

Kahara picked out a white linen, loose-fitting shirt for Gary. "This is what I want for dinner," she said teasingly, as they headed to the register.

They walked to the Caribbean Café on the way back. The diner looked unchanged since last year. The gentle breeze floated through the yellow and brightly flowered umbrellas covering each of the uniquely designed cast iron patio tables. Kahara sat down while Gary went to place their order. The café drew patrons not by the sight of its splintered green-framed counter, but because of its appealing aroma of baked bread, jerk chicken, and fried plantain. Kahara sat there with her chin resting in her hand, and thought back to when she was in that very same spot the year before, having dinner with Gary and his friends, and interviewing Thomas Johnson. Gary returned with two orders of jerk chicken. "I remembered," he said, setting a large mango frost drink in front of her.

Kahara smiled. After eating, she clasped her hands together and rested her chin in them. "Remember when we first came here and we were sitting at this table," she said. "I took your chin with the tip of my finger, looked at you and said you had some sexy, sad eyes." She placed her hand gently under his chin again. "You still do."

He grabbed her hand and squeezed it. "I swear, I couldn't figure you out. There you were, clearly flirting with me."

"I'm flirting!"

"Yeah, what was that about sad eyes, askin' me to dance, tellin' me to come see your film when it's finished."

"What about you?" she said. "First you're flirting with me, then, next thing I know, you run downstairs. Not five minutes later you're dancing with some twenty-year-old."

"Let's not talk about dancin', okay Ms. Jenkins? Let's not even go there, because when Gigantor was feelin' you up, I thought, They must be goin' together, they gotta be. You didn't carry yourself like a sister that would let—"

"Okay, okay you're right. Let's leave the dance floor alone," she said.

He smiled at her. "I remember that Sunday morning. I just had to scoop you up in my arms, you looked so broke apart."

Kahara smiled sadly, and sighed. "Yeah, I was," she said. "Back then, I definitely was broken apart. Not by him, but by my own issues. My own mess." She toyed with her straw. "You still got that picture of Lisa Fayson?"

"Yeah, somewhere."

"Boy, you don't know how much I wanted to rip that picture up."

"Don't tell me you were jealous even before you nailed me."

"Nailed you! You the one callin' a woman after four months beggin'." She looked down at her drink and smiled. "I can't believe you remembered my mango frost."

After leaving the diner, they dropped off their packages at the hotel, and went for a long romantic walk along the beach. They sat on a blanket, talking for about an hour as they looked out over the black ocean. Kahara lay back on the blanket. "I am lovin' this," she said, looking up at the sky and stretching her arms up. She turned to him. "What do you want to do later?"

"You want to check out the party tonight?" Gary asked.

"Yeah, sure," she said. For some reason, though, the thought of running into Marshall made her a little nervous. Before arriving in Virginia, she felt the prospect of running into him, with Gary firmly perched on her arm, would be the perfect revenge. But after having such a wonderful day with Gary, she didn't want anything to spoil it, least of all spotting an ex-one-night stand. They arrived at the festival party at around ten o'clock.

The club was huge; about as big as the one they were at the night before, minus the palm trees and other tropical-island effects. As they walked around, Kahara spotted a few of her classmates and introduced them to Gary. Gary, in turn, introduced her to some of his associates from Norfolk who were attending the festival, as well as a few from Los Angeles. Kahara was disappointed she did not spot Sergio or Keith, who were both due to arrive that Thursday. They continued networking for a while, then headed out onto the large, sunken dance floor.

As Gary and Kahara danced, she looked up and noticed Marshall standing at the entrance of the dance floor looking down at the crowd. Her stomach dropped. He looked different, sporting a beard and mustache, hair still cropped close to his head. Kahara wondered whether Gary had seen him. She felt a little afraid he would view her differently, still feeling guilty for going to bed with Marshall so soon, especially after making Gary wait. As Kahara danced with Gary, her expected feelings of triumph were replaced with uncertainty. She thought she was 180 degrees from the person she was last year, but somehow, the sight of Marshall catapulted her back to that lonely, scared, dejected woman who stumbled out of the closing night party without an escort. A slow record came on and Gary, as if sensing her loss of confidence, pulled her close.

"You gonna wear that gown I got for you?" he said into her ear.

"Yeah," she said, relieved to take her mind off of Marshall. "It's very pretty. Thanks again."

"You okay?" he said, leaning back a little.

"Yeah, sure. Why?"

"I don't know," he said, pulling her close again. "You just seem a little disjointed. I noticed your guy up there."

Kahara's body froze. "He's not my guy, I thought you were."

"So they tell me," he said, teasing her to try to lift her mood.

"*They* told you that, huh? What else did *they* say?"

"I love you."

The statement caught Kahara off guard, but it was just the reassurance she needed at that point. Kahara hugged Gary close. "I love you too."

She breathed a sigh of relief when Marshall left a few moments later. Leaving the dance floor, they ran into Keith and Sergio, chatted with them for a while, networked with a few other people, and then left about a half-hour later.

As they rode back to the hotel, Kahara felt a mixture of relief and excitement. Relief that she had seen Marshall without any major reaction from Gary, and excited that they were returning to the room for what she hoped would be another lovemaking session.

"Let's have sex on the terrace again," Kahara said, as they entered the room.

They took a shower together, and went out onto the terrace. Gary, decked in his robe and Kahara in her new peach gown, with the robe covering it. The beach was dark and only the dim lights from the balconies lit the area. Gary pulled Kahara close to him as he sat in the patio chair. He kissed her stomach, and eased his hands up to her breasts, circling her nipples with his fingertips. Kahara felt herself becoming wet. He slid his hand between her thighs and began massaging her already slippery lips, parting them so he could stroke her clitoris.

She held onto his shoulders, barely able to stand as he brought her to orgasm. She quickly helped him apply the rubber, then straddled his lap and eased her hips down onto his rigid penis. He squeezed her behind, lifting it up and down until they both climaxed. They went inside and tumbled into bed, completely exhausted, the long day catching up with them. Gary draped his long arm around Kahara's waist as they slept.

She awoke the next morning and lay there, soaking in everything she had experienced so far. The entire trip, save for the presence of Theresa and Marshall, was like salve on a wound. She readied herself for class while Gary slept, and nudged him before she left.

"Meet me outside of class?"

Gary turned over, rubbed his eyes, and looked up at her. "Naw babe, remember I've got to meet with Chuck about the tour. This is major bucks K. We're talking six months of steady work for me and some of the guys that contract with me. I gotta do this. I want to make a good impression on this brother. It could lead to a lot of future gigs, too. I'm supposed to have lunch after the meeting with him, his wife Cynthia, and Theresa."

Next Time

Kahara's body slumped a little. She had to keep reminding herself that while she was there to relax and do a little networking, Gary was there trying to trump up more business.

"Tell you what," he said. "If we're in the area around the time your class lets out, you can come with us. Otherwise, let's see...otherwise meet me here at 2:00 p.m.."

"You sure?"

"Yeah, yeah," he said, with some hesitancy in his voice. "That'll work."

"Alright," she said, stepping back from the bed a little.

Gary rolled over on his side and looked up at her. "Come here."

She looked at him apprehensively. "What do you want?"

"Come closer," he said, reaching out and easing his hand around the back of her thigh, pulling her towards him.

"Gary, I gotta go. I gotta get to class."

"I got something to teach you, it'll only take a few minutes," he said, squeezing her thigh.

"No, if I'm late, I'll be locked out of class."

Gary's face registered his disappointment. "Okay, you're right. Go do what you gotta do."

Kahara bent over and kissed him. "I'll see you later. Listen, if you must masturbate, do it in the shower, or wear a rubber. You don't want the cleaning lady finding all your stuff on the sheets. Remember, this isn't one of those cheap shacks down south."

Kahara ran for the door, just as Gary picked up a pillow and threw it at her. He missed her by an inch. She opened the door quickly and scampered out, laughing.

As she walked down the hall toward the elevator, she smiled, thinking about the last crack she made to Gary.

Her smile faded though, as she thought about Theresa, and whether she and Gary would get together after class. She realized, however, that he needed time alone to mingle and make connections.

Kahara's class didn't let out until twelve forty-five that afternoon. She felt a little frustrated as she rushed out, wondering if Gary had come by at twelve-thirty, but left, seeing she wasn't there. She ran into Keith, Sergio and a few other people from Chicago, and hung out with them for a while, before heading back to the room at one forty-five. She turned on the TV, confident Gary would be there any minute.

At about two-fifteen, then two-thirty, that confidence gave way to concern. Kahara got up and walked out to the terrace, looking down at her watch. It was ten after three. Kahara sighed hard as she looked outside. Where was he? She shook her head, thinking that Theresa had probably maneuvered a way to divert him from getting there on time.

At around four o'clock she became angry. She could have stayed with her friends from Chicago and the other filmmakers, but where was she? Waiting for Gary and Theresa. She hated her. It amazed her how Gary could not see that this woman was after him. She turned on the TV deciding to give him until four-thirty.

At four forty-five, Kahara left the room, fuming. She attended the last portion of the seminar on Film Production, hoping she'd run into him there. On her way in, she passed Marshall. He did not make eye contact with her, and she did not speak. She continued toward the front of the room and sat down. Just who she needed to see at that point—Marshall. Kahara had no intention of speaking, but she thought he might have at least attempted to say

Next Time

hello, especially after not calling her back the year before. It bothered her, but if he didn't volunteer an explanation, there was no way she was going to lower herself to approach him.

When the seminar ended, Kahara walked to the back of the room and stood, waiting, but there was no sign of Gary. She looked at her watch. It was 6:30 p.m. She left and stood in the lobby. Keith and Sergio saw her, and invited her out to dinner. Kahara turned them down, opting instead to return to the hotel room to see if Gary would show up, or if he had at least left a message. When she entered the empty room, she looked to see if the message light was blinking. It wasn't.

Kahara sat down on the bed and smoothed over the sheets. "Where the hell are you?" she said, looking around the room.

After a half-hour, Kahara decided to walk over and join her filmmaker friends, who had mentioned going to the Caribbean Café. The evening breeze was soothing, but she didn't feel it, her thoughts consumed with where Gary might be. When she reached the café, Sergio, Keith, and two other filmmakers were there.

"Thought you'd be with your boy," Keith quipped.

"Yeah, I did too. He had a meeting that must have run long," she said, taking a seat. She picked up the menu.

"You'll never guess who's here," Sergio said.

"Who?" Kahara asked.

"Don Thompson the producer. I gave him a copy of my screenplay."

"That's great Serg," Kahara said.

"Yeah, I'll tell you how great it is once he makes me an offer. I'm firing my agent."

"Why?" she asked.

"It's not working out. I need someone in L.A."

"At least you have an agent," Kahara said. "Keith, when do you start work on your next film?"

"Sometime in October, if my money's right. You want to help?" Keith was working on his third short film.

"Sure, what do you need?"

"Everything. Just show up the day of the shoot. I'll find something for you to do."

After eating, she went for a walk with them around Virginia Beach, then headed back to the hotel for a networking session. She returned to their room later, to look for any signs of Gary. The room was dark when she entered. At this point, her anger began to melt away to concern. Where was he? Suppose something had happened to him? Kahara paced the floor, trying to figure out what to do. She called Theresa's room. No answer. She hung up and left, deciding if he'd be anywhere, he'd be at the festival party.

Kahara took a cab to the club where the party was being held. The huge two-level structure was jam-packed with people when she arrived. This wouldn't bother her ordinarily, but on a night when she was trying to find someone she was worried about, it was especially annoying. As she pressed her way through the crowd, she passed Marshall. He looked down at her, saying nothing. She kept going without acknowledging him. Her mind catapulted back to the previous year after the seminar, when Gary was trying to talk to her, as she was busy obsessing over the woman Marshall was talking to. How the tables had turned.

Twenty minutes had passed and still no sign of Gary. She went from one end of the club to the other. No luck. Her heart began beating fast as she thought about what could have happened to him. Suppose he had been in a car accident? She could picture him laid up in a hospital somewhere unconscious, while she was there at the party looking for him.

Kahara climbed the stairs and searched the second level. Nothing. As she stood there looking down at the crowd of people dancing below, her eyes teared up a little. Where was he? She went to the back of the upper-level bar and looked for him there. Still no sign. She stood there, trying to determine what she should do next. After a moment, she walked back to the balcony area and looked down at the dance floor.

To her relief, she spotted Gary in the middle of the dance floor with none other than Theresa. The two were dancing next to Cynthia and Chuck. Kahara imagined the four of them together all day, Theresa pretending Gary was hers.

Kahara began breathing hard, trying to fight the rage that was building up inside of her. As she had rushed back to the hotel repeatedly all day, and all evening, looking for him, worrying about him, thinking he was lying somewhere half-dead, where was he? With Theresa, of course. She watched, as her most capable competition, dressed in a cream-colored, sequined dress, pulled her usual stunt—spinning around, shimmying her svelte rear end, then twirling back around, touching him lightly on the shoulder. For his part, Gary moved like a man who didn't have a care in the world, as though he could care less where she was, or the fact that he had promised to meet her at two o'clock, and it was now well after nine-thirty.

Kahara watched the four of them as they headed toward the bar. With each step she took down the spiral staircase, she became angrier and angrier. Her feet hit each step harder and harder. Her pencil-thin heels gave way under the pressure. Kahara tripped over her own feet, twisted her ankle, and landed hard on her rear end. Embarrassed, hurt and angry, she thanked the man who helped her up, brushing off her skirt and continuing on. This was supposed to be her correcting a past wrong—her showing the world that she had a man who was ten times better than the man-boy who had sexed her then ignored her the year before. Instead, this seemed like a repeat of the previous year. Gary, like Marshall, gave her a great time the day before, and then completely ignored her the next day.

As Kahara neared the bar, she breathed deep, trying to maintain her composure. Theresa spotted her first. Kahara gave her a cold stare. Everything was welled up inside of her at that point—Theresa insisting on joining them at the last minute for dinner, her snide remarks, her pulling Gary away when she visited him in Norfolk—and now this. She had had enough. Gary looked over at her and smiled.

"What happened to you earlier today," she snapped.

"Look, I couldn't get away. I left you a message at the hotel. I figured—"

"You're lying." She said, cutting him off, and then turning to Theresa. "I want you to leave him alone. You got that? I want you to leave him the hell alone, and find yourself—"

"Katari, I don't understand—"

"Look bitch, I'm sick of you mispronouncing my name. I said, leave him the fuck alone. Get a life—get a man—and stay the fuck away from mine."

Kahara turned and limped away. She realized in that instant she'd just blown her relationship. She walked toward the ladies' room, not realizing that Gary was following close behind her. He grabbed her arm before she had a chance to enter. Kahara whirled around to face a scowling Gary.

"Where the hell do you get off talking to her like that?"

"Why did you stand me up?"

"I *told* you if I wasn't there at twelve-thirty to go on—I'd catch up with you later."

"No, NO! You said if you weren't there when my class let out you'd meet me at two."

"I left you a message."

"You're *lying*. There was no message."

"You just screwed my relationship with her and the people she was trying—"

"You're not in a relationship with her, you're in a relationship with me."

"Not for long," he said, turning away.

Kahara followed behind him, still limping. "What the hell is that supposed to mean Gary?"

He turned around, the vein in his neck bulging. "It means I'm sick of arguing with you, I'm sick of dealing with your jealousy. If you can't handle the fact that I have female clients, maybe you need to get with someone else. What about your boy? He's still here. You two can pick up where you left off last year."

"Fuck you Gary—this has nothing to do with Marshall. You want to cut and run—go ahead. Go on back in there and let her feel you up some more. I'm not going to stand around and watch this shit."

Kahara turned quickly and half-walked, half-hobbled out of the club. She looked back, hoping Gary would follow her again, but he didn't. She stood outside for a moment, and then hailed a cab. Her mind flew back to April of last year, when she walked back to her hotel room alone after being blown off by Marshall. She sat in the cab, tears rolling down her face, as she replayed the heated exchange she'd just had with Gary. Why did she explode at Theresa like that? Why didn't she wait until she could confront her offline, without Gary or others around? Now she had made a complete fool of herself and shattered her relationship in the process, which was exactly what she felt Theresa wanted.

When she got back to the hotel, she wrapped some ice in a towel, and applied it to her throbbing ankle. About a half-hour later, she undressed slowly, and climbed into bed. She curled up on the left side of the bed and cried herself to sleep.

Kahara awoke abruptly at 1:00 a.m., and looked around the room. No Gary. Anger filled her as she thought of him with Theresa. She stared up at the ceiling. "Come back home," she said softly, turning over on her side again.

A half-hour later, she heard the door open. Her heart calmed with relief. Kahara lay there not moving, uncertain as to what to say. Should she be angry that he was coming in so late, nervous that he might want to break things off, or apologetic for what she had said to Theresa? She lay there motionless, as she heard him undress, and then go into the bathroom to brush his teeth. As she lay there near the edge of the bed, she tried to think of what she was going to say if he tried to talk to her, since she was too nervous to initiate any conversation. She felt Gary as he climbed into bed. He did not come near her. For a moment, they both lay there silent.

"Kahara, are you awake?"

"Yeah," she said reluctantly.

"We need to talk," he said.

Kahara pushed herself up from the bed. "What do you mean, strolling in here at one-thirty in the morning?"

"Look, I was in no mood to be around you, after that stunt you pulled. I spent the rest of the evening trying to clean up the mess you made."

"You spent until one-thirty cleaning up mess, huh? Does cleaning up include fuckin' her too?"

"I can see right now we're not going to get anywhere with this. I have a big meeting tomorrow. I'm going to sleep."

"Oh, another all-day meeting with her? This bullshit—you should have stayed with her if you were going to spend all of your time with her."

"The meeting is not just with her, it's with—damn, I am so *sick* of this. Sick of your jealousy and sick of this up and down bullshit we keep going through. Either we're arguing or we're screwing—it's getting old."

"Ok, if it's so old, why don't you go back over there with her—you've been with her all day, you might as well be with her all night too. Just get the hell out."

"No problem." He stood up, cut on the light, and began putting on his trousers.

"Gary, if you leave and go over there with her, you can kiss this whole thing goodbye."

Gary zipped up his pants, then sat back down on the bed, his back to her. "Maybe that's what we need to do," he sighed. He paused for a moment, "I'll be honest with you. I don't have much left after this. I told you how important the relationship with Chuck was, and what did you do?" He shook his head. "I mean, look at us, we can't even have an intelligent conversation. I don't have the energy for this anymore. I can't keep going through this. This isn't a vacation for me—this is what I do for a *living*.

I can't have you spoiling that. We've never been on the same page about this since this whole thing started. I'm sorry Kahara, but I really don't see this working."

Kahara was stunned. She breathed in hard. "If that's what you want, fine. Go back. Go back to those weak-assed women you're used to. You can't take a real woman with an opinion and a backbone."

Gary got up and walked over to the terrace. "If, by 'backbone,' you mean somebody who embarrasses me by cussing out my clients—no, I don't want that."

"Well, if you don't want it then just go. Leave."

Gary came over to the bed and sat down. "Look, we're adults—let's act like adults. I'll stay here tonight, and I'll get another room tomorrow. I'll pay for this one, don't worry."

At this point, Kahara didn't want him to go, but she didn't want him to stay either. She didn't know what to say, so she said nothing. As Gary undressed and got back into bed, she curled up into a ball crying silently, staying on her edge of the bed until early that morning.

Almost too despondent to go to the screenwriter's workshop, Kahara dragged herself out of bed at seven-thirty and went into the bathroom to take a shower. Gary was still asleep when she came out. She looked over at him, her body dripping wet, hoping he would wake up, see her, become aroused and call her over into his arms. But he didn't move. He hadn't come near her at all while they were asleep. Kahara might as well have been a large boulder sleeping next to him. At least that's how she felt.

As she stood there drying off, she was a mixture of sadness and sexual arousal. He looked so peaceful and sweet lying there, that she felt like crawling into bed with him, snuggling up to him, and making him touch her—making

Next Time

him want her again—forgive and forget everything that happened the night before. Start over again. But there was a finality in his voice—a sense of deep disappointment, no doubt fueled by Theresa. Every time she thought about that whole exchange, Kahara felt a weight pulling inside of her stomach.

It was raining outside, and the room had a gloomy, grayish hue. Kahara stood there for a moment after drying off, and watched him as he slept, his long body stretched out on his back, one hand above his head, the other draped along his side. A tremendous sense of sadness swept over her. She remembered back to how miserable and dejected she felt the previous year Sunday morning, before returning to Chicago. It was only drizzling then, but it was raining now, and the hotel room had a sad and gloomy look to it. The same way it did over a year ago.

Kahara thought back to when Gary first brought her the red t-shirt, the morning before she left. How handsome he looked, and how stupid she had been to ignore him for Marshall. She felt very alone now—very isolated. While she wouldn't have wanted him to have spent the night with Theresa, in a way it was more painful having him there. It would be easier if he weren't so mature about everything. Losing a jerk wouldn't be as much of a sting. Kahara wiped away the tears that had started to form, got dressed, and left for class.

Chapter 25

As she sat in class, she bent over periodically to rub her sore ankle. Some of the swelling had subsided. After class, she ran into Sergio and Keith. Noting her downcast mood, they offered to treat her to lunch at the Caribbean Café. Her heart sank as she sat there remembering yesterday, when they dined there, and the previous year, when she, Gary and his friends were there. Keith looked up at her as he ate his meal.

"What, you on a starvation diet? Eat!"

"I'm not hungry," Kahara said, pushing away her meal.

"What happened—somebody get shot?" Keith asked.

"If she doesn't want to eat, she doesn't want to eat," Sergio said, sounding annoyed. "Must you get in everyone's business?"

"As a matter of fact—yes. What business is it of yours whose business I get into? Why don't you just mind your own damn business?" Keith turned back to Kahara. "Why aren't you eating?"

"Keith."

"Sergio, shut the fuck up. I directed my question to Kahara. No one is talking to you."

"Can't you see she doesn't want to talk about it? Leave it alone."

"Again, why—do—*you*—care?"

Even in the midst of her depression, Kahara found their bizarre arguing amusing. Of course, that was their dynamic. They would fight furiously, but still remain friends. She only wished Gary had the stamina to survive a relationship like that.

Kahara sighed. "Keith, I'm okay. But I really don't want to talk about it."

"See, I told you," Sergio chided.

"You ain't told me shit. You always gotta be right about every damn thing. Kahara, you don't want to talk about it—fine. Tell the chump, what's-his-name—Gary, to get over it, whatever it is."

"Oh wow, now there's some truly meaningful unsolicited advice," Sergio said, shaking his head.

"Excuse me, but was I talking to you? Did I address you directly?"

"Not that I recall."

"Well then, why are you injecting yourself into this conversation when clearly your input is not needed or sought after?"

"Especially when she's getting such great advice from you." Sergio quipped.

They finished their meal in silence. Keith looked at Kahara, then at Sergio. Sergio shook his head no at Keith.

"I ain't said shit. Why you shakin' your head at me?"

"I know what you were about to say," Sergio said.

"What are you, a psychic now?"

"Well, what were you going to say to her?"

"I was going to ask her if she wanted to check out the Matt McGaw flick, if that meets with your approval."

"No, I'd rather go to the seminar," Sergio said.

"I wasn't asking you, I was asking her."

"No Keith, I'm not really—I'm going to check out the seminar," Kahara replied.

Keith rose out of his seat. "Ah hell no, I can't take another seminar. You on your own there. Come on Serg, let's go."

"I said I wanted to check out the seminar," Sergio said.

"Then go check out the seminar. I don't give a shit. I came here to see films—not listen to a lecture. Kahara, you gonna be okay?"

"Yeah, I'm fine," she said, sitting up, trying to perk up for their benefit.

"So man, what you gonna do?" Keith asked.

Sergio sighed. "I guess I'll go to the movie."

Keith threw his hands up. "After all that." Keith turned to Kahara. "Listen, if you don't go to the awards show with him tonight, give us a call."

"Yeah, I'll do that," Kahara said, thinking wistfully back to last year. *No way,* she thought. No way was she going to return to the scene of the crime, remembering how depressed she was the year before at the awards banquet. There was no way she was going to take a chance on running into Gary with Theresa.

Keith and Sergio headed to the theatre, leaving Kahara alone. She sat in the café by herself, her chin in her hand, picking at a meal she had no intention of eating. She threw away her lunch, purchased a mango frost, then headed for the seminar at the Avenda Hotel.

As she walked along, she thought about Marshall and Gary. Two rejections in two years. Both unfair, and both individuals got off scot-free. There was Marshall, without even the decency to speak, apologize, or even acknowledge her existence. And now, Gary. A feeling of resentment, toward men in general, began to well up inside of her.

Next Time

Ignored by one, and dumped by another, Kahara began to feel used and thrown away. Two years in a row. Two failures. Now, as she entered the seminar, all she could do was wonder who may have heard her make an ass out of herself the night before.

If anyone in her screenwriter's workshop had overheard her outburst against Theresa, or the argument with Gary, they didn't say anything to her about it, much to her relief. Why did she make such an ass out of herself? But the underlying question was, why did Gary stand her up? He never answered that. What was he doing until one-thirty in the morning with Theresa? He never answered that either. Why did Marshall think he could just fuck her and dump her like she never existed? If she ever had the opportunity to talk to him, she would confront him with that question.

As she walked into the seminar, her temples felt flushed. She passed Marshall on the way in. He was sitting by himself in the back row. Kahara headed toward the front and took a seat. As the speaker droned on, she became angrier and angrier, thinking how relaxed Marshall looked when she passed him on the way in.

She wanted to confront him, but was afraid of making an ass out of herself yet again. But why not? Why not hold him accountable for his actions? Why should he get off scot-free? Kahara got up out of her seat and limped hard toward the back of the room where Marshall was sitting. She hurried past him, chickening out at the last minute, walking outside and heading toward the bathroom.

On the way there, she spotted Gary in the distance, talking to a few people, one of them being Theresa. Anger filled her. Kahara entered the bathroom and tried to compose herself, feeling embarrassed and awkward, as though she should have acknowledged Gary. But he was breaking up with her, so why should she? He had apparently moved on. Damn him. And damn Marshall. She pushed the restroom door open hard, and walked firmly on her sore ankle back to the seminar. Once inside, she spotted Marshall, still sitting alone in the back.

Her first impulse was to confront him. But as she stood watching him stretched out lazily, the idea of approaching him, walking up to him, making the first move, especially after he didn't even speak, somehow seemed demeaning. She walked quickly past him, ten rows ahead, not looking back, and took a seat. She inhaled deeply, regaining her composure. Part of her wanted to go back and *demand* an explanation from him. Another part of her wanted to go outside and beat the hell out of Theresa.

As she sat there with her arms tightly folded, staring straight ahead thinking, she didn't notice Marshall as he sidled up to her row. She looked up, startled, as he took a seat next to her. He nodded an almost silent hello.

"Nice of you to speak after over a year," she snapped.

He sat there, saying nothing. There were few people sitting in their row, but the rows in front of them were almost full.

"I see you're by yourself now, huh?" he said, noting her abandoned status.

She looked at him, studying the smug look on his face.

Kahara didn't want to make an ass out of herself again, but she was angry. Angry with Gary for dumping her, and angry with Marshall for ignoring her.

"You don't have anything to say, do you?"

"Not really. Is there an issue?"

Kahara shook her head. "Is there an issue? Yeah, there's an issue. You had sex with me then blew me off. That's the issue."

A woman in the row ahead of them turned around briefly. Kahara shot her a "mind your own business" look, and she immediately turned back around. Gary walked by, looked back at the two of them, and continued on.

"Friend of yours?" Marshall said, with just a touch of sarcasm in his voice.

"It's like it never happened, isn't it? You blow me off the next day. You don't return phone calls, emails."

"Too busy."

"Bullshit, Marshall. You ignored me on purpose. Somebody must have really burnt you in the past."

"Nobody got burnt. You just gotta be careful when you do these things."

"Who's got to be careful?" Kahara asked. She looked up and saw Gary coming back toward them. He passed by once again without saying a word.

"You," Marshall said, turning around, watching Gary as he walked out. He turned back around, slid down in his seat, stretching his legs out in front of him. "And me too. We're both adults. We knew what we were doing. I never stated I was looking for a relationship."

"You intimated it."

Marshall shrugged. "Some of that's necessary in order to seal the transaction, but you women know that. How old are you again?"

Kahara sat silent for a moment, feeling incriminated. Who was she really mad at—Marshall or herself? His rhetorical question about her age stung deep. It further underscored how much older she was than he, and it was a painful reminder that at her age, she should have been more savvy than to fall for his frat-boy routine. Yes, she was mad at herself, and had beaten herself up over the situation for months. Kahara had long ago accepted responsibility for her recklessness and had corrected the behavior that got her into the situation with him in the first place. But none of that excused him.

She sat rigid in her seat and took a deep breath. "You know what Marshall, the next time you just want to fuck someone—just say it, okay? Be honest. Tell them, 'I don't want to get to know you. I don't want to be your friend—I just want to fuck.'"

Another woman in front of them turned around, but Kahara kept going. "'I don't want your picture, your phone number. I don't want to exchange ideas, thoughts, dreams. I just want to fuck. And after it's over, I'll treat you like a used tampon okay, because that's all women are to me.'"

"Sound bitter. You must be having personal problems. Why you taking them out on me?"

Kahara understood now why he sat next to her. The statement he made about her being alone clicked. After seeing Gary with Theresa, he probably figured Gary dumped her—the same way he did the year before.

Kahara sighed hard. "So you came over to gloat, huh?"

Marshall shrugged with a slight smirk on his face.

"Well, I'll tell you what. Whether I'm having problems or not is none of your damn business. This has been sitting inside of me for over a year and it felt good to finally get it out. Don't strike up a conversation with a woman about how much you like kids and how affectionate you are when you're in a relationship, when you know good and damn well that all you want to do is fuck her and dump her. Have the decency to tell her that so she can make an informed decision."

Next Time

"So you're saying I misled you?"

"I'm saying you pissed on me. And I don't like it."

A man turned around this time. Kahara shot him a mean glance. The blanket had been pulled back. She'd been rejected twice in two years and her rage didn't have room for embarrassment. She was past that.

"You mean pissed off."

"No, pissed on," she said. She rose up and looked down at him. "But I feel better now. Much better."

She turned and limped off before he could respond. A few more people in the row in front of them turned around to get a look at Kahara before she left. Marshall sat there with a perturbed and embarrassed expression on his face.

As she exited, she saw that Gary was still outside talking to Theresa and some other people. Kahara looked over at him, shot him a mean look, and continued to her room, trying unsuccessfully not to hobble. Once inside, she placed her purse on the table, sat on the bed, and stared out the terrace window.

The encounter with Marshall left her feeling vindicated. She didn't like the idea that the people around them heard the conversation, but at this point what did she have to hide? It was more important to get it out of her system. Kahara knew no more now than she did before, about why Marshall never contacted her, but at least she had the opportunity to confront him. And although his answer was anything but satisfactory, she got a chance to tell him how she felt, which was all she really wanted anyway.

So much had changed in the last year. In some ways, she felt as though she was right back where she started a year ago, but she still felt satisfied. In the past, she would have berated herself about her faults, but no more. *She* was the judge now—*no one else*. Was she wrong for the way she talked to Theresa? Yes. But would she kowtow and beg Gary to stay in the relationship? No. Absolutely not. She wasn't perfect, but neither was he. They both had issues they needed to work on, and if he was willing to throw her away, then he wasn't worth the effort.

"Left me a message huh?" Kahara said out loud, looking over at the phone. She picked up the receiver and checked the voicemail. To her surprise, there were four messages on the machine. One at 11:00 a.m. Saturday from Arnita, and three messages that Friday—a message at 6:00 p.m. from Phil, Gary's business associate, and two messages from Gary, the first at two-fifteen that afternoon, stating that he would come back to the room at five o'clock, and another message at six-thirty, stating he would see her at the party that evening. The message light wasn't working.

Kahara sat there holding the phone in her hand. While she felt bad about exploding and knew she needed to reign in her famous temper, she also knew that Gary needed to reign in his tendency to dismiss prior commitments when he was going after a client.

Kahara got up off the bed after a while and walked out onto the terrace. Leaning over the railing, she looked at the beach and thought back to happier times. Back to the night at the restaurant with Gary, back to their lovemaking sessions on the terrace, and back to her walk on the beach with him two days ago—it seemed like two years ago now. The thought of that beautiful Thursday brought a sad smile to her face.

She heard a noise behind her and looked back toward the room. Gary was standing there, apparently having entered without her hearing him. He walked out onto the terrace with her. He looked a little shy, as though he didn't know how to approach her. Kahara turned back around, looking toward the ocean. Gary walked over and stood next to her. "What happened to your meeting?" she said, still staring out at the beach.

"I cancelled it."

"Why?"

"I wanted to see how you were doing."

"What? You saw me with Marshall and thought I had him up here?"

"After what he did to you last year, I can't imagine you'd even go there. I could tell by the expression on your face that you weren't too happy, so I assumed you must have been telling him off."

"Yeah, I seem to be a pro at that lately," Kahara sighed. She watched a flock of seagulls take off in flight over the ocean. She turned toward Gary. "Look, I owe you an apology, and Theresa too. I had no right to spout off the way I did. I was so worried about you and when I saw you with her I—"

"Listen, I've been thinking. I was wrong, and not just about last night. I do use my job as an excuse a lot of the time for canceling our plans. That needs to stop. I should have tried to hook up with you sooner yesterday. There was a problem with the phone—the voicemail malfunctioned. I found out this morning after you left."

"I know. I just found out."

"I got so wrapped up trying to snag this new client, that I pushed everything else aside. You had a right to be angry—at me and at her. Just to let you know, I did speak to her about you."

"You did," she said skeptically.

"Yeah, I did. I told her that you were a permanent part of the picture and I wanted her to stop the cat fight."

Kahara stood back on her good leg, hand on hip. "What did she say?"

"She agreed that the name mispronunciation was uncalled for. That didn't give you the right to call her a bitch."

"She is."

"K—"

"But you're right, I had no right calling her that," Kahara said. "Even though that's what she is," she uttered under her breath. "You both had me pissed off that night."

"Next time, bring it to me okay? I can take a punch."

Kahara balled up her fist, punched him lightly on the arm, and smiled. "I guess you can."

Gary pulled her close to him and planted a kiss on her forehead. "Friends?"

She pulled away from him. "Is that all?"

"You give me a chance, and I'll show you what else." He took her hand and began leading her off the terrace.

"Wait a minute, wait a minute," Kahara said, before they entered the room. "What were you doing until one-thirty in the morning with Theresa?"

"What! Oh come on Kahara. I wasn't just with her. I was with two other people. We didn't leave the club until one o'clock. Don't tell me we're going to have another fight about her." Gary looked at Kahara and shook his head. They both began laughing. After a few minutes, they went inside and settled into some afternoon lovemaking. They lay there afterwards, resting up before the awards banquet that evening.

"You know, I think it's time we started planning for that documentary we talked about working on," Gary said.

"I thought you said we should wait until we've been together a year-and-a half?" Kahara said.

"What's eight months?" he smiled.

She laughed. "Yeah, I guess you're right."

"Plus, we'll need to have products if we're going to do that marketing project you were talking about for black films."

"So you really want to work on that with me?"

"Yeah, what better place to start than with your own films?"

Kahara hugged him and smiled. As she lay next to him, she thought back to last year, and how on that particular Saturday evening she had slowly begun to realize that Marshall no longer wanted to have anything to do with her. She smiled to herself, and then looked over at Gary who had fallen asleep. The circle was now complete.

ABOUT THE AUTHOR:

A native of Chicago, Cheryl Matlock's writing inspirations started in elementary school and were stimulated by ideas as diverse as horror movies and jazz music. Through her maturation process, Cheryl's tales drifted from horror towards romance and drama. Her experiences broadened as her family relocated to Evanston, Illinois during her sophomore year of high school. Her creative expressions provided repose from the isolation she felt after being removed from familiar surroundings. A graduate of Roosevelt University in Chicago, Ms. Matlock continued writing fiction, poetry, and prose through and beyond her college years. Cheryl also has a background as a filmmaker. She has produced and directed three films. Her latest film, Keepin' It Real, was screened at two California black film festivals (San Francisco and Hollywood) and two in Chicago (Black Harvest and Visions Blu). She is currently working on a short film and another novel. For additional information, please visit: www.cmatlock.com.